A Town Called Library

Jan-Andrew Henderson

Black Hart Entertainment

Edinburgh. Brisbane

A Town Called Library.
ISBN-978-1-64570-603-8 (Print)
ISBN-978-1-64570-604-5 (eBook)

The Division of Youth

The worldview of the Division of Youth is clear and simple so that each worker can easily understand and follow it.

Each worker is one of a Type and each Type is given a task in life.

Types are identified by their physical appearance.

Each Type knows its place in the Order of Things.

Different Types are encouraged not to mix, in order to keep their purpose clear and their minds pure.

The Code of the Division of Youth

Mike 3 shuffled a pile of carrots around on his tray. He hated carrots.

He looked up at the other 49 Mikes in the enormous food court, all performing the same motion. Every Mike loathed carrots. But they'd eat them in the end because food was never wasted in the Division of Youth. And because Mrs Brown told them to.

Set in the roof were two cameras so she could keep an eye on the hall, while a screen on the wall flashed up inspirational messages. Today's was…

Avoid clichés like the plague.

The boy watched the others at his long table, all identical. Short in stature. Sandy hair. Snub noses. Thin lips. Green homespun tunics and caps. The only way to tell them apart was by the numbers they scrawled on their wrists each morning in black marker pen.

Normally, the Mikes didn't talk at mealtimes. There wasn't much point. They all had much the same thoughts and feelings and their daily routine never varied. But this was a farewell dinner.

Tomorrow, everyone in the Division of Youth would turn sixteen and graduate. It wasn't their real birthday but nobody cared. In just twenty-four hours, they'd leave the Fort, enter New Eden and see the outside world for the first time. There, they would join previous generations, taming a wilderness and rebuilding the human race. They had been preparing for this moment for two years.

"How do you feel about finally getting out of here?" his neighbor asked. Mike 3 didn't have to look at the boy's arm to know it was Mike 32. Mike 32 always sat next to him.

"Same as you, I guess," he replied.

"I gotta admit, I'm a tad nervous." Mike 32 slid a carrot from his plate and sneakily pinged it under the table. "But mostly, I'm over the moon."

He punched his companion on the shoulder.

"The moon, huh? We'll finally see it. And the sun as well. Mrs Brown says it feels like being prickled with happiness."

"I know. I sat next to you in the lesson."

"I can't wait to look at the sky! You think it's bigger in real life than the pictures Mrs Brown showed us?"

"Wait till we see a bear for the first time," Mike 3 countered. "I bet *that's* bigger in real life than the pictures Mrs Brown showed us."

"You seem a mite out of sorts." Mike 32 narrowed his eyes. "Got the jitters about this?"

"What I got is a mouth full of horrible veg."

"Ah." His neighbor nodded sympathetically. "We'll eat meat soon. When we get to New Eden, I intend to kill the first bear I see."

"You'll most likely have to get in line." Mike 3 jerked a thumb at his 49 duplicates. "Poor bear's gonna have more holes in it than a pepper shaker."

"I sense you want to be left alone to reflect on this momentous occasion." Mike 32 nodded sagely. "I might just do the same."

He turned to the boy on his other side.

"How do *you* feel about Graduating?"

"I'm a tad nervous. But mostly, I'm over the moon."

Mike 3 watched the rest of the Types in the hall, each at their own enormous table. 100 identical Sierras. They were the farmers. 30 identical Uniforms, pushing and shoving each other. They were the explorers and protectors. 20 identical Tangos. They were the engineers and builders. 17 identical Echos, filing their nails. They were the medics and general administrators.

And, at the top table, three identical Alphas. The leaders.

Six Types of worker, each with a specific role to play in New Eden when they graduated. That was the order of things and Mike had always accepted it.

Until an hour ago.

An hour ago, Mike 3 had seen a ghost.

He'd been walking from his quarters to the main hall when he had the feeling of being watched. Mikes were hunters and fishers and never ignored their instincts, so he glanced over his shoulder.

A girl was standing at the end of the corridor, staring at him.

One glimpse was enough to tell him something was very wrong. There were only three female Types in the Division of Youth. Echos were pale, blonde beauties. Sierras short and dark. Tangos gangly, with mousey brown locks.

This girl had a freckled face and long red hair.

She raised a slim hand, put a finger to her lips and ducked out of sight.

It took a few seconds for Mike to recover, then he sprinted after the apparition. But, when he turned the corner, the next passageway was empty.

He hadn't imagined the girl, no doubt about that. More worryingly, she seemed familiar. Not just the hair and face but the gesture she had used. Problem was, nobody in the Division of Youth looked like that.

Nobody in the Division of Youth had *ever* looked like that.

"Coming to play Lacrosse?" Mike 32 interrupted his thoughts. "It's our night to have the hall."

The others were clearing the space so it could be used for recreation. Usually, Mike 3 enjoyed running around with them, though the game always ended in a draw. Right now, he needed to think.

"Broke the string on my bow," he lied. "Best go and repair it if I'm gonna beat you to that bear."

He left the food court and crept back along the silent corridor, listening for the slightest unfamiliar sound. Darting into his room, he pulled a hunting knife from the wall. He switched off the light and sat in his single chair, facing the door.

Should he tell the leaders what he had witnessed? Types didn't usually mix, but this was surely an exception. Then again, what if the Alphas thought he was crazy? They wouldn't trust him out in New Eden and he'd end up digging ditches with the Sierras, rather than hunting.

He couldn't take that chance. Which left Mrs Brown.

Alphas might be in charge of the Types but Mrs Brown had given them life. She provided heat and light and the air they breathed. Her replicators supplied the children with fruit and vegetables, so there was enough for everyone to eat. And she was their teacher.

Mrs Brown had told all Mikes the best way to kill a bear, skin a deer or spear a fish. Which was pretty vital information since there were no actual animals in the Division of Youth.

He swung his chair to face a screen on the wall.

"Mrs Brown?"

The monitor flickered to life. It showed an expanse of tilled land dotted with log cabins and flanked by thick forest. Smoke rose from some of the chimneys and tiny Sierras could be seen in the distance gathering crops. This was New Eden. Their future. It was only a simulation, as there were no cameras to see outside, but it always reassured him.

Yes, Mike 3? Mrs Brown's voice was calm and robotic. **I see you're not playing with the others. Graduation nerves, I presume?**

"Question." He thought for a moment, unsure of how to start. "Ehm… Is there anyone in the Division of Youth who *isn't* a Type?"

He felt stupid even asking.

Of course not, boy. Mrs Brown said sternly. **There are only Alphas, Mikes, Echos, Sierras, Tangos and Uniforms.**

Exactly the answer he expected. So, what exactly *had* he seen? He took another stab in the dark.

"Question… Is there anything alive in the Division of Youth that *isn't* human?"

Sure. There are Brussels Sprouts.

That was no help. He wondered if he should just leave things as they were. Then a thought struck him. What if this was some kind of graduation test to see how he handled the unexpected? You wouldn't ignore a strange creature out in New Eden. You'd try to find out what it was.

A knowing smile played on his lips. He had this sussed.

"Question. Is there anything in the Division of Youth, alive or not, that has freckles and red hair?"

Mrs Brown's tone changed immediately.

You Graduate in one day, Mike 3, she barked. **If you want to see New Eden, best leave that topic well alone.**

The boy recoiled as if he had been slapped.

"Sorry," he stammered. "I will. I'll leave it alone."

Sensible child. Mrs Brown said approvingly. **You're over-excited, is all. Get some rest. Would you like to hear some music to help you sleep?**

"Yes, please." Mike tried to keep the tremor out of his voice. "I'd like Greensleeves. It's my favorite."

Prefer a bit of Honky Tonk Piano, myself. But it's your choice. The picture on the screen switched to a night sky with twinkling stars. **Happy sixteenth birthday for tomorrow. Sleep tight and don't let the bugs bite.**

Mike lay on the bed and put his hands behind his head, trying to quell his unease. He closed his eyes and breathed deeply.

No more thinking. It didn't matter what he had seen. He didn't care. The only important thing was getting to New Eden.

Music began to play softly. Mike twitched. This wasn't Greensleeves. It was a girl singing.

Ring around the roses
A pocket full of posies.
Ashes A-tishoo!
We all fall down.

The teenager could have sworn he'd never heard the tune or lyrics before. Yet, somehow, he had.

"Mrs Brown? This isn't what I asked for."

The computer didn't answer. Hairs rose on Mike's neck and he slowly opened his eyes.

A girl with red hair filled the monitor, staring down at him.

-3-

"Gnaaaah!" Mike 3 flung himself off the bed and scooped up the knife, sliding backwards on his butt, weapon held in front of him.

"Don't have a heart attack, hunter." The girl put one freckled finger to her lips again. "Think I'm going to jump out of the screen?"

"How did you get *in* there?" Mike lowered the blade.

"You've made Mrs Brown suspicious." The teenager said reproachfully. "Good job she has her hands full with the big day tomorrow."

"Who *are* you?"

"I'm the girl you saw in the corridor. How many redheads are you familiar with?"

"Where's Mrs Brown?"

"Like I said, she's busy preparing for graduation. Made it easier for me to hack into her systems unnoticed."

"She would never allow that."

"No, she wouldn't." A hint of pride tinged the girl's voice. "So, obviously, she doesn't know and I'd like to keep it that way."

"This *is* a test, isn't it?" The boy got up and paced the room in agitation. "I knew it. I'm being assessed somehow."

"It's no assessment. You caught me by surprise and that kinda forced me to get in touch. If the truth be known, I'm pretty relieved. I could do with a friend."

Her brow furrowed.

"You haven't told anyone you saw me?"

"Not yet. Though I got to say, I'm sorely in need of guidance." The boy tried to regain his composure. "Where did you *come* from?"

His jaw dropped.

"Are you from New Eden? Are you from *outside*?"

"I wish. But I've never seen the sun or felt the rain on my face." The girl looked at him sadly. "Don't you remember me, Mike?"

"I never set eyes on you before today."

"You sure? Aren't I familiar? Didn't that song you heard ring any bells?"

"No. Well… maybe". Mike put his head in his hands. "I don't *know*."

"What's the first thing you *can* recall?"

"Pardon my impertinence, but I don't see what that has to do with anything."

"Please, Mike. This is important."

"Ehm… I must have been about thirteen." The boy thought back. "All the Types had come out of their tanks and Mrs Brown was telling everyone about New

Eden and how we were going to be trained to survive there. It's a bit fuzzy."

"I'll bet it is," the girl tisked. "All right. Let me show you an image and you say the first thing that comes into your head."

She vanished and some sort of identification card flashed up on the screen. Under the words **Homeland Security** was a picture of a pretty, gray-haired woman.

"Who's this? Quick! Don't think!"

"Mrs Brown." Mike blurted out. "No, wait! It can't be." The boy shook his head. "Mrs Brown isn't a real person. She's a computer."

"It is Mrs Brown. And she used to be a person."

"Please stop," the boy moaned. "Why are you doing this to me? Pick on another Mike. We're all the same."

"You're not." The girl looked puzzled. "You're very like them, I admit. But not quite. A bit more of a loner. Slightly slower to smile. A mite smarter, perhaps."

"Did you let me spot you on purpose?" Mike narrowed his eyes.

"That's what I mean!" the girl beamed. "You're clever. And seeing me has jogged a few memories, I'll bet."

"Not in the slightest. I don't know you and I wish you'd go away."

"You *have* to remember your past. If not, you'll go through the airlock to New Eden tomorrow with the rest of the Types, no matter what I say."

"I reckon that's going to be the case, anyhow." Mike folded his arms defiantly. "You've no idea how sick I am of carrots."

"Hah! I do like you." The girl appeared on the screen again. "You have a sense of humor."

"I don't find *this* funny, Juliet."

"It's working!" The teenager clapped her hands, delighted. "All you need are the right triggers!"

"*What's* working?" the boy snorted.

"Mike?" Juliet laughed. "If you never saw me before, how come you know my name?"

-4-

The boy staggered to the toilet. Juliet waited patiently until he came out.

"I threw up," he said wanly.

"Understandable. But hardly inspiring in a hunter."

"I'm all confused." Mike wiped his mouth with the back of his hand. "How could I know your name? What's happening to me?"

"You lost your memory, like all the other Types. You just need the correct stimuli to jog it back. Sights and sounds that Mrs Brown is careful to make sure you never experience." Juliet screwed up her face. "It's a bit traumatic to do things this quickly, but I only have a small window while she's otherwise occupied."

"I'll be facing wolves and bears with nothing but a bow and arrow in a couple of days." Mike snorted. "Will I find it more traumatic than *that*?"

"You might well do." Juliet tilted her head. "Let's try something else. Do you recall your mother and father?"

"That's how things worked in *olden* days," the boy pointed out. "Not any more. Like I said, all the Types came out of tanks, me included."

"Hold on to your natty green hat." The girl vanished. "I found this in Mrs Brown's data banks."

A photograph appeared on the monitor. A thin man with sandy hair had his arm around a pretty woman in a purple outfit. They were smiling at each other. Pressed between them was a little boy clutching a teddy bear.

Mike's jaw tightened. The faces were familiar. The bear even more so.

"I remember that dress." He crept up to the screen. "It felt all soft and silky."

The words caught in his throat.

"It smelled of lavender."

The boy reached up, index finger, pinkie and thumb outstretched, and pressed his palm against the glass.

"Careful!" Juliet appeared back on the monitor. "You're getting me all streaky."

"It means *I love you* in sign language."

"Aw, shucks."

"It wasn't meant for you." He withdrew his hand and looked at it in astonishment. "How the hell do I know sign language?"

"Because your mother was deaf." The girl watched him, her expression unreadable. "That's her, in case you hadn't guessed. With you and your dad."

"I *had* a mom and dad. I did!" Mike flopped down on the bed. "What happened to them?"

He put his head in his hands.

"There are dozens of Mikes," he protested. "We can't all have…"

"Here's the last trigger," Juliette interrupted. "I don't think it's one you could *ever* forget."

An eerie wail emanated from the speakers on either side of the screen, building in volume. Mike looked around in terror.

"The sirens!" he clasped a hand over his mouth. "Where's my oxygen mask?"

And, suddenly, he remembered everything.

Part 2

The Le Mans bug

The Renaissance took place in chaos and plague.

Shiva Ayyadurai

The Le Mans bug first appeared at Brandenburg International Airport in Berlin. By the time those infected began dying, the plague had been carried by unsuspecting passengers all over the globe. It killed so quickly, planes on some of the longer flights simply fell out of the sky.

It was the last blow to a world already devastated by climate change, conflict and pollution.

Many fled for the hills. Others boarded up their homes. Some danced in the streets, declaring it was God's will. When the disease had passed, there would finally be enough food, land and oil for the blessed few who were left.

The Le Mans bug killed them all.

Across the planet, machinery stopped and the lights went out as the human race was extinguished.

Almost extinguished.

For, deep underground, four giant forts survived.

Waiting for the day it was safe to go outside again.

-6-

Harvey Stoddart, Fort New York State's head technician, watched on the monitor as a small group was led down the corridor towards the control room.

"Helluva chance for us to take." He turned to the head of security. "Opening the Fort's blast doors for a van full of kids. Christ. How did they manage to get a military escort?"

"Orders from Willard Chain himself, apparently," the Security Chief replied. "They cut it a bit fine but they've been scanned and aren't infected." He tapped the monitor. "Rumor is, one of them is Chain's own kid. No idea which one, though. Didn't even know he had offspring."

"That would explain it, all right," Harvey said grumpily. "What about the others?"

"A few lucky stragglers whose parents were already working here. The plague spread so bloody fast, I'm surprised they made it. People left out there are desperate and throwing themselves at our defenses. We had to let the dogs loose."

"There was no need for that." Stoddart reprimanded. "This place can withstand an army and the plague will reach them pretty soon."

The door slid open and a handful of teenagers entered. Some sauntered in, looking curiously around. A couple hung back, shy and uncertain. The white-coated men poring over various consoles gawked at the little group.

"Come on, Mike." A gray-haired woman wearing a matching tweed skirt and jacket ushered them along. "Sierra? Move it."

The children did so. Mrs Brown's tone carried no-nonsense authority and she had a large handgun strapped to her slim waist.

"Really?" Stoddart marched over and confronted the woman. "How come you're marching your wards all over the place instead of billeting them in one of the ready rooms?" He peered angrily over his glasses at the children. "They look about eleven."

"They're thirteen." Mrs Brown said. "I'm giving them a tour of the facility."

"Why?"

"Cause I'm sick of their questions." She swept a wiry lock from her forehead. "I thank you in advance for volunteering to explain how the control center works."

"Say what, *now?"*

"They're asking things about this place and I don't have answers." Mrs Brown surveyed the room. "Never had much time for technology."

She plonked herself on the nearest chair and crossed shapely legs.

"You just carry on. I'm quite interested in the setup, myself."

"You can't waltz in here like you're on some school trip," the head technician fumed. *"We're the hub of a top-secret facility."*

"I got clearance." Mrs Brown flashed him her Homeland Security badge. *"Anyhow, who are the kids gonna blab to? Their imaginary friends?"*

The children shuffled awkwardly on the spot.

"Just rattle off some random facts and send em on their way to the tanks." The security chief nudged him. *"What's the harm?"*

The head technician shot Mrs Brown a dirty look.

"All right, you lot," he said curtly. *"My name is Dr Harvey Stoddart. I'll tell you a bit about the function we perform here. Then you can go play tag or whatever kids do when they're not on their iPads."*

"Ipads don't work no more," Sierra said dolefully.

Stoddart removed the horn-rimmed glasses and tucked them into the pocket of his lab coat.

"We call this complex the Fort and it's essentially a very large... no.... a giant underground shelter. There are four Forts in total and their exact locations are secret but I guess there's no harm in telling you this one is in New York State. After all, you're already here."

He sighed loudly.

"And a bunch of other people seem to have found the entrance, as you probably saw."

The children listened solemnly, remembering the desperate throng their escort had driven through.

"There's also a Fort in the west and two in the south," Stoddart added.

"Just my luck to end up in Yankee central," Mrs Brown drawled. "I'm a Texas gal, myself."

"I'd happily transfer you back," a lab worker grumbled under his breath.

"If I may continue," Stoddart pressed on. "The Forts were built by a billionaire called Willard Chain, to withstand any sneaky foreign attack. They're filled with the brightest and best scientists and the latest technology - some of it so new, it's still experimental. We were working on ways to save the human race from the mess it got itself in."

"What ways?" Mrs Brown asked.

"Chain had a breakthrough with a compound called WC-57, which could enhance human abilities and make us more suited to harsh living conditions. Unfortunate name though, I admit. And it still needs some... eh... adjustments before it'll work properly."

A large, stocky boy yawned loudly.

"Show some respect, Uniform," Mrs Brown cautioned.

"Why are you calling them by international phonetic symbols?" the technician asked.

"I'm a bodyguard, not a nanny." The woman stretched. "Got no interest in remembering their real names."

"All rightee." Stoddart raised a bushy eyebrow and bent over the teens, who all shrank back. *"It's a good job the Forts were built because, down here, we're safe from the Le Mans bug."*

He eyed Mrs Brown.

"They have heard about the plague, haven't they?"

"No. They missed the human race dying because they were busy playing tag."

"I'm just asking."

"Don't sugarcoat things for them, neither." Mrs Brown urged him on. *"They're thirteen, not four. I already explained the situation as best I could."*

"Poor buggers," Stoddart muttered, turning back to the children.

"We've learned a lot about the plague in a short space of time. Had to really."

"Question." A little hand shot up.

"Yes?" the technician snapped, annoyed at being interrupted. *"Sierra, isn't it?"*

The girl nodded enthusiastically.

"How come it's called the Le Mans bug?"

"Because it only takes twenty-four hours to kill you. Same length of time as the famous race." Stoddart smiled thinly at Mrs Brown. If she didn't want things sugar-coated, he was only too happy to oblige.

The woman simply shrugged.

"We've determined it was created deliberately," he continued. *"Most likely by some unfriendly country. We concluded this because the Bug is incredibly*

contagious and it doesn't kill plants or animals. It's obviously been genetically modified, so only humans are susceptible."

The teens stared at him, wide-eyed.

Stoddart coughed and adjusted his tie, suddenly feeling guilty for his lack of tact.

"The good news is that the plague will eventually burn itself out." His tone softened. "We've given it five years, just to be on the safe side. There will be no people left, of course. But we can restart the human race using the inhabitants of the four Forts."

"Where's my mom?" One of the girls began to sniffle. "We've only seen the people in this room."

"Echo?" Mrs Brown interrupted. "It's not good manners to cry. The boring man is trying his best."

Stoddart's lips tightened.

"The Fort has replicators that can duplicate plants and animals," he continued. "But it's not fair to keep everyone cooped up for half a decade, so most of the people here have been put in suspended animation tanks, where they won't even age. The Fort is fully automated, and the scientists in this room will join them soon. You'll be going too."

Stoddart warmed to his tale. After all, he had been instrumental in creating the system and wanted someone to boast too. Even if it was only kids.

"I've programmed the computer to re-animate 300 of our adults in five years. Then they'll leave and start building a New Eden for us. They'll tame the wilderness, just like those pioneers of the old west."

He glanced at Mrs Brown again. She gave him a thumbs up.

"Every five years, after that, the computer will reanimate another 300 people. They'll join the existing community and make it stronger and larger. It's a slow process, but there are thousands of them snoozing away. If we released everyone at once, there wouldn't be enough crops to feed them all."

He winked.

"This is a very long-term project but we can't exactly afford to make a mistake, eh? Best to take it slow and steady."

He spread his hands as if expecting applause.

"Never fear. Someday, we'll have the country up and running again."

"Question." Another hand was raised.

"And you are?"

"Mrs Brown calls me Alpha." The boy folded his arms. "Are you sure the animation tanks will work properly? You said a lot of the technology was still experimental and I doubt those have been used before."

Stoddart was taken aback. This one was clever.

"We've done tests and being woken from suspended animation causes memory loss." The head technician rubbed his chin. "So... eh..."

"So, we might not remember anything, ever?" A red-headed girl interrupted. "Is that it?"

"God, she's smart as well," Stoddart whispered to Mrs Brown

"Got it in one, Juliet," the woman replied caustically.

"I mean, none of us will forget things we've been taught or come naturally," Stoddart reassured them. "Like how to speak and read books."

"Hah!" Uniform declared proudly. "I can't read too well as it is."

"But Juliet is right. The memory loss might be fairly severe." The head technician brightened. "However, the right sound and visual triggers will bring total recall to everyone, and the computer will put those into effect when we wake."

He gave a reassuring smile.

"There's absolutely nothing to worry about."

"Thank you, Harvey. That was very illuminating." Mrs Brown got to her feet. "For me, at least."

"The name is Dr Stoddart."

Mrs Brown ignored him.

"Mike?" One of the boys had his back to the others. "What's so important you couldn't take two minutes to listen to this gentleman's rambling lecture?"

"There's a red light blinking on the screen." The boy pointed. "It wasn't there a few seconds ago."

The color drained from Stoddart's face.

"That's impossible," he gasped. "It can't be!"

Chairs were knocked over as the white-coated men sprinted to their positions, frantically pushing buttons.

"Fill me in, Harvey!" Mrs Brown gathered the frightened children to her side. "Right now."

"Someone is hacking our system!" Stoddart's fingers were a blur on the keyboard in front of him. "They've released samples of Le Mans bug into the suspended animation tanks." His voice rose an octave. "And the Fort's life support system!"

Sirens began to go off and the teens looked around in terror.

"Can we vent it?" Sweat broke out on Stoddart's brow. "Force it back out?"

"We're too late!" a scientist yelled. "In a few moments our air supply will be contaminated."

"Break out the oxygen masks!" The security chief darted for a closet and began pulling breathing apparatus onto the floor.

"Give masks to the kids as well," Mrs Brown commanded over the hubbub.

"Sorry! There's only enough for us."

Echo began to sob again. The woman put a protective arm around her shoulder.

"In that case, give them your *masks."* She unholstered her weapon. *"I'm sworn to protect these children."*

"Don't you understand?" A brawny man with a black beard brushed past her. *"We need the oxygen. We have to get the situation under control."*

"Can you contain this?" Mrs Brown fixed Stoddart with a piercing stare. *"I want the truth."*

The technician looked at Echo, crying into her protector's jacket.

"No." He shook his head miserably. *"It's too late."*

"Then give your masks to the kids. And one for me, til I figure something out."

"Sit back down and shut up, lady." The security chief spun round to his companions. *"All you men, put on your breathing apparatus."*

Mrs Brown raised her weapon and shot him in the back of the head. There was a stunned silence as he slumped to the ground.

"Sorry, children," The woman apologized. *"Wish you hadn't seen that."*

She motioned with the pistol for the scientists to step away.

"Harvey? Get breathing apparatus on the young 'uns. Alpha? Be so good as to assist him."

The child ran over and began to help.

"Keep a mask for yourself, technician." Mrs Brown instructed. *"We'll need you."*

"For what?" Stoddart couldn't take his eyes off the blood, slowly spreading across the tiles. "This is Game Over."

"What's the furthest part of the Fort you can seal off? One with no people? I saw airlocks everywhere."

"Thought you didn't understand technology?" the man rasped.

"I pick things up fast."

"The agriculture section on the lowest level. We follow the green line on the floor to get there." Stoddart pulled a mask over Mike's face. "It has a skeleton staff but they'll have headed for the safety bunkers soon as the sirens went off."

The technician's face hardened.

"It won't do them any good. All those people in one place. Infected air..." His voice trailed away.

"Children." Mrs Brown opened the control center door. "Get ready to run like you never ran before."

"Wait!" Stoddart turned to the bearded scientist. "We have banks of WC-57 in storage. Release them into the suspended animation tanks. It might give the occupants a fighting chance."

"It's no antidote and it still has massive flaws!" the man protested. "You saw what it did to the dogs we tested."

"Hardly matters now, does it? Use it all. They're dead otherwise."

The sirens continued to wail.

"What about us?" the bearded scientist pleaded. "You can't leave everyone to die."

"You had samples of the Le Mans Virus here, huh?" Mrs Brown glared at the scientists.

"Of course! We were trying to find a cure."

"Really?" The woman leveled her weapon at Stoddart. "You build these Forts and fill them with the rich and privileged. Soon as you do, a man-made plague comes along and kills everyone else."

"It's just a coincidence," the bearded man cried.

"Was it a coincidence you happened to have suspended animation tanks for the occupants to ride it out?"

Stoddart hung his head.

"This infection is global, so it sure as hell wasn't released by some terrorist." Mrs Brown pushed her charges and the head technician into the corridor, weapon trained on the scientists.

"These children deserve a chance. You people don't."

With a disdainful scowl, she backed out of the door, Then they ran.

The sirens continued their deafening howl. The teens and Mrs Brown sprinted through the Fort, Stoddart stumbling behind. The oxygen tanks were too big for the thirteen-year-olds. They bashed against the backs of their legs and they had to hold the masks over their faces with one hand to stop them slipping off. Echo fell and was pulled to her feet by Uniform, who held on to her arm and yanked the smaller girl forcefully along.

Eventually, they reached the Agricultural Section and collapsed on the floor of its anti-chamber. Stoddart sat down at a console, pulled off his mask, and began tapping keys. The airlock slid closed with a whoosh.

"I think we got here in time," he panted. "I'm isolating this section and rerouting circuits, so it's a self-contained unit. We won't be attached to the main computer, so this area can't be hacked. Hopefully."

"Harvey." Mrs Brown pointed. "We're about to have company."

Above his head was a monitor. People streamed down corridors, elbowing each other out of the way, screaming and crying.

"News travels fast." The man peered at the stampede through his fingers. "Everyone not in suspended animation is heading this way."

The man winced as several people fell and were trampled underfoot.

"Can we keep them out?" Mrs Brown asked pointedly.

"Airlocks open automatically when you approach them. We can retreat into the main hall and lock the antechamber door but they'll break through by sheer weight of numbers."

"If we can see them," Alpha said. "Surely they can see us?"

Mrs Brown stared at him.

"Remember the old nursery rhyme I taught you?" the woman whispered. "About a plague from long ago. I showed you how children used to act it out?"

They nodded tearfully.

"Do it now. Your lives depend on it. Follow their lead, Harvey."

She turned her back to the monitor and began to mouth softly.

Ring around the roses
A pocket full of posies.
Ashes A-tishoo!
We all fall down.

The group clutched at their throats, pretending to choke. Then they fell to the ground and lay still.

"I got cramp," Echo hissed.

"Shut up!" Juliet slapped her.

Stoddart and Mrs Brown staggered around theatrically for a few seconds, almost standing on the prone figures. Then, they too, fell over and played dead.

The crowd on the screen surged to a halt, looking at the monitor above the door.

"They have the plague! They must have been infected when they arrived!"

With a wail, they turned and fled back to the safety bunkers. The screen flickered briefly and went black. Stoddart jumped up and got on the console again.

"Well done, kids." Mrs Brown stood up and helped the little group off the floor.

"But we're trapped in here," Stoddart said morosely.

"How long until the plague burns itself out?"

"Nobody knows for sure. I'd venture a couple of years, at least."

"Yeah. The kids really didn't need to hear that." Mrs Brown beckoned to Alpha. "You're the oldest, aren't you?"

"Yes, ma'am. By a whole two months and four days."

"Why don't you take the rest and explore?"

"Can I see the hothouses, Miss?" Sierra asked solemnly. "I'm awful fond of flowers."

"Sure you can, honey." Mrs Brown patted the girl on the head. "As long as you count turnips as flora. And you, Mike? Good call, spotting that red light. You have sharp eyes."

The boy straightened up proudly.

"Off y'all go. Behave, now."

The teens shuffled into the nearest corridor. Echo was still crying, though the others were in too much shock to register emotion. As they closed the door, Juliet stopped and peered at the adults through a small glass panel.

"I wish I knew what they were saying," she remarked to Mike. "I bet they're talking about us."

"I can read lips," the boy volunteered.

"You can?"

"My mom is deaf. Was deaf." His eyes filled with tears. "What's happened to our parents, Juliet? They must have been in the tanks."

"Tell me what Mrs Brown is saying and maybe we'll find out." The girl put a finger to her lips and waved the others away.

"You guys head off and explore. We'll catch up."

Mike stood on his toes, looked through the glass and began to translate.

Mrs Brown and Dr Stoddart were sitting on the floor.

"How do we survive this, Harvey?"

"Didn't figure you for an optimist." The head technician pouted. *"Short answer is, we don't."*

"Why not?"

"The airlocks aren't foolproof. We can't keep the Le Mans bug out for more than a couple of days."

"Get on that console and find a way."

"Yah, mien Fuehrer." But he did as he was told. Mrs Brown watched over his shoulder.

"I'll be damned." Stoddart spun round. *"Come with me."*

Juliet and Mike jumped back as the door opened and the technician marched through. They followed him as he strode down the passageway, Mrs Brown bringing up the rear.

"That's our salvation."

Stoddart led them into a huge chamber. The rest of the children were clustered in a bunch, staring at the spectacle. Round Perspex tanks stretched away as far as the eye could see, all of them empty.

"These are our replicators," the head technician explained. *"Built to provide enough food until we could grow our own outside."*

"What do they replicate?"

"They can clone anything that's cellular-based, like plants from the hothouses. But also those."

Stoddart indicated seven bigger tanks set against one wall. Each held a different animal suspended in clear fluid. Two horses, Two cows, Two pigs. A brace *of chickens. Tango had her face pressed against the glass, making clucking sounds.*

"I guess this is what Noah's ark would have looked like," Mrs Brown snorted. "If Doctor Frankenstein had built it."

"You're missing the point," Stoddart said patiently. "These are suspended animation tanks. What's more, they're on a separate system from the human ones, using filtered air from vents on the surface."

"You mean?"

"If we turf out the animals and use them ourselves, we're saved!"

A grin split his face and the teens gave a small cheer.

"With me, Harvey." Mrs Brown practically pulled Stoddart back the way they had come, shutting the door behind them. Juliet and Mike followed at a distance, then took up positions at the window again.

Stoddart couldn't contain his elation.

"The rest of the Fort is doomed but we can make this area fulfill the same function as the whole complex." The technician punched the air.

"We get in the tanks. We don't age. The computer re-animates us in five years. The Le Mans bug will be gone and we can make our way through the dead area and into New Eden."

He spotted Mrs Brown's crestfallen look.

"What are you so po-faced about? A few minutes ago, it was End Times for all of us."

"On old woman, a lab rat and seven kids with no memory." Mrs Brown snorted. *"How are we gonna survive in a wilderness?"*

"You're not old."

"I'm sixty-two."

"Woah! That is getting on."

Mrs Brown grimly tapped her gun.

"Though I have to say, you don't look your age."

"Got that right."

"Anyhow, we have time on our side." Stoddart slid down next to the woman again. *"There won't be any animals left but there are plenty of vegetables to eat and seeds to plant. With the proper triggers, the kids will get their memory back - though it might be best if they don't remember* this *part of their lives."*

"Wouldn't mind forgetting it myself."

"We don't have to go out right away. We could re-animate them in three years and then take another couple to teach them proper survival skills."

He looked down at his pot belly.

"Well, you *probably could."*

"Trained or not, they'll still just be seven kids." Mrs Brown pursed her lips. *"The original plan for the Fort was to release 300 adults, with livestock to boot."*

She closed her eyes.

"They wouldn't stand a chance."

"There might be another solution," Stoddart said. "But I suspect you won't like it."

"I aint exactly over the moon about our present situation."

"The computer is programmed to extract DNA from the animals and clone them in the replicators."

"Are you suggesting we do it to the kids instead?"

"I don't like it any more than you," Stoddart shot back. "But we're talking about the survival of the human race."

Mrs Brown was a practical woman, so she nodded tersely.

"Go on."

"We clone your group," Stoddart said cautiously. "Make more of them. 300 if you wanted. Yes. We could follow the original agenda and make 300 clones. Train them up and lead them into New Eden."

"I sense a catch."

"There are two, actually." Stoddart ran a hand through his unruly locks. "Replicators can reproduce living tissue, but it's degenerative. Put simply, you can't duplicate a clone."

"Explain."

"The original kids would have to stay in suspended animation until their clones got New Eden up and running properly. That could take a few generations."

"Better than getting eaten by wild animals or starving to death." Mrs Brown said acerbically. "What's the other problem?"

"*You probably noticed there are only seven suspended animation tanks but nine of us. Two people would have to stay outside.*"

"*And die when the plague finally gets past the air-lock.*"

"*In a nutshell.*"

"*No problem. There's one girl I don't like and a spoiled madam who cries and complains all the time. I reckon she wouldn't be too much use outside.*" Mrs Brown slapped Stoddart on the leg. "*Get working on it.*"

"*Who is she talking about?*" Mike stepped down from the window. "*Which of us are gonna die?*"

"*It's not too hard to guess,*" Juliet replied angrily.

"*I believe she means Echo and me.*"

-8-

A few hours later, Mrs Brown gathered everyone together. Stoddart had emptied the suspended animation tanks and incinerated the animals, removing a horse's leg before he did so.

"You might be able to carve weapons from the bones," he explained. "They're cellular material, so you can replicate them. "

The teens were grimy and tear-stained, except for Juliet. She had washed her face and carefully combed her long, red hair. Mike couldn't stop looking at her. Even at thirteen, he could see she was almost as pretty as Echo.

"You're about to go into suspended animation, kids." Mrs Brown said nonchalantly. "When y'all come out in Three years, you'll be the same age as you went in."

"With no memories," Alpha said bitterly.

"You can't have all that many at your age," Mrs Brown scolded. "You'd rather hang around here and die of plague?"

"No, ma'am."

"Question, Mrs Brown." Juliet put up her hand. "There are only seven animation tanks."

Stoddart suddenly busied himself inspecting one.

"Who's getting left behind?"

"Always the perceptive one, huh?" Mrs Brown smoothed down her skirt. "I'm afraid you and I are staying, kid."

The girl's lip trembled but she remained silent.

"What do you mean, you're *staying?" Stoddart spluttered.*

"You really think I'd take a child's place?" the woman said reproachfully. "That would never sit right with me, technician. You'll have to teach em yourself. Please impress on them the value of good manners and personal hygiene."

Juliet stared up at the adults with wide green eyes.

"Aw, Jeez." The technician patted her head. "Get in the tank, girl. Before you bust a gut trying to look cute."

"Thank you, Mr Harvey, Sir," Juliet replied gratefully.

Mrs Brown ran a hand down her face.

"I can program the agricultural section's systems to do everything automatically, just like the main complex would." Stoddart's shoulders drooped. "Was just too chicken to admit it cause I didn't wanna expire yet."

"A couple of weeks with these horrors would soon change your mind."

Once the teens were inside the cubicles, Stoddart sealed them and switched on life support. As clear fluid rose around him, Mike watched the adult's lips through the glass, fighting to stay conscious as long as possible.

"What now, Technician?"

"Once the rest of the Fort has... expired, I'm gonna put on an oxygen mask and go back to the main section."

"What for?"

"I'm pretty sure you were right, back in the control center," the technician said quietly. "Willard Chain claimed he wanted a safe haven while he worked on his serum to make people hardier and stronger."

"You reckon it was a fib, huh?"

"WC-57 had... problems. I presume he decided on a more radical solution."

"The Le Mans bug?"

"Yeah. Instead of altering the existing population, why not just destroy it and start again, using only the smartest and best?"

"The irony is, we managed to finally perfect the serum, only a few days ago." Stoddart shook his head miserably. "There are a few vials of it in the command center safe."

"Then I'd sure like to meet this Willard Chain." Mrs Brown cracked her knuckles.

"He was at a conference of top scientists in Berlin on Tuesday. Then, they flew back to their respective *countries, taking the plague with them. Chain must have been the original carrier."*

Stoddart laughed harshly.

"At least he had the guts to die for his own beliefs."

"And what went wrong here?"

"I honestly don't see who could have had the resources or know-how to sabotage us. But it happened, so I'm going to go to the main control center and try to raise the other Forts."

Stoddart continued sorting through the tanks.

"If I can't, I'll head outside." His eyes misted. "I'll grab the perfected samples of WC-57 and see if I can drive to Fort Carolina with them. I doubt I'll survive but I get to see green grass one last time."

He sniffed loudly and fastened the top button of his collar.

"Is my tie straight?"

"You look fine."

"Don't want to meet my maker all scruffy. Though that's the least of my problems, considering what we've done here." He took a deep breath. "You wanna come with?"

"I'll stay with my children as long as I'm alive." Mrs Brown looked skeptical. "Can the computer in this section really handle all you'll set it to do?"

Stoddart stroked his chin, staring at her.

"What?"

"The people who paid to be in the Forts had more money than Midas, so it's equipped with technology that would boggle your mind."

He gave a thin smile.

"Including a human/computer interface."

"What's that, when it's at home?"

"Another of Chain's many inventions. The man was a genius."

"I presume you mean evil genius. But go on."

"I scan your brain patterns and incorporate them into the computer's processors. It was supposed to me running the whole show, but you put paid to that."

"My heart bleeds."

"It doesn't matter." Stoddart waved his hand dismissively. *"The main computer will carry out its functions anyway, not that there's anything left for it to do. I can't imagine the people in the tanks are still alive."*

He tapped his long nose.

"But the agriculture section is now completely self-reliant. If I scan you, you'd run it."

"What? Are you saying I'll become *the computer?"*

"You'll physically die when the Le Mans bug gets in," Stoddart replied brusquely. *"But, yes. You'll basically be the computer and it will kinda... eh... adopt your personality."*

"I don't have much of one, in case you hadn't noticed."

"Then the two of you are a match made in heaven," the technician said snidely. *"Point is, your simulation can teach each generation of replicants survival skills before it sends them to New Eden. In a more... human manner."*

"Couldn't I take over the whole complex if I'm the computer?"

"How many times do I have to tell you? The agriculture section is now completely separate from the rest of the Fort."

"Fifty should do it. Like I say, I'm old fashioned."

"It's not ideal." The man looked defeated. *"I mean, I wish there was a way for you and me to survive..."*

His voice trailed off.

"You did your best." Mrs Brown winked at him. *"I guess you're not such a bad guy, Harvey. If I was ten years younger..."*

"Maybe twenty years," the technician grinned feebly.

"Back in the day?" Mrs Brown patted her hair. *"I'd be too much for you to handle."*

"You still are." Stoddart chuckled. *"C'mon. I'll hook you up to the system."*

"I'm called Eve, by the way." Mrs Brown held out her hand. *"Evelyn Brown."*

"Nice name." The technician shook it. *"Better than Harvey. Makes me sound like a pet rabbit."*

"Question." The woman held on. *"I'm happy to replicate six of the children. But not Juliet. She stays in*

the tank forever, unless there's a dire emergency. Is that possible?"

"If it's what you decide." He squinted at her. "You really don't like that kid, huh?"

"I assure you, I'm not that narrow-minded," Mrs Brown replied heatedly. "But I know things you don't. I want the new human race to be better than the old one."

She tapped the glass of Juliet's tank.

"This girl can never be part of it."

Graduation

You can design and create and build the most wonderful place in the world. But it takes people to make the dream a reality.

Walt Disney

-9-

Mike slunk back into the bathroom.

"You throw up again?" Juliet asked when he finally emerged.

"No. I wanted time alone to think."

"What've you thunk?"

"I been hit by a bombshell, no denying." Mike 3 plonked himself on the bed. "But I don't see it changes anything."

"Doesn't change anything?" The girl was incredulous. "Aren't you mad at finding out you're a replicant?"

"I prefer the word Type. And we already *know* we weren't made the old way. That's why we all look the same." He patted his chest. "But I got thoughts and feelings... even memories now. I'm as human as the original Mike."

"Who's still stuck in suspended animation."

"What he doesn't know won't hurt him," the boy objected. "Harvey told Mrs Brown it would take a few generations to get a settlement up and running properly. Eventually, somebody from New Eden will report back and she can let him out."

"Exactly how many generations do you think have gone there?"

"I dunno. Two or Three?"

Juliet gave a thin smile.

"Mike, Mrs Brown has been sending Types through the airlock for almost 200 years. Nobody has *ever* come back."

The boy's eyes widened. But he had been taught to be pragmatic. In fact, it had been drummed into him.

"Maybe it's tougher out there than she thought."

"Maybe they're not reaching their destination."

"We'll all find out tomorrow," Mike said defiantly. "I don't see what else we can do. I'm certainly not getting left behind because you got a hunch."

He tapped the screen indignantly.

"Where do you fit into all this, anyhow? How are you able to hack into Mrs Brown's systems? She said you were never to be replicated, so why have you turned up now?"

"I still have no idea why she wouldn't replicate me," Juliet said sadly. "Why on earth did she detest me so much?"

"I honestly don't know her reasoning."

"Neither do I. It was a topic she absolutely refused to discuss."

Mike suddenly felt sorry for the girl. He'd always found it frustrating, stuck conversing with people who thought exactly as he did. He never considered being an individual might be worse.

"I reckon she changed her mind, if you're around now." He tried to sound reassuring. "Do you know why?"

"I do. Though, I'd prefer to tell you face to face." Juliet clasped her hands together. "Why don't you meet me by the airlock in ten minutes?"

"Huh?" Mike was taken aback. "Why would I go there, of all places?"

"I found the code that lets us into the antechamber where the airlock is located. We can enter the rest of the Fort together, undetected, and see precisely what's going on. We might even be able to look outside!"

"Are you completely nuts?" The boy almost fell over. "That's... that's... just not right!"

"I'll tell you what's not right. 200 years passing with no word from New Eden." Juliet tilted her head. "What's the problem? We go into the main section and look around. If everything is fine, we come straight back and nobody will ever know. If things are not what they seem, we can warn Mrs Brown and the Types."

Her fingers were laced together so tightly the knuckles shone white.

"You'll be a hero and Mrs Brown might not hate me anymore."

"I... *can't*."

"Then I'll go myself, though I've no training in weapons or hunting." The girl stuck out her chin. "If I don't come back, be sure and tell Mrs Brown I died trying to save the children she *really* cared about."

Mike remembered how much he liked Juliet. He hadn't known her long but she was still the funniest and most intelligent person he had ever met.

If he went with her, she ought to favor him over the others when they reached New Eden. After all, Mrs Brown said children there would have to be made the old way. Juliet might even become his partner. Which, he had to admit, gave him a nice feeling.

But none of that mattered, really, if he was honest with himself.

This defenseless girl was willing to sacrifice herself for people who didn't even know she existed. If he was too lily-livered to help, how would he fare against a bear or a mountain lion?

This was his test.

"All right. I'll see you in ten minutes." He fastened the knife to his belt. "If there are any vegetables where you are, smear them on your skin."

"Thank you, Mike!" The girl unclasped her hands gratefully. "Eh… Why am I to do that?"

"So you don't smell like prey if we do get outside." Mike tucked the knife into the sheath by his side.

"Not carrots, though. I *hate* carrots."

-10-

The girl was waiting by the anti-chamber airlock. They stood facing each other for a few seconds, uncertain how to act. In real life, Juliet was even better looking than on screen, though she still seemed completely alien to someone who had grown up knowing six sets of features. It made her exciting. Exotic.

She stepped forwards and put her arms gingerly around the boy, kissing his cheek. He hugged her awkwardly, ready to leap away. Mrs Brown strongly discouraged physical contact between different Types.

"Your hair's going up my nose," he complained. "And you smell funny."

"I took your advice." Juliet stepped back, pulling a clove of garlic from her pocket. "This is pretty strong."

"Indeed it is." The boy wrinkled his nose. "It'll sure keep us safe if we run into vampires."

"Very droll. We'll talk properly once we go through and start walking." Juliet turned to a console on the wall and tapped a few buttons. "Or running, depending on what's waiting for us."

"That does *not* fill me with confidence."

With a click, the anti-chamber door opened and they stepped into a room lined with blank screens.

"Here goes nothing."

They approached the airlock and it slowly slid open. They stepped through and it softly closed again.

Mike took in his surroundings.

It was a corridor, identical to any in the Division of Youth. But the only illumination came from red emergency lights set in the ceiling. Shadows hunched in corners and spread out of alcoves like sinister black wings.

"Where are we going?" Mike whispered. He was sure there wasn't any reason to stay quiet, but he'd been taught not to take unnecessary risks.

"Glad you're being cautious." Juliet pointed to another door. "The blast doors are this way."

"You know where they are?" The boy raised an eyebrow. "How?"

"The green line on the floor, remember?" Juliet took Mike's hand and the boy felt an unexpected thrill at her touch. "C'mon."

After a hundred yards, Mike suddenly stopped.

"Wait." A shiver ran up his spine. "Are you sure we can get back? After all, this section is run by the main computer."

"So what? There are sensors set into the walls that will automatically open the airlock again." Juliet grinned. "The blast doors to the outside work on the same principle. We should be able to stroll right out."

"I'd feel better if they had handles."

Still, it was too late now. Mike allowed the girl to lead him further into the labyrinth. They crept through the gloomy passageways, the air musty and stale, irritating their throats.

"This place is truly creepy but I'm not seeing anything hazardous."

"Don't sound so sorry about it."

"If you don't think it's too impertinent a question, why did Mrs Brown revive you after all this time?" The boy asked. "Seeing how she disliked you so much."

"The Fort wasn't designed to last 200 years without maintenance, and the equipment is breaking down." Juliet nodded to the emergency lights, some of which had already gone dark. "My mom was a computer whiz and I guess I picked up her talent. I was the only person in the Division of Youth with a chance of patching up Mrs Brown's circuits. That's why she reanimated and coached me."

"I thought she didn't understand technology?"

"Mike. She *is* a computer."

"Still, you were thirteen when you got put in suspended animation." The boy turned a corner and another corridor stretched in front of them. "No offense, but how much help could you be?"

"Like you, I needed training, but I'm a natural. Mrs Brown had nobody else to turn to, but she made sure I was locked away from the other kids. I live in a section that never gets used. Been on my own for two years."

"Jeez!" Mike stared at her. "Hope you had a hobby."

"You could say that." The girl smiled slyly. "I've learned a lot, repairing Mrs Brown. Enough to be able to hack into her systems undetected. Open locks. Find out things I wasn't supposed to. That's how I got *my* memory back."

"But two *years*? I would have gone crazy."

"I don't care for people. Prefer my own company." Juliet shrugged. "I still don't understand why I wasn't cloned like the rest of the Types, though. I know Mrs Brown didn't like me but she refused to discuss it."

They reached the end of the passage.

"There's no evidence of anything amiss. The place is empty." Mike shivered. "Though, I wouldn't like to see the safety bunkers."

"I thought, if I found proof of my suspicions, Mrs Brown would be grateful." Juliet pushed open the next door. "Finally let me mix with the other kids. It looks like I was wrong. There's obviously no danger."

"Juliet." Mike reached out and turned her head. "Is this the main food court?"

The girl looked.

"Oh, my."

The gigantic auditorium was filled with tables bathed in the sickly red light.

And, spread across the floor, were hundreds of broken bones.

-11-

"I didn't want to be right." Juliet staggered back. "I hoped I'd be mistaken. I really…"

Mike clamped a hand over her mouth.

"Stay here and keep quiet," he whispered, pulling the knife from his belt. He threaded his way through the piles of white debris to a door on the other side of the hall. Juliet shuffled from foot to foot, glancing apprehensively around.

The boy pulled it open and stuck his head gingerly into the gap. He closed it softly, then made his way back.

"No sign of life," he whispered. "Keep your voice down, just in case."

"These bones used to be Types from the Division of Youth." Juliet hissed. "Check out the weapons."

Bows, knives and swords were scattered everywhere.

"Looks like a battleground."

"Mrs Brown told us that moisture causes decomposition." Mike knelt by a pile of remains. "That's why you store a kill in a dry place. But the air in here *is* dry."

"You're giving me a *science* lesson?"

"It means there should be mummified flesh on those bodies. There isn't and they're in bits."

He picked up a leg bone and ran his finger along it.

"Imbedded with teeth marks." He dropped the shard in revulsion. "Whatever killed these people *ate* them afterwards."

The teenagers sat on two righted chairs, as far away from the carnage as they could get.

"Any idea what happened?" Mike nudged the girl's leg.

"What does it look like?" Juliet was pale. "The Types reverted to cannibalism."

"They might have fancied a snack in the food court on the way to New Eden." The boy replied sarcastically. "But I reckon a cereal bar would have done them till they got outside."

"They couldn't *get* outside."

"Is this another hunch?"

"No. It's on the wall behind you."

Mike slowly turned.

Computer won't let us out.

The message was smeared and faded with age but still legible.

It had been written in blood.

"I'll bet it's because they were clones," Juliet said wearily. "Sorry if you don't like the word."

"But Types are identical to real humans."

"Obviously not to a sophisticated scanning system," the girl replied sourly. "If the main computer didn't recognize them as human, it wouldn't open the blast doors for a replicant any more than it would an ant."

She kicked out miserably at one of the bones.

"Two hundred years and nobody ever got into New Eden. They starved to death in this crappy place."

"You may be right about the computer." Mike was staring ahead. "But you're way off base about the Types."

"It turns my stomach, too, but all the hothouses are in the Division of Youth. There wouldn't have been anything in the rest of the Fort to eat."

"I'm telling you, they didn't do this to each other." Mike pointed up.

The roof of the food court was latticed with girders, each embedded with arrows.

"If they were fighting among themselves, why were they shooting *upwards*?"

"Don't frighten me, Mike."

"You're not the only one who's scared." The boy's face paled. "This is a kill zone."

"I don't know what that means, but it doesn't sound good."

"It's a trick used by predators who hunt in packs. One or two herd their prey into a large, enclosed area, like a canyon. Once they're trapped, the rest attack."

He stared upwards.

"Whatever annihilated the Types was hiding in the rafters." Mike removed his cap to get a better look. "But what kind of creatures could climb like that? Or leap twenty feet to the ground without getting hurt?"

He got up and searched around.

"All the weapons here are ours. These *things* took on 300 Types and beat them using what? Their teeth?"

"You remember what Harvey said?" Juliet snapped her fingers. "In the control center, all those years ago."

"I was a bit preoccupied running for my life."

"Before that."

Mike thought back to the heated argument between Stoddart and his subordinate.

"We have banks of WC-57 in storage. Release it into the suspended animation tanks. It might give the people inside a fighting chance."

"The scientists flooded the suspended animation tanks with Willard Chain's serum," he groaned.

"The Le Mans bug didn't kill them, after all?

"No. But the dose was far too large. It made them immune from a plague targeting humans, all right." The boy paled. "Immune, cause they weren't human anymore."

"It all fits." Juliet thumped her palm. "Every five years, Mrs Brown sends 300 replicated kids out of the

Division of Youth. At the same time, the central computer releases 300 adults from suspended animation, only they've been turned into mutants of some kind. Its scanners don't recognize *either* group as being human." Her voice trailed away. "So, the computer won't let any of them out."

"Instead, they annihilate each other."

"You know what this means? Even if we warn the others, and they actually *believe* us, we'll still be stuck in the agriculture section."

She leaned her head back against the wall and sighed.

"We're never going to see New Eden."

"Maybe we could dig a tunnel," Mike began.

"Through reinforced concrete, up half a mile to the surface?" The girl said bitterly. "With what? Spoons?"

"Could *you* hack into the main computer system?" Hope sparked in the boy's eyes. "Override its defenses and open the blast doors?"

"I'm good, but not that good. It took me two years to get round Mrs Brown's security encryptions."

Mike felt a cold lump forming in the pit of his stomach.

"Juliet?" he said slowly. "If Types have been getting sent here for 200 years, odds are *some* of them would have survived the mutant attacks. Why didn't they retreat back to the Division of Youth?"

"They most likely did." The girl wouldn't look at him. "But the sensors wouldn't let them back through the airlock either. It's made of foot-thick steel, so Mrs Brown wouldn't know they were there, even if they were hammering on the other side."

She gripped the boy's hand.

"Which means we're trapped too."

"No, we're not." Mike pulled her to her feet. "It's Graduation tomorrow and Mrs Brown controls the agriculture section. When she opens the airlock to let the other Types through, we'll be waiting right there to warn them."

They jogged back the way they had come until they reached the doors.

"Make yourself comfortable." Mike sat down with his back against the metal. "It's gonna be a long night."

The airlock opened with a pneumatic whoosh and the boy toppled into the Division of Youth.

"Well, *that* was easy." Juliet stepped over him with a sigh of relief. "But I don't get it."

She tilted her head quizzically.

"If the airlock opened for us, how come no other Types ever made it back?"

-12-

They made their way to Mike's room and sat on the bed until they had stopped shaking.

"We gotta bite the bullet, Juliet," Mike said reluctantly. "You ready?"

"In no way, shape or form."

"Me neither." He stood up and straightened his jacket.

"Mrs Brown?"

Yes, Mike 3? The familiar image of New Eden appeared on the screen. Then it faded to black. **Juliet? What on God's green earth are you doing there?**

The girl looked at the floor.

You were warned never to mix with the Types.

"We've been in the main part of the Fort." Mike stepped in front of his companion. "Everyone you ever sent through is dead."

There was a long pause.

Explain.

They told her everything.

The teenagers waited patiently until the computer spoke again.

My apologies, Juliet. Mrs Brown actually managed to sound contrite. **I have to commend you for your actions, even if they were sneaky and underhand. As for the main computer? I was right never to trust technology.**

"What should we do?" Mike asked.

Go to room 40 tomorrow at 7.00 hours. Await my instructions. You too, Juliet. In the meantime, return to your quarters.

"Can't I stay with Mike?" The girl pleaded. "I'm afraid."

You need to pack a bag. Besides, I won't have any hanky-panky in the Division of Youth. You can save that for New Eden.

"New Eden?" The teenagers looked at each other. "We… can't *get* there."

I been around forever and a day. Mrs Brown said calmly. **I have a solution. Just be sure you're in room 40 tomorrow.**

The screen went blank.

When they arrived at their destination next morning, the pair found five other Types already seated at desks. They stood when Mike entered and stared in amazement at Juliet.

"Mike 3, I presume?" A tall, blonde youth with wide shoulders walked over and shook the boy's hand. "I'm Alpha 3. That was some stunt you pulled last night."

The boy couldn't tell if his leader's tone was admiring or reproachful.

"And you must be the infamous Juliet." Alpha 3 bent and kissed the back of her hand.

"My, my." Juliet batted her eyelashes at him. "What a charmer."

"You know about her, Sir?" The boy gasped.

"Mrs Brown had a long talk with me after your escapade. With all of us, in fact."

The others nodded in agreement.

"This is Uniform 3, Echo 3, Tango 3 and Sierra 3." The boy swept his hand in an arc. "Not hard to see a pattern emerging, huh?"

"She told you *all* the situation?"

"Yup. And it's pretty grim." Alpha patted the boy's shoulder. "On the plus side, Mrs Brown has triggered our memories and filled us in. Thanks to you two, we know the score."

"You see anything in the Fort we could use against them mutants?" Uniform barked.

He was a burly teenager with a shaved head. He held up his sword, carefully fashioned from the horse's thighbone.

"Modern weapons, for instance?"

"Nothing we don't already have."

"You should have taken me instead of him," the boy said belligerently to Juliet. "Uniforms are the explorers and *real* fighters."

"Put a muzzle on it, Uniform 3." Alpha snapped his fingers. "Plain speaking is a virtue, but you're capable of starting a fight in an empty room."

"That I am, Sir."

"I think what you done was totally brave, Mike 3," Sierra piped up.

"Wasn't nothing." The boy blushed bright red.

Let's save the recriminations and congratulations for later. Mrs Brown's voice drifted out of a speaker on the far wall. **Everybody sit down again.**

They did as they were told. Echo reached out and touched Juliet's red locks.

"How good would *I* look with hair that length?" she said enviously. "We're ordered to keep ours short."

"An open face is an open book. That's what Mrs Brown tells us." Tango patted her own plain bob. "Sides, I get split ends."

Enough, Mrs Brown commanded. **I'm going to give y'all the low down and I don't want any interruptions until I'm done. Understood?**

"Understood, Ma'am." Alpha waved the others into silence.

As you are now well aware, I have been thwarted in my attempts to start a new human race. So, we have to make the best of the bad hand we been dealt. The good news is that you seven *can* get out to New Eden.

An excited murmuring broke out among the teenagers.

What part of not interrupting did you fail to understand?

"Quiet everyone," Alpha commanded. "Carry on, Mrs Brown."

I didn't make it public knowledge, but yours was the final generation of Types. Nothing in the Fort was built to last two centuries without maintenance, including me. Juliet has been instrumental in keeping me going these last couple of years, but the suspended animation tanks are falling apart and nobody has the skills to repair them.

She paused to let what she was saying sink in.

If I kept the original children inside any longer, they'd die. So, I let them out to join the replicants of this generation.

Mrs Brown tutted.

Replicants. I never did favor that term. You're all human in my eyes. Well, if I had eyes.

It was Juliet who cottoned on first.

"The kids in this room aren't Types, are they?" she spluttered, looking at her companions. "The Threes are the *originals*."

And you're the original Juliet, Mrs Brown said evenly. I couldn't take to you, girl, but I wouldn't let any of my charges die. I swore an oath.

"Why didn't you tell us this before, Ma'am?" Alpha queried.

Don't like favoritism, neither. Y'all would get swell heads if you thought you were different from your peers. But you *are* different, I realize that now. And so does the

main computer in the Fort, otherwise it wouldn't have allowed Mike and Juliet back into the Division of Youth. If you can reach the blast doors, it has no choice but to let you out.

The children grinned at each other.

Then you're on your own, I'm afraid. I wouldn't lay great odds on your chances of surviving the wilderness, but it's better than staying here.

"Question." It was Juliet again. "How do we get past the creatures in the Fort? Won't there be a new generation of *them* getting released?"

I presume so. There were thousands of people in suspended animation.

"We could wait for them to starve to death," Tango volunteered. "I get peckish if I even miss breakfast. Most important meal of the day, you know."

They're changed in a way I have no info on, Mrs Brown countered. **It's possible they might last for months without food. You go tomorrow.**

"I'm willing to fight," Uniform said. "But, if the 300 kids in previous generations got wiped out, I don't rightly fancy our chances."

There's an alternative route through the Fort. The black line rather than the green one. You can sneak through while the creatures are otherwise occupied.

"Otherwise occupied?" Mike bit his lip. "What exactly would be occupying them?"

"No!" Sierra jumped up, knocking over her chair. "You're still sending the other Types through the air-lock. You ain't gonna tell them about the mutants!"

As you proved, they'll never see New Eden, and there's nothing I can do about that. Mrs Brown's voice was dispassionate. **There are other Forts, true, but I've no idea if they still exist. For all I know, you're the only hope the race has.**

"That's inhuman," the girl snarled.

So are the Types, apparently.

"We have to warn them!" Mike ran to the door and pulled the handle.

It was locked.

"I can't agree to this, Mrs Brown." Alpha came to help him, Uniform right behind. They couldn't budge it.

You'll be in charge if you make it outside, Alpha. But this decision isn't your call to make.

"Can you override her?" Mike turned to Juliet in desperation.

"I can sure as hell try."

She got on the wall console and began quickly typing in numbers.

I'm ready for her this time. Mrs Brown said. **She won't pull the same stunt twice.**

"Think so, you old cow?" The girl's brow furrowed in concentration. "You should have taken the chance to know me better."

The lock clicked open. Then it closed again.

Quit it, Juliet.

Juliet kept typing.

There was another click.

"Now!" She shouted. "Go now!"

Mike and Uniform slid the door open a few inches and squeezed through. It whooshed shut and locked again.

The boys pounded on the surface.

"Not budging." Mike pulled Uniform away. "It's up to us to warn the other Types. They'll have gathered in the hall."

"Affirmative." Uniform sprinted off down the corridor. "Keep up, hunter."

"No problem." Mike raced after him.

"I've had plenty practice running recently."

-13-

The Exodus had already begun. Types were lined round the hall, wearing backpacks and chattering animatedly to each other. They paid no attention as the pair stumbled in.

"One Alpha has already gone," Mike cursed. "He's leading the others."

"That's the protocol. One Alpha to lead the way, another in the middle and the last bringing up the rear." Uniform pointed to a blonde youth pacing up and down. "He's looking pretty confused that one of his own is missing."

"How do we play this?" Mike hesitated. "We should have thought of a strategy."

The Alpha spotted them and advanced on the pair. He had a two marked on his wrist.

"You're late," he scolded, near to panic. "Have you seen Alpha 3?"

"Sir. He ain't coming." Uniform saluted. "Some of us have discovered that the doors to New Eden can't be opened."

"Don't be dumb. Mrs Brown gave us the all-clear." Alpha dismissed them with a snort. "If you know the whereabouts of Alpha 3, fetch him right now."

"Uniform's right, Sir," Mike joined in. "There's no way outside."

"Morons." Alpha turned and waved for the line to speed up. "I'll deal with you two later."

"This is hopeless!" Mike hissed. "He's never gonna believe us. Maybe we should try another avenue."

"Sir!" Uniform barked.

"What is it *now*?" The leader whirled round. "Can't you see I'm…"

Uniform punched him square in the jaw and he crumpled into a heap on the floor.

There was an astonished silence.

"Ah." Mike raised an eyebrow. "The subtle approach."

"Everybody listen up!" Uniform marched into the center of the room. "You are to return to your quarters immediately. Graduation is canceled."

Ignore them. Mrs Brown's voice burst from the speakers. **They've got a bad case of nerves, is all.**

"I'm a Uniform. I'm not afraid of anything." The boy glared at his duplicates. "You know that. I'm one of you."

Carry on through the antechamber to the airlock, Mr Brown insisted. The line began to move again.

Uniform 3 pulled out his sword.

"I will *kill* the next Type who leaves this room," he bellowed.

The remaining Uniforms drew their own weapons in unison. Within seconds the boy was surrounded by a ring of bodies.

Don't hurt him. Mrs Brown commanded. **I won't hold with any bloodshed.**

"Uniform 3 is telling the truth!" Mike shouted. "What's more, there are monsters on the other side of the airlock."

The Types ignored him and kept shuffling along.

"I've been there myself!" the boy raised his voice even more. "It's a trap. You'll die if you go through."

Don't listen to him, children. It's perfectly safe.

One boy broke away and ran over to him.

"What are you doing?" he pleaded. "You'll never get to be a hunter, carrying on like this."

It was Mike 32.

"I'm not lying!" Mike 3 grabbed him by the shoulders. "I went through the airlock last night with a girl called Juliet. There are bodies everywhere. Nobody has ever made it to New Eden."

"Stop all this crazy talk." The Type pulled away. "There's no such thing as a Juliet. Just get in line with me. Please!"

"Don't go, Mike 32. I'm *begging* you."

Uniforms. Escort those two out of the hall. If they don't want to go to New Eden, it's their funeral.

"I'll see you on the other side, huh?" Mike 32 punched him awkwardly on the shoulder. "I'm afraid as well but I been waiting for this moment all my life."

A pair of protectors grabbed Mike 3 by the arms while another escorted Mike 32 back to the line. Uniform 3 was being forced backwards to the door, still swinging his sword.

"Mrs Brown is lying!" Mike screamed as he was dragged away. "Can't you wait? What's the harm in staying one more day? Don't you want to LIVE?"

He was flung into the corridor. A few seconds later, Uniform 3 landed on top of him and the door slammed closed.

"Could've gone better." The burly protector scrambled up.

Mike glared at him.

"What did you expect?" the boy retorted. "Uniforms are trained to follow orders without question. *I* never disobeyed before."

"There must be another way to stop this."

"Not unless you can chew through the wall."

"They're my *friends*."

"Mine too." Uniform pulled the boy to his feet. "And they're about to die so we can make it to New Eden."

He dusted himself down.

"So, we're *gonna* make it." He picked up his sword and slammed the weapon into its scabbard. "I'm the last of the protectors and, if any mutant gets in my way, I will mess that sucker up."

He turned and stormed off down the corridor.

When they reached room 40, the door slid open. The Threes gathered around them expectantly.

"We couldn't stop it." Mike sank into a chair. "The Types have gone into the main complex."

I'll wait an hour, then unlock the door of the antechamber. Mrs Brown broke in. **When I do, it's your turn to go through the airlock. By that time, the Types and the mutants will be fighting and you can circumvent them. Got that?**

The children sat sullenly, refusing to answer.

You hate me. I understand. If I was human, I'd hate myself.

Silence.

This is the only viable option if you want to survive. The Types have been told to take the direct route – the green line. You take the black line. It's longer but ends up at the blast doors as well.

"What makes you think we would stand a better chance?" Juliet said finally. "Won't the monsters check both ways?"

I honestly don't know. Depends on how clever they are.

"Let's scrape together every spare weapon we can find," Uniform said. "Mike isn't as good as me..."

"Yes, I am."

"But he knows how to use a bow and knife," The boy ignored the interruption. "The rest of you will have to bunch behind us and hope for the best. You agree, Sir?"

"I do." Alpha nodded.

By all means, take your weapons. You'll need them outside, where there's no technology. But I imagine you could use something more potent in case you run into the enemy.

"An army of 300 Types would have been just the ticket," Juliet said bitterly. "If you hadn't already sent them to be slaughtered."

Don't be churlish. Without that diversion, I imagine every corridor would be crawling with mutants. The alternative route goes past an armory and that may just tip the scales in your favor.

"An armory?"

It's got guns. I'm sure you remember them from the movies.

"Why didn't you tell the Types that?" Sierra raged.

Because *you'll* need them. I'm assuming the creatures don't use weapons, after listening to what Mike said. You'll have to hope the armory is untouched.

"At least we can kick some real butt," Uniform said. "Once I work out which end of a gun to point."

He looked around at his companions' shocked faces.

"What? I only been trained to use a sword and spear. I'll learn."

"On your feet, everyone." Alpha beckoned to the others. "This isn't how we wanted things to be, but it is what it is."

He faced the screen.

"Goodbye, Mrs Brown. I wish I could say it's been a pleasure knowing you. Turns out it wasn't."

On y'all go. Times a wasting. Mrs Brown's voice was impassive. **Mike? You stay behind for a moment.**

The others gawped at him.

"Follow me, people." Alpha ushered them out. "We can grab our packs on the way. Mike 3? Catch up as soon as you can."

"I'm just Mike now, Sir."

"Of course. Guess I'll have to get used to not having a number myself."

Alpha left without a backward glance.

Sit down, boy.

Mike did so.

I asked you to stay behind because you seem like a decent and moral type.

"Ma'am, I'm not a Type."

Figure of speech. You seem like a decent and moral *sort*.

"Thanks. I can't say the same about you."

Touché. Mrs Brown bristled. **Do you remember the advice I've always given?**

"Of course." It had been drummed into the boy for years. "Civilization is built on good manners and consideration for others." He laughed cynically. "Oh. And always follow orders."

Turns out, I've changed my mind about that last bit.

"Preaching to the converted, Ma'am." Mike returned to his chair. "What did you want me to stay behind for?"

Delaying the inevitable, I guess. Once you are gone, I'll be by myself for the first time in two centuries.

"Am I supposed to care?"

It's strange. I find I don't want to be alone.

"You can't rightly complain after the ordeal you put Juliet through for two long years." The boy shot back. "Besides, you're a computer. You don't have feelings."

True. But neither does Juliet.

"Why do you hate that girl so?" Mike threw up his hands. "She risked her life to try and save the Types."

People like her are risk-takers, agreed. But it's purely for their own benefit, regardless of the consequences to anyone else. Juliet wanted out. And she won't let anyone stand in the way of what she wants.

"And this observation is based on what, exactly?"

Do you know who her father was?

"She never mentioned him."

His name was Willard Chain. The man who designed the Le Mans bug.

Mike swallowed hard.

According to Harvey Stoddart, it was Chain who wiped out the human race. Juliet's father was more of a monster than the creatures waiting for you.

"All right, her dad was a mass murderer," the boy admitted. "It's not her fault. She was *thirteen* when it happened."

He got to his feet and made for the door.

"Please let me out."

There's more to it than that, Mrs Brown said softly. All the kids had to take a barrage of tests before they were considered for entry to the Fort. Juliet failed one spectacularly. If her father hadn't been so important, she would never have been allowed in.

"How could she fail?" Mike stopped. "She's smart as a whip."

This was a psychological test, measuring empathy. Juliet has none.

"I don't believe you."

I read her evaluation myself. She's clever, funny and likable, no denying it. She can laugh, make jokes and cry. But it's all an act.

"Stop it."

Juliet has no feelings or morals of any kind. That's why I kept her in suspended animation for so long. I didn't want a girl like that getting into New Eden.

"I'm not listening."

Deep down, she's more like me that I care to admit, Mrs Brown insisted. And you just saw what kind of actions *I'm* capable of.

She gave an almost human sigh.

Mike. Juliet is a psychopath.

The Main Complex

Mounting evidence shows that small modifications in when and where genes are switched on are all that's necessary to trigger dramatic shifts in anatomy. These changes can lead to the appearance of beaks, turtle shells and jaws.

Sujata Gupta. *New Scientist Magazine*

-15-

Mike caught up with the others at the open airlock. They looked at him quizzically.

"Saying my goodbyes," he said simply.

"And the crowbar in your hand?"

"You'll see."

Nobody had a comment to add. An era was over and that was that. Their focus was on surviving what lay ahead.

"Juliet, Sierra, Echo and Tango? Stay in the middle. Uniform and I will lead." Alpha handed Mike an extra backpack. "You cover the rear, hunter."

"Will do." The boy pushed his crowbar into the track under one side of the airlock, preventing it from fully closing.

"Just in case any clones make it back from the carnage," he explained.

"Very astute," Alpha nodded his approval.

"Here's the black line." Uniform stamped his foot. "Move fast and keep your eyes and ears open."

They jogged silently through several sets of corridors until Alpha raised a hand.

"We've arrived."

They stood outside a room with **ARMORY** written on it. The lock looked like it had been chewed apart.

"Mutants have obviously been here at one time." Alpha cautiously swung the door open. "Let's see if they left anything."

"Guess those creatures really *don't* need weapons." Uniform gave a low whistle. "Or can't remember how to use them."

One wall contained handguns, already in holsters. The others were lined with rifles and semi-automatics. Juliet took one down and studied it.

"Seems simple enough. You pull the trigger to fire." She picked up an ammo clip. "I guess this bit goes in here and you replace it with another when it runs out of bullets."

"Found instructions, too." Tango had a semi-automatic in one hand and a manual in the other. "Apparently, each gun has a safety catch that won't let you fire when it's on. How thoughtful."

"Just as well," Uniform snorted. "You're pointing the barrel at your face."

"The handguns are different," Alpha hefted one in his hand, feeling the weight. "I remember my dad getting all excited about their revolutionary design. He even let me try one."

"Nothing like liberal parenting," Mike grunted. "They look like the revolvers cowboys carried in old westerns."

"They work on the same principle, only they don't use ammo," Alpha explained. "When you cock the hammer, the chamber captures air and compresses it into a tiny missile.

He demonstrated.

"Pull the trigger or fan the hammer with your other hand. Like this."

There was a soft whoosh and a hole appeared in the armory wall. Alpha grinned at his companions' astonished expressions.

"Internal pressure forces the ball of air out of the barrel."

He spun the weapon around one finger.

"It's quiet, accurate and never runs out of bullets."

"That is *so* cool." Uniform took down a holster and strapped it on. "How come the bigger guns don't operate the same way?"

"Pressure guns don't have the range of a rifle and automatic weapons fire too quickly." Alpha fastened a holster round his waist and slid the revolver into it. "But it's lethal in close quarters, just like a normal pistol."

"All these guns are two centuries old," Echo said doubtfully. "How do we know they'll still work?"

"They're built to last, like almost everything in the Fort, and they've never been used." Juliet scratched the stock with her thumbnail. "Treated plastic, rather than wood and metal. Won't rust or rot." She gave a sardonic laugh. "Only complex stuff, like replicators and computer circuits are breaking down."

"Everyone take a handgun as well as something bigger," Alpha commanded. "They'll be a godsend if we make it outside."

"So will this." Mike took a rifle with a telescopic sight from its rack and sighted down the barrel. "Beats a bow and arrow for hunting any day."

He whistled softly.

"This bad boy is most definitely coming with me."

Alpha waited impatiently until the teenagers had familiarized themselves with their chosen weapons.

"Let's go, folks," he urged. "Nobody needs to be Hawkeye. Just point the thing at what you want to kill and jerk your finger."

"Sir? We should find the Types who went ahead and lead them back here." Sierra hung back. "These guns might give them a chance against the enemy."

"That wasn't a suggestion, Sierra. It was an order."

"Begging your pardon. You're in command in New Eden and the Division of Youth." The girl stood her ground. "This is in between. I figure it don't count."

"Know your place, farmer!" Uniform thundered. "You're talking to an Alpha."

"You aint the only Alpha in this hellhole, Sir," Sierra reminded the leader. "You think Alphas 1 and 2 would abandon *you*? I got sisters I grew up with, trapped in the dark somewheres. It pains me to leave them to such a nasty fate."

"Maybe the Types *could* get outside," Mike said. "If they were with us."

"I'm not willing to take that chance," Echo broke in. "I'm going straight to the blast doors, no matter what anyone says."

"Tell us what to do, Sir." Uniform swung his semi-automatic up. "I'll keep everyone in line."

"I declare, this is a peculiar situation for me," Alpha said nervously. "I see both sides of the argument and I have to admit, I'm not happy about either."

He tapped slender fingers together, clearly unsure of what to do. Finally, he took a deep breath.

"I say we vote."

-16-

"*Vote?*" Uniform almost choked. "This is a decision on our survival, not a beauty contest."

"First time for everything, I guess." Alpha looked stonily at the others. "But you all have to abide by the majority decision."

Mike suddenly realized the leader didn't want the responsibility for the fate of the Division of Youth resting solely on his shoulders.

"Once we're outside, I'm in charge again," Alpha continued. "Otherwise, I'll have Uniform knock some sense into you. Understood?"

They nodded.

"All right, Sierra. Say your piece."

"We save our friends."

"Tango?"

"Mrs Brown told us to head straight to the blast doors. We should do what she says."

"Echo?"

"Yes. Head for the blast doors."

"Juliet?"

"I think it's too late to rescue anyone." The girl cocked her weapon. "I'm for pressing on."

"Uniform?"

"Whatever you say, Sir."

"I'm asking your opinion."

"Protectors don't run from a battle," the boy replied unexpectedly. "We help the Types."

Alpha faced Sierra, arms folded.

"I only had two friends, farmer, so we were pretty tight. You're right. I don't suppose they'd leave me to die." He came and stood next to her. "I say we fight."

Everyone turned to Mike. With a cold horror, he understood he held the deciding vote. Now he knew exactly how Alpha felt and it was a horrible sensation.

Once choice meant leaving his friends to die. The other risked ending what little was left of humanity.

The Threes waited expectantly. Mike was of a mind to side with Juliet. If what Mrs Brown had told him about the girl was true, she would be the only one to have based her decision on cold, hard logic.

But he *wasn't* like Juliet.

The boy put his rifle on the floor and spun it. It revolved a few times, then slowed, finally coming to a stop with the barrel pointing at Echo.

"We head for New Eden."

"That ain't a choice," Uniform shot Mike a look of distaste. "It's a cop-out."

"And a smart move." Alpha sounded relieved. "Wish *I'd* thought of it."

They set off again, the leader in front. But his step was less sure. This had been the boy's first big test of leadership. He'd failed to rise to the challenge and he knew it.

Uniform was in a black mood, too.

"I got my eye on you." He punched Mike in the arm as they ran. "Don't be thinking you're some kinda big shot cause you impressed Alpha with a sneaky trick."

"Save your breath, big guy," the boy shot back. "I'm not afraid of you."

"Hold on." Alpha stopped again. There was another door with **DISPENSARY** written on it. This lock had also been torn apart.

"Grab medicines and antibiotics, helper. We'll need them."

"I don't wanna go in there," Echo wailed. "I'm too pretty to die."

"Uniform?"

The protector kicked open the door and shoved the protesting girl inside.

"Sorted, Sir."

"I meant, *escort* her."

"Whatever you say."

"My backpack's too heavy now." Echo emerged a few minutes later, glowering at Uniform. "I'm carrying more drugs than Walgreens."

"Stop whining and press on."

-17-

After a dozen more corridors, the teenagers' breathing had become as ragged as their nerves.

"Aren't we there yet?" Echo wheezed. "I'm hot and sticky and I need to sit down."

"Quiet." Uniform skidded to a halt and crouched. "I heard something up ahead."

He unslung his gun and the others knelt behind him, pointing their weapons into the gloom.

"Rest your rifle on my head, Sierra," Tango suggested. "It'll steady your aim." She wiggled her eyebrows. "I'd make a good general, wouldn't I?"

"We're unarmed and come in peace," Uniform shouted loudly. "Please don't hurt us."

He glanced over one shoulder at his companions.

"Soon as whatever it is gets in range, start shooting."

A figure edged round the corner.

"Huh?" Uniform lowered his rifle. "This guy's no mutant."

He was right. The man looked normal, though he wore some kind of skin-tight, black fabric, similar to a wetsuit. He was holding one shoulder and the teenagers could see blood seeping through his fingers.

"I…" He sank to his knees, wincing in pain. "I'm…"

He tried to rise, swaying alarmingly. Then he toppled over with a groan.

Sierra ran towards him.

"Get back here!" Uniform commanded. "Send Echo instead."

"But he's hurt." The girl crouched by the prone figure and shook him. "What you trying to say, mister?"

The adult opened one malevolent eye.

"HUNGRY!"

He grabbed Sierra and stood in one fluid motion, lifting the girl off her feet.

Echo screamed.

The man's jaws widened, revealing a gaping maw ringed by pointed teeth layered with mucus.

Sierra reacted instinctively, slamming her handgun into the massive mouth. The creature gagged and tried to pull the weapon out, still holding on to the terrified girl with one hand. She kicked out, wriggling furiously.

"Shoot him!" she pleaded.

"You're in the line of fire!"

"Then shoot *me*!"

The monster grabbed her head and squeezed. Sierra's eyes bulged and she shrieked in agony. Mike raised his rifle and aimed, but the struggling girl was still in the way.

The point of a sword burst through the mutant's chest. The creature dropped Sierra and scrabbled at the wound.

"Think *that* hurt?" The farmer reached up and pulled the trigger of her pistol. "Try *this!*"

The gun made a quiet *phut*, muffled by the top of the creature's exploding head. Gray matter splattered across the ceiling and the monster crumpled to the floor and lay still.

Behind it stood Mike 32, still holding a bloody sword.

The Threes crowded around the boy, laughing and hugging him. Mike 3 shook his hand warmly.

"I never expected to find you alive." He grinned from ear to ear. "Didn't think you'd listen to me."

"I thought you were crazy at first," Mike 32 admitted. "But I got suspicious when I noticed an orange hair on your shoulder."

"You calling me a carrot top?" Juliet fumed. "My hair is *flame*-colored."

"Allow me to make introductions," Alpha said. "This is Juliet. How she got here is a long story and we don't have time to recount it."

"Course. But, when I saw that hair, I knew Mrs Brown was keeping *something* from us." Mike 32 stared at the girl. "So, I kept harping on at Alpha 1 and it made everyone jittery." The boy's smile disappeared. "Some of them went into the recreation hall but more hung back. When we heard shouting and screaming, we split up and ran. I been wandering around on my own ever since."

He eyed the weapons enviously.

"Are you going back for the others? Help them fight the monsters?"

"No," Alpha replied bluntly. "We're too heavily outnumbered. Anyhow, we took a vote."

Mike 32 considered this.

"I don't blame you."

"Time's a wasting people, Uniform urged. "We've gotta find the blast doors."

"They're in a big hall, two corridors away." Mike 32 said quietly. "But they won't open."

Echo bit her lip.

"Lead us in the right direction, huh?" Mike turned his twin gently round. "Let's have another go."

The boy led them the last hundred yards until they came to a door with a flickering sign above.

"That's an awful small word to convey so much," Sierra remarked.

Exit.

-18-

The blast doors were huge. Two blocks of dull gray metal, the width of several men, and twenty feet high.

"There are the sensors." Juliet pointed to a gold strip above them. "The doors should open automatically when we pass them."

"What if they still don't work?" Echo bit a knuckle.

"I'm sure they will." Tango propped her gun against the wall and marched towards the formidable barrier. "After all, today is my birthday and I made a wish."

"Well, that's jinxed us for sure," Juliet muttered.

The Threes held their breath. Tango spread her arms.

"Open Sesame!"

The blast doors stayed firmly shut.

"All this sacrifice for nothing." Sierra's shoulders sagged. "What a damned shame."

"They're probably just a bit rusty. I'll be more polite." Tango took a step forward. "Open Sesame. *Please*."

Nothing.

The teenagers joined her, placed their hands against the cold metal and pushed, to no effect.

"Could we shoot our way through?" Echo wondered out loud.

"They're called blast doors for a reason." Uniform slumped on the floor. "Our guns won't even dent it. They'd just alert the mutants to our location."

"Could we hit the sensors?"

"Then it will never open, genius."

"Do we retreat to the Division of Youth?" Mike asked.

"The only thing we had back there was hope, and that's most definitely gone." Alpha checked his revolver. "Now I'm madder than a wet hen and spoiling for a fight."

"Go out with all guns blazing, huh?" Uniform fastened the top button of his tunic. "Fine by me. I'll kill so many of those creeps, they'll be paddling in their own blood."

"There must be another way!" Echo wailed.

"Aw, I bet we'll beat them easily." Tango did a little boxing shuffle. Her heel caught the rifle leaning against the wall and it toppled over. Uniform grabbed at the gun and missed.

The weapon went off. A short, sustained burst that sprayed bullets across the door. The noise reverberated deafeningly round the hall and the teenagers clasped hands over their ears until it had faded away.

"Butterfingers." Tango picked up the weapon and inspected it for damage.

"You damned idiot!" Uniform slapped her arm. "You read the manual! The safety catch goes *on* when you ain't in immediate danger!"

"I'd say we're in immediate danger now, moany face." Tango lay down on the floor and raised the gun to her cheek. "Anyhow, I saved you the trouble of going looking for mutants."

"Uniform, you're the protector," Alpha said. "Take charge."

"I hate to admit it, but Tango's right." Uniform lay down beside her. "Get in a line on the floor. There's only three ways into this hall, all through small doorways. It'll be like shooting fish in a barrel."

"And when we run out of bullets?"

"Switch to handguns."

"What if they're not powerful enough?"

"Start calling the creatures rude names." Uniform snarled. "Whaddya think? I'll use my fists and teeth if that's all I got left."

He laid out two magazines in front of him.

"May I say, it's an honor to fight alongside y'all. Except for Tango. She's a moron."

"What? You've never made a mistake?"

"Yeah. I should have shot you back in the armory."

Then they heard howling.

It was high pitched and ululating, almost girlish in tone. A gibbering cacophony rising in crescendo, far away but heading steadily towards them.

The teenagers' blood turned to ice.

"Don't waste your ammo." Alpha was ashen. "And, despite what Uniform said, you might want to save the last bullet for yourselves."

Echo began to cry again.

"I don't understand why the doors won't open!" Mike 32 was pacing up and down behind them. "I wanted so much to see the sky."

The others slowly turned to look at him. For a second, the Threes had almost forgotten he was there.

"I think the penny just dropped." Juliet nudged Mike 3. "Suddenly, we're all thinking the same thing."

"No, we're not."

"Yeah," Uniform whispered. "We are."

"He won't leave," Sierra said. "Would *you*?"

Mike 32 was so consumed by his own misery, he didn't even notice they were talking about him.

"Make him go away, Mike." Juliet gritted her teeth. "Do it before Echo or Uniform kill him."

The boy clenched his fists and took a deep breath.

"You want to see the sky, Mike 32?" He got up and beckoned to his double. "Then do exactly as I say."

"What do you mean?"

"From the sound of it, the mutants are coming from the left. Go across the hall and into the corridor on the right. Shut the door."

"Are you serious?" The boy's lip trembled.

"Trust me, please." Mike took him by the shoulders. "Count to ten, slowly. Then come back in. The blast doors will be open and you have to make a run for them."

"I don't understand."

"You *know* I don't have time to explain."

"All right." The boy's eyes filled with tears. "I owe you my life, after all."

He walked across the giant hall, a small forlorn figure, then vanished into the passageway.

As soon as he was gone, the blast doors slid open with a near-silent hiss and light flooded the hall. The Threes drew a shuddering collective breath.

"I know. *I know*." Mike's voice cracked. "He's a clone. The doors wouldn't work while he had a chance of getting out."

"All of you." Alpha leapt up. "Grab your ammo and high tail it."

The teenagers scrambled to their feet.

"Leave 32 the automatic weapons," Mike growled. "We can keep the handguns and my rifle is all we require for hunting."

"Don't be dumb." Uniform scooped up his magazines. "The kid would be a goner if he had a tank."

The rest copied his actions, too ashamed to look at the hunter.

"Tell them to leave him some weapons!" Mike pointed his rifle at Alpha's head. "Give him that chance or I swear to God, your life ends with his."

"Steady on!" Juliet gasped.

Alpha stared down the rifle barrel, eye twitching. Mike didn't waver.

"Do as the hunter says," he commanded. "Drop the heavy artillery and let's go."

As they stepped through the opening, Mike 32 appeared back in the hall.

"I counted…" The boy stopped and goggled. "The sky! I can see outside!"

The blast doors began to slide shut.

"Run!" Tango shouted. "You can make it!"

The boy broke into a manic sprint, arms and legs pumping. Mike and Sierra grabbed the blast doors and attempted to stop them closing, their feet slipping on the smooth floor. They had as much chance as insects trying to stop a rolling boulder.

"Quicker, hunter!" Alpha urged as Juliet and Echo frantically beckoned to him.

The boy doubled his efforts. His eyes bulged and his breath came in terrified spurts. He was fifteen feet away. Then ten. Then five.

"Oh God, *faster*!"

32 reached out with one hand as the doors slid closed with a thud, trapping him inside.

"Aw. No! *No*!" Mike 3 burst into tears.

Sierra put her arms around him until his sobbing subsided.

"That was a tough call." She let go and pointed. "But look."

They were in some kind of enormous hanger. At the end was a light they had all but forgotten, layering the floor in lattices of purest white. Outside the opening, they could see a swathe of blue, so bright and unblemished it seemed unreal. The other Threes moved towards it, transfixed.

"You told him the truth." Juliet took Mike's arm and tried to lead him out. "He saw the sky."

"Just long enough to know what he missed." The boy pushed her away.

"You did what you had to do."

"I left him to die." Mike slammed his fist against the immovable blast doors and Juliet flinched.

"He was doomed, anyhow." The girl said. "It was him or us."

"*You* don't seem too bothered."

"I didn't *know* him." Juliet was stung. "Mike, I never met any of the Types, remember? I been on my own for two years."

Now it was the boy's turn to feel bad. Juliet had stayed to comfort him when the rest had wandered off.

"We could go back in…" he began.

"As many times as you like," the girl said patiently. "But the result will always be the same. You know the computer is never gonna set any clone free."

Mike *did* know. No amount of scheming or wishing would change that fact. And he had been bred to be practical.

"All right. Let's get outside." He brushed away tears and offered her his arm.

"See what all the fuss is about."

-19-

Alpha led the others towards the hanger entrance, his throat tight. Partly it was because of leaving Mike 32 to his fate. Partly it was anticipation.

Mostly it was fear.

He felt wind on his face. Not stale like the air in the Fort but hot and scented. He sucked in lungfuls until he became dizzy.

"I'm not sure I can go out there, Sir." Tango appeared by his side. "Forgot my sunscreen."

"Are you for *real*?"

"I'm kidding, silly." She broke into a run.

"Must be nice to live on planet Tango," Alpha grunted.

The others followed the lanky figure up to the hanger lip.

Then they stopped, stunned. Hardly able to comprehend what they were seeing.

The hanger was built into the side of a craggy scree, the only part of the Fort visible from the outside. Behind it, imposing mountains rose steeply to jagged peaks.

In front of them clumpy grass, studded with wildflowers, unfurled to a paddock far below. There had been a wire fence ringing the complex at one time but now it was rusted and in ruins. A stream meandered through the vista, sparkling in the sunlight. Behind that, a forest stretched to the right and a long basin slewed left. Both ended at a range of hills, pixilated with haze.

And, above that, was the sky. It was cloudless, cobalt and went on forever. Forwards. Up. Sideways.

"Everything is so *big*." Echo sat down and clutched a handful of grass in each hand. "I feel like I'm going to float away."

Tango lay on her back and stretched out spindly arms and legs, sighing contentedly. Uniform stuck his sword in the ground and sat next to it, chin on one knee and a small smile on his face.

Sierra pulled off her cap and raised her hands to the sun.

"It's glorious," she said simply.

"Good farming land?" Alpha inquired. From the corner of his eye, he caught Mike and Juliet emerging, blinking, from the dark maw of the hanger.

"Can't rightly tell from up here." Sierra shielded her brow with one hand. "There's a river for irrigation and trees and hills mean protection from the elements. But, away from the water, it looks pretty brown and dry."

"We don't want to live so close to the Fort, do we?" Echo shuddered. "Not with those things still inside. Isn't that dangerous, Uniform?"

"We're the first living beings to make it out in two centuries." The protector tipped his sword over. "I reckon we're safe."

Mike wandered past, Juliet still on his arm. Their expressions showed the same shock and awe as the rest of the party.

"Impressive."

"Very. Think you could hunt here, Mike?"

"For sure." The boy pointed to a bend in the river where the water slowed and formed a wide pool. "That's a natural watering hole. Should attract plenty animals and it looks shallow enough to wade across."

He frowned.

"In fact, it's almost too perfect."

"It isn't called New Eden for nothing."

"I mean, there's something's odd about the layout." Mike scanned the forest. "I just can't put my finger on it."

"Have you got anything *constructive* to add?" Alpha didn't bother to hide his exasperation.

"Yeah. Tango should construct a stockade in case there are predators in the woods."

"Later, honey. I'm working on my tan."

"A few more weapons would have helped," Uniform added unhelpfully.

"Those semi-automatics were loud, wasteful of bullets and useless for hunting." Mike's black mood descended again. "A bit like you, I imagine."

"Cut it out, you two," Alpha said sternly. "Uniform? Learn some tact."

"My new middle name, Sir."

"As for you, hunter? You ever point a gun at me again? Better be prepared to use it."

"Sorry. It's just... well... you saw Mike 32's face when the doors began to close."

"We all lost people." The leader's tone softened. "You put what happened out of your mind, hear? We've got to leave the past behind and concentrate on the present or, most likely, we'll lose more."

The others stared at him.

"Sorry to be indelicate but you know it's true." The leader shouldered his pack. "There was supposed to be 300 of us but there's only seven. We were meant to join a thriving community, only it doesn't exist. That's a couple of big inconveniences to be getting on with."

He started down the hill.

"Let's go make camp and figure out how the hell we're gonna stay alive."

New Eden

Only those who risk going too far can possibly find out how far one can go.

T. S. Eliot

It's important for the explorer to be willing to be led astray.

Roger von Oech

-20-

They worked until the sun began to sink below the horizon, the skills Mrs Brown had taught kicking into action. Uniform collected wood for a fire to keep wild animals away. Tango constructed a makeshift lean-to and fashioned rough beds out of desiccated moss. Echo emptied the rucksacks and took an inventory. Mike caught a brace of fish, scaled them and put them on spits to roast. Sierra filled their canteens from the stream and collected roots and berries round the edge of the forest.

Juliet looked lost.

Alpha sat on a rock near the edge of the clearing, staring into space.

"Got the leader role down pat, don't he?" Sierra complained.

"I'd be happier if he joined in." Uniform agreed, rubbing sticks together until the moss smoldered into life.

"Taking time to think always leads to trouble."

Once darkness had fallen, they huddled around the fire. Mike roasted the fish and passed them pieces. He took a bite and sat back appreciatively.

"Wow. This tastes *great*."

"Don't eat too much," Echo warned. "Our systems aren't used to this kind of food."

She popped a tiny sliver of blackened flesh into her mouth.

"Forget I spoke." She tore a chunk loose and began to devour it. "This stuff is delicious. Shame I'm on a diet."

"I'd rather have had meat." Mike looked puzzled. "But there didn't seem to be any game in the woods. Yet there's a watering hole not fifty yards from us. I don't understand why no animals are using it."

"Probably cause they ain't seen a human in two centuries," Sierra said. "We scared them away."

"Maybe."

They finished eating then stared into the flames, still trying to come to terms with where they were and what they were doing. The hunter stared up at the moon Mike 32 had so badly wanted to see and felt as black inside as the sky above.

"Night's scary." Echo hugged her knees. "There's lots of weird noises."

"Those are just crickets," the boy reassured her. "They're harmless."

Far off in the distance came a plaintive howl. Uniform reached for his sword.

"Most probably a coyote," he informed them. "Not so harmless."

"I'm not sure it *is* a coyote," Mike argued. "It doesn't sound quite right."

"Ten minutes in New Eden and you're an expert on animal noises?"

"*You're* the animal making most noise around here."

"Stop scaring Echo." Juliet admonished. "Whatever it is won't come near the fire." She looked around apprehensively. "Will it?"

"Nah, the sound is miles away." Mike grinned. "Even if it wasn't, Uniform's sitting nearest the woods."

"It's time we made plans." Alpha wiped fishy hands on the grass by his side. "Decide what to do next."

"That's a no-brainer." Uniform sighed contentedly. "We begin our own community right here and restart the human race."

"Can you build us places to live, Tango?"

"Of course." The girl pulled an ax from her backpack. "It'll take a while and they won't be very big. Might be a bit drafty. And most likely let in some rain."

"In other words, we'd be as well sheltering under a tree."

"Only one of me, chief. It takes at least six Tangos working together to make a log cabin."

"Can you teach the others?"

"Happily. Problem is, we only have one ax."

"I give up. What about farming, Sierra?"

"The valley floor is overgrown with shrubs and grass."

"That's bad?"

"The land will have to be cleared and irrigation channels dug before I can plant anything." Sierra crumbled gritty soil through her fingers. "Otherwise, it'll be too dry for seeds to take hold." She nodded towards the forest. "That's why the conifers have a brown tinge."

"But not impossible?"

"Plants take a while to grow. It'll be months before we can harvest any vegetables or crops."

"I'll teach everyone to hunt," Mike chipped in. "Please don't plant any carrots, Sierra."

"I can't dig ditches on my own," the girl continued. "Or till the soil myself, neither, even if Tango manages to put together a plow."

"I'll give it a go," the girl replied enthusiastically. "It might even work."

"We'll all help." Juliet offered.

"Not if you're learning to build and hunt, you won't." Sierra poked the fire with a stick, refusing to look at her companions. "We were supposed to have horses, remember?"

"I sense you have more to say." Alpha studied the girl. "Out with it."

"All right. In these circumstances, I ain't too keen on being a farmer. That plain enough for you?"

"Hark at her!" Uniform laughed out loud. "Didn't take the dirt grubber long to get uppity."

"Oh, oh," Juliet muttered. "Rebellion in the ranks."

"A farmer is what Mrs Brown bred you to be," Alpha said gently.

"It's what Mrs Brown *told* me to be," the girl shot back. "None of the Sierras ever wanted to work the land. Some of us were even gonna run away when we got outside."

"It's all you're good for, girl." Uniform curled his lip. "We each gotta play the part we been given."

"Really? What part are you gonna be playing? Swanning around with a big sword, sticking it into things?" Sierra spat on the ground. "What's Juliet good for, come to think of it? There's no technology out here."

"Less of your lip, Sierra!" Alpha scolded.

"She has a point," Juliet said quietly.

"You get to explore, Uniform." The farmer's anger bubbled to the surface. "Mike gets to hunt. Alpha can sit around giving orders. Me? I'll end up breaking my back, day in day out. You think that's fair?"

Flames flickered across her face, deepening the shadows of her misery.

"What if I get injured? What happens to your pretty little garden of Eden then?"

"Sierra's right." Juliet rubbed her arms. "No matter how good our intentions, we're spread too thin to start a community."

"Nobody claimed it was going to be easy," Alpha said uncertainly. "Nothing worth doing ever is."

"I've got an idea." Juliet threw the remains of her fish into the fire and watched it crackle. "Why don't we head for the nearest Fort?"

"Shouldn't take long. It's in the hill behind you."

"You know what I mean."

"It could be the other Forts worked exactly how they were meant to," Tango agreed. "Then I wouldn't have to build *anything*!"

"You mean Forts that are hundreds of miles away." Alpha rolled his eyes. "In *secret* locations we were never told."

"Eh, yeah. Those."

"They may not even exist," Uniform added. "Ours didn't do too well, huh?"

The Threes thought about that.

"I know this location is far from perfect. It's obviously too arid." Their leader patted the ground. "But it must have been chosen by the Fort planners for a reason. Mrs Brown told us climate change was altering the whole world. For all we know, it's turned most of America into a desert."

"I love sand." Tango wiggled her toes. "Reminds me of the beach when I was little."

"It's too risky to move, is all I'm saying." Alpha spread his hands reasonably. "As far as we know, we *are* the human race. So, we need to survive and there isn't much doubt that right here is our best chance."

He stood up, hands on hips.

"History starts again right now, and *we'll* be shaping it. You realize how important that is? Our lives will be damned hard, no denying. But it's a sacrifice I'm prepared to make. The Threes are going to be remembered, millennia from now, as the founders of New Eden. People who toiled selflessly and tirelessly to create a society that actually works."

"I'm not all that keen on toiling selflessly and tirelessly either." Echo held up carefully manicured fingers. "Think what it will do to my nails."

"Don't be a party pooper." Tango clapped her hands. "That was a very pretty speech, leader."

"It *was* good, wasn't it?" Alpha sat down again. "I've been practicing all day."

He yawned and stretched.

"Let's get some shut-eye. The fire looks big enough to last till morning."

"I'll take first watch." Uniform pulled his sword from the ground. "Wake you in a few hours to take over, hunter?"

"You got it."

"No. I'll take first watch." Juliet stood up. "As Sierra pointed out, I don't have any real role to play here."

"I didn't mean it like *that*."

"All the same, it should be me." Uniform rubbed his eyes. "I'm trained in this kind of thing."

"Yeah." Sierra snorted. "I'm sure you were great at defending the Division of Youth from midnight pilferers."

"If a critter comes along that's big enough to kill us, I'm fairly confident I'll spot it," Juliet added curtly. "Then you can come to my assistance."

"Fair enough." Uniform tipped his cap at her. "Thank you, Juliet."

"You're welcome. I'll be on that little hillock to the left." The girl picked up a blanket and vanished into the dark.

"Is she ok?" Alpha turned to Mike. "She seems uncomfortable around us."

"Juliet's not a people person, far as I can gather," the boy replied, thinking again about what Mrs Brown had said. "She's used to being on her own."

"Then let's get some sleep."

The Threes lay down on their moss beds. Exhausted, they were out cold within minutes.

Next morning, they were woken by Echo screaming.

-21-

"Sound's coming from that way." Uniform was on his feet in an instant, sword in hand. "Echo took over the watch just before dawn."

He looked at the empty hillock.

"I *told* her not to move from that spot."

Then he was off and running, the rest close behind.

They found Echo in a leafy clearing, standing next to an olive-green truck, lodged in the remains of a perimeter fence that had long since collapsed. The vehicle was half-hidden by weeds and covered in ivy, but they could still see the words **US Army** stenciled on the side. There was rusted wire wrapped round the wheels.

The passenger door was open.

"What are you playing at?" Uniform pulled her away from the vehicle. "Why did you leave your post?"

"It was getting light and Juliet was awake. I got bored and thought I'd have a look round."

"I did wake up," The girl admitted. "But I must have drifted off again."

"Lord's sakes." Uniform slapped his broad forehead. "We'll be lucky to last a week at this rate."

"It was *horrible*." Echo burst into tears and buried her face in Alpha's chest.

"Eh... there, there." The leader patted her blonde locks awkwardly. "It's just a truck. Unexpected, sure, but hardly horrific."

"That's what I thought. So, I managed to open the door." She clutched him tighter. "There's someone inside."

"Check it out, Uniform." Alpha tried to prise the girl away. "I'm kinda tied up here."

The boy vaulted onto the running board and peered inside.

"There's a driver, but he's been dead a long time." He waved away musty air. "He's pretty much intact and even got some remnants of his clothes. I guess being sealed in the cab meant animals couldn't get to him."

"Who is he?" Echo wailed. "What the hell is he doing here?"

"Tell you what. I'll ask him." Uniform stuck his head into the vehicle. "Nope. Says he won't talk till you stop sniveling."

"Remember what I said about tact, protector?" Alpha cautioned.

"Oh, come *on*, Sir! You don't just walk off when you're on guard." The boy backed out and jumped down. "She could have gotten us all killed."

"I'd say she's learned her lesson."

"I hate this place," Echo sobbed. "I wish I was back in the Division of Youth."

Juliet was staring at the truck.

"It can't be." She scrambled into the cab and rummaged around on the floor.

"Damn!" She cursed. "His arm fell off and hit me on the head."

A withered limb came flying out of the door and landed next to Echo. She shrieked again and Sierra suppressed a giggle.

"I'm getting to quite like Juliet," Uniform said breezily.

"I wanna see too!" Tango wormed her way into the vehicle and began rummaging around.

"Jeez. This is worse than being in charge of a bunch of rodeo clowns." Alpha finally wriggled free of Echo. "Searching for anything in particular, girls? Or just starting a valet service?"

"There's an empty oxygen tank in here. And this." Juliet emerged and handed a sheaf of papers wrapped in waterproof cellophane to the leader. "They look like blueprints of the Fort."

"How in God's name did such sensitive info get in a truck parked outside?" Alpha studied the bundle in astonishment. "Could he be the guy who sabotaged the place all those years ago?"

"You couldn't be more wrong." The girl opened her other hand. "I spotted this on the floor."

In her palm was a rectangular enamel badge.

Dr H. Stoddart.
Head Technician.

"No way!"

"I'm afraid so." Juliet passed the pin around.

"I think we just found our old friend, Harvey."

They buried the technician in a sunny clearing. Alpha let Mike conduct the ceremony while he comforted Echo.

"If it wasn't for you, Mr Stoddart, none of us would be alive. Though, to be honest, you might have helped kill the rest of the human race. Anyhow, thank you for saving us and may God rest your soul. Amen."

The boy crossed himself.

"Oh. And I straightened your tie. The little scrap that was left."

Juliet raised an eyebrow.

"It was important to him," Mike said sheepishly.

-22-

After the ceremony, Uniform herded the others back to camp while Alpha searched the truck properly and Mike scoured the brush for anything useful that might have been dragged off by animals.

At the campsite, Juliet spread the blueprints carefully over a rock and read them. They were brittle with age but undamaged.

Mike and Alpha appeared in the clearing.

"Find anything interesting?"

"No. But I've been thinking," Mike replied. "Stoddart drove out of the Fort and straight into the surrounding fence. He demolished it but it looks like the vehicle got tangled in the wire and wouldn't go any further."

"So?" Uniform was sharpening his sword on a stone. "After the plague, there wasn't anyone alive to keep out."

"Alpha found a key for the gate in his pocket." Mike held out a tarnished sliver of bronze. "Why didn't he just get out and unlock it?"

"He was afraid of the Le Mans bug, of course."

"He was already a dead man, but the plague would take 24 hours to actually kill him." Mike stared at the key in his hand. "He ruined the fence with his truck, so why didn't he get out and wriggle through a hole? Why did he spend his last hours sitting in a truck?"

He furrowed his brow.

"I'm missing something important. I just know it."

"What about you, Sir?" Tango inquired. "Discover any more goodies?"

"Nothing of consequence," the leader said sharply.

"Sorry I spoke, grumpy."

"Put the blueprints away." Alpha tapped Juliet roughly on the shoulder. "I need everyone out looking for edible fruits and berries."

"I wouldn't know a raspberry from poison ivy." The girl snapped. "The Fort is my area of expertise."

She glanced up.

"Harvey's truck has been in the open for two hundred years and there isn't a bit of rust on it. It's almost all plastic, like the guns."

"And?"

"According to these blueprints, there are identical trucks back at the complex. They're in a depot near the hanger and might still work. There's fuel there as well."

She tapped the plans.

"And there are storerooms in the Fort with supplies. Including canned food."

Her eyes widened.

"The mutants came out of suspended animation, so they had no memories. Or they were in a primal state.

Either way, they probably didn't touch the stuff, just like they ignored the weapons and medicine. Wouldn't even realize what it *was*."

"That's ironic. Starving to death cause you don't know how to work a can opener."

"The point is, there are enough provisions in the Fort to equip an army, never mind seven of us."

"We can't go back in," Echo stammered. "What if the monsters are waiting on the other side?"

"If they were too close, the blast doors wouldn't open." Mike pointed out. "The computer refuses to let them out, just like the Types."

"We could go in quickly and quietly to find what we need using these blueprints." Juliet warmed to her idea. "Load provisions and fuel into a truck and drive out again."

"Just like that, huh?"

"I admit, it'd be a bit... eh... risky."

"Suicidal is the word you're searching for." Alpha scratched his cheek. "Yet we could sorely do with more supplies. What do you think, protector?"

"Farther into the Fort we go, more chance we have of being eaten." Uniform studied the map. "Mike and I could probably scout the first few corridors, grab a few things and get out fast. Anything else is too hazardous."

"The mutants might be savage but they know how to hunt," Mike agreed. "We'd have to wait a few days before trying the same trick again, or we might walk into an ambush."

"We need a truck!" Juliet dug in her heels. "With transport we could go anywhere. Even look for the other Forts."

"We decided to stay here, remember?" Alpha's face clouded. "I don't want to hear any more nonsense about moving somewhere else."

"It's surely worth taking a chance," the girl persisted. "This is a golden opportunity…"

"Enough!" Alpha snapped. "*I'm* in charge here."

"I know that, but…"

"See here, red." the leader hissed. "You're the closest thing we have to dead weight, so keep your opinions to yourself."

The others looked away, embarrassed.

"We're gonna build a community on this spot, like we damned well agreed and that's the end of it. You wanna strike out on your own, get walking."

The boy turned his back on Juliet.

"Or you can go with the other girls and find roots and berries. Mike? Uniform? We need meat." He strode off. "Tonight, we'll discuss the best way to make a quick sortie into the Fort. *Uniform's* plan."

As he walked, Alpha's shoulders began to shake. He quickened his pace and disappeared into the woods.

"Who died and made *him* King of the Hill?" Juliet muttered.

"Everyone else in the world, Jules."

"I've never heard of a leader losing their temper." Echo shuffled nervously from foot to foot. "Was he... *crying*?"

"Shoot. I really didn't need to see that." Uniform shouldered his sword. "Coming hunter? I most definitely feel the need to kill something."

"So long as it isn't me." Mike picked up his rifle. "You cut into the woods and I'll skirt the edge. See if we can trap some game between us."

"C'mon." Tango took Echo's hand. "A good haul of juicy berries will cheer everyone up. You two joining us?"

"Presently." Juliet silently folded up the blueprints and began to pack them in her rucksack. Sierra waited till everyone had gone, then crouched next to her.

"Could I trouble you for those?" She looked around. "Everyone is gonna be busy for a while and that'll give me some time."

"Are you saying you *agree* with my idea?"

"Hell, no! It's idiotic. But that don't give Alpha the right to disrespect you or condemn me to a life of back-breaking toil." Sierra glanced at the Fort entrance, high on the hillside. "So, I'm going in. I ain't asking anyone else to risk their life, but I'd rather die than spend my days bent double in some field."

"You don't need the blueprints." Juliet tapped her head. "I already got them memorized."

She stood up.

"Assuming you want a hand, that is."

"You know it." Sierra gave her companion a dazzling smile.

"We sisters are gonna boost ourselves us a truck!"

Mike was waiting for them at the Fort entrance, lounging against the wall. Juliet and Sierra quickly pretended to be looking for berries.

"Cut the innocent act." The teenager sighed. "Soon as I saw you two menaces conspiring, I figured you were up to no good."

And because Mrs Brown warned me Juliet was a risk-taker, he thought. *Who won't let anyone get in the way of what she wants.*

"You gonna go running to Alpha?" Sierra squared up to him. "Tell on us?"

"He's the last person I'd confide in right now." Mike shook his head. "When he came out of Harvey's cab he was all shook up and shoving something under his tunic. He's hiding it from everyone."

"You ain't talking me outta this," Sierra said adamantly. "Just pretend you never saw us."

"Actually, I'm coming with you." Mike unslung his weapon. "There's something wrong with this valley. I can't work out exactly what, but I got a really bad feeling. I reckon we might have to move and move fast."

He turned to Juliet.

"You have a cunning strategy, brainbox?"

"Run for the armory and grab more guns. Next stop, the storerooms."

"That'll be a 'no', then."

"Load the provisions onto a vehicle and fill it with gas." Juliet ignored his sarcasm. "Then drive right out."

"Assuming the trucks still work. And the mutants?"

"There's a big difference between unsuspecting kids armed with primitive weapons and a wary hunter carrying a rifle." Juliet gave a disarming smile. "I've every confidence you'll keep us covered."

"I'll certainly do my utmost, ladies." The boy bowed gallantly. "Let's go before I chicken out."

"Thank you for helping us," Sierra said gratefully. "You *are* pretty brave."

"Not as brave as you two," Mike smiled. "But, obviously, just as dumb."

Juliet walked towards the blast doors and they rolled open. Mike crouched down and took up a defensive position.

"What the hell?" He lowered the rifle.

There was an empty truck sitting on the other side of the door.

"Wow!" Juliet hoisted herself into the back. "It's already loaded with supplies and fuel."

"How did it *get* here? It didn't drive itself."

"Ain't gonna look a gift horse in the mouth." Sierra yanked open the cab door. "The keys are in the ignition."

She hesitated.

"Eh. Do any of us know *how* to drive?"

"Right-hand pedal is the accelerator." Juliet jumped down. "Then point it where you want to go." She climbed into the driver's side. "I remember mom telling me that."

"Guys?" Mike repeated. "How did the truck *get* here?"

"There's a scrap of paper on the seat." The girl picked the note up and read it. "Oh, crap."

"What's wrong?"

"It's for you, Mike."

"Let me see."

Dear Mike 3.

The creatures in here are strong and fast but they're not indestructible and we killed a few. I rounded up all the Types I cood find and we emptyed the armory. We loded a truck and tryed to drive it out but the blast doors still won't open. I don't understand why but I rekon you do. You fooled me yesterday but I'm sure you had a good reason cause you're my best frend.

We're going back to the Division of Youth. The airlock will keep the monsters out and there is plenty of food. But we are stuck there.

Pleese come back and save us, Mike 3. I no you woodnt leave me to die.

Yours affectionately
Mike 32.

"He's still alive." The boy crumpled up the note. "We have to go get him."

"Did you read it *properly*?" Juliet tugged at Mike's sleeve. "Nothing's changed. Your crowbar trick let them back into the Division of Youth but they can never leave."

"We'll jam the entrance." Mike looked around wildly. "We can use the truck!"

"The blast doors must weigh tons," Sierra said sadly. "They'd cut this vehicle in half. Even if it didn't, that would let the monsters out as well."

"Remember what Alpha told us about writing the history of the new human race?" Mike seethed. "Is *this* how we want it to begin? By leaving our companions to die?"

"You can't save them if you're dead too." Juliet turned the key in the ignition and the engine roared into life. "The Types are safe for now and we are, most definitely, *not*."

The truck bounced out of the hanger and onto the grass. Mike followed and the blast doors slid closed behind him.

"I *will* find a way to release you." He stared at the immovable barrier. "I *swear*."

"We're heading downhill." Sierra's voice drifted out of the cab. "Brake's, the middle pedal, you said?"

"I'll get in the back." Mike stopped to take in the view. He blinked rapidly and waved the girls on.

"Actually, I'll catch you up."

The vehicle kangarooed down the slope, engine revving madly. Mike stared at the panorama, mind whirring.

Then it clicked.

There was a perfect watering hole at this point of the river. Herbivores would trample saplings on their way to the water and they'd graze away any plants on the flat area as they went.

But the valley floor *wasn't* being grazed anymore. As Sierra pointed out, the terrain was stubbled and overgrown and a whole day had passed without one animal coming to drink.

Flat valley floor. Watering hole but no wildlife drinking. Steep hills on Three sides and a forest on the fourth. Trees thick enough to hide large predators until they were in attacking distance.

The boy put a hand to his mouth.

This was another kill zone.

-24-

Parked by the river, Sierra and Juliet were in ec-stasy.

"We found bottles of Cokey Cola in the back of the truck," Sierra shouted gleefully as Mike came puffing up. "I remember Cokey Cola. It used to fizz out my nose when I drunk too much."

"Pour it away," the boy commanded. "Pour the Coke out and fill the bottles with gas. Then stuff rags in the top."

"There's bottles of water too!" Sierra protested. "Can't we use *those*? We'll just refill them from the river."

Mike glanced in the back. The water containers were plastic.

"The bottles have to be glass. Hurry up!"

"Do as he says." Juliet laid a hand on Sierra's arm. "What's the matter, Mike?"

"Honk the horn. Get the others back here, pronto."

"No need." Alpha emerged from the trees, Uniform behind him. "We could hear your engine a mile away."

In the distance, Mike could see Tango running to-wards them.

"I absolutely *forbade* you to go into the Fort." Alpha's face was purple. "I was *clear* about it."

"But we've got fuel and food," Juliet retorted.

"Any guns?" Uniform asked hopefully.

"The Types have them," Sierra piped up. "Some of them are still alive, Sir! They've retreated to the Division of Youth. They're making a stand!"

Alpha hesitated, indecision and anger flickering across his handsome face. Tango reached them, doubled up and out of breath.

"Pour out the Coke and replace it with fuel," Mike repeated. "Stuff the tops with rags. Now!"

"Why are you making Molotov cocktails?" Uniform asked, suddenly alarmed.

"You're fixing *drinks*!" Alpha's eyes bulged as he saw the bottle in the girl's hand. "Why don't you put on a sparkly *dress* since you're obviously in the mood for celebrating this mutiny!"

"Molotov Cocktail's a homemade bomb, Sir," Uniform interrupted.

"You heard the engines a mile away." Mike wiped sweat from his lip. "Listen…"

"No, YOU listen," Alpha rasped. "I swear, I been disobeyed for the last time."

"I mean, *listen*." Mike cupped his ear. "The birds have stopped singing."

He licked his finger and held it up.

"Wind's blowing away from the forest."

"Cut the mountain man crap." Alpha slapped his arm down. "Sierra, Juliet, get out of the truck." He held out his hand. "You, hunter? Give me your rifle."

Mike lifted the weapon to his shoulder. This time, the leader refused to back down.

"I warned you," he snarled. "If you ever pointed a gun at me again, you better be prepared to use it."

He drew his revolver.

"Now, give me the weapon."

Mike fired.

Alpha flung himself sideways, throwing both arms over his face.

There was a scream of rage at the edge of the woods and a creature burst from the trees. It was almost the height of a man, with short, matted hair and a drooling, black muzzle - eyes glowing points of hatred.

And the beast had tusks. Two curved, yellowing scythes protruding from hairy cheeks, each capable of opening a human from groin to neck.

Mike ejected the spent bullet from its chamber and fired again.

The creature stumbled but kept going. Spotting Uniform's sword, it skirted the boy and headed towards Alpha, still lying prone on the ground.

Mike fired one last time.

The creature's legs gave way. It crashed into the dirt, sending up a shower of broken twigs, then lay still.

"What *is* that thing?" Alpha spluttered, getting shakily to his feet. "It's… it's… *huge!*"

"Is it a wild boar?" Sierra was frantically pouring Coke from the bottles and passing them to Juliet to fill with gas. "It don't look like the pictures I saw back in the Division of Youth. The legs are too long."

"It's not a boar." Mike walked over and kicked the dead animal. "It's a dog."

"I had a dog once." Tango goggled at the prone monstrosity. "It didn't have tusks, though. It was a Pug."

"*No* dog is that size." Juliet shook her head. "No dog *looks* like that."

"The scientists on the complex tested WC-57 on them." Mike pumped another round into the chamber. "Remember what that technician said when Harvey wanted to flood the suspended animation tanks with the serum?"

You saw what it did to the dogs we tested it on.

"I'm betting those are the descendants of the creatures the Fort released."

"*That's* why Harvey tried to drive through the perimeter fence rather than get out and unlock the gate." Juliet began to stuff rags into the bottle tops. "They would have torn him to pieces."

"With the fence down, they escaped and they've had 200 years to breed without anyone to cull them." Mike pointed to the scrub brush carpeting the valley floor. "It's why the meadow is overgrown. They've killed every herbivore in the area and now they're searching further afield for food."

"Please let them have got lucky," Sierra prayed.

"Oh, they did," Mike replied. "The rest are bound to have smelled our campfire last night and be on their way back."

He kicked the dead hound again.

"This one's an outcast. Either he challenged the leader and got injured or he's a runt. He stays on the outskirts of the pack. It means they're close."

"A runt! He took three bullets to kill."

"Exactly," Juliet said. "Imagine what the others are like."

"I'm trying not to picture it."

"What do we do?" Tango took a swig of Coke before emptying the rest of the bottle. "Bwaaaaaaaaah!" She let out a huge burp. "Pardon *me*!

"We need to get out of here." Alpha brushed twigs from his tunic, trying to regain his composure. He looked at his companions and frowned.

"Where the hell is Echo?"

"She's in the woods somewhere." Tango scanned the trees. "Maybe she went to powder her nose."

"Why does that girl keep wandering off?" Uniform fumed. "We gotta find her."

"Don't have time." Mike cupped his ear. "Listen."

The Threes could hear the sound of yapping and snarling drifting down the valley.

"Dogs can't climb trees," the boy continued. "Echo can. If she has enough sense to think of it."

"Should we do the same?" Alpha asked.

"Only if we don't intend to ever come down."

"Uniform?"

"The hunter might be a jumped-up runt himself, but he's the animal expert."

"Agreed. Your instructions, Mike?"

"Everyone into the back of the truck. Sierra? Uncap a fuel drum and pitch it over the side. Then I'll drive into the river.

"Dogs can swim, can't they?"

"They can." Mike vaulted into the cab. "But, if they get that close, we're all pooch chow."

The Threes clambered into the flatbed and Juliet handed them a Molotov Cocktail each. Sierra pushed an oil drum over the side and watched the contents soak into the grass. Mike bounced the truck into the river while the others clung on for dear life.

The dogs appeared at the end of the valley. Tiny, bounding dots, quickly growing in size.

"Sweet lord, there are dozens of them." Alpha drew his revolver and the others followed suit. "Get ready to fire on my command."

"By the time these creatures get in range, it'll be too late." Mike stuck his head out of the cab window. "We have to frighten them away with fire."

"What about Echo?"

"She'll be OK," the boy promised. "The wind's blowing away from the forest. Light the rags on the Molotov cocktails."

"We don't exactly have time to rub sticks together."

"What? Nobody has *matches*?"

The beasts loped towards them, speeding silently through the meadow.

"Look for something! The Types can't be so dumb that they'd have loaded Coke and not something to start a fire!"

"They might if an Echo was given the job."

The teenagers began madly opening the packs in the back of the truck.

"Hurry!"

"Got some!" Juliet tore open a cellophane-wrapped box using her teeth. With trembling fingers, she struck one and lit each person's Cocktail.

The hounds were close enough now that the teenagers could see their lolling tongues and the wind ruffling through their fur. Some had tusks. Some horns. Some spiny ridges cresting their backs.

"Throw the bottles as close to the oil drum as you can!"

They stood up and launched the missiles. The Cocktails landed in the scrub brush near the bank and exploded with a muted *whump*.

A wall of flame shot up as the spilled gas ignited.

The dogs skidded to a halt, then turned and fled, yelping, into the trees.

The teenagers gave a yell of triumph.

"Ehm. Those flames are spreading pretty fast." Juliet pointed. "And they *are* heading towards the woods."

Burning ash began to settle on the teenager's clothes.

"It was a calculated risk." Mike stuck a finger in the air again. "It's possible I calculated wrong. The wind has changed direction."

"Pour our water bottles over the supplies." Alpha took charge. "The packaging will protect them. Then everybody into the river."

The Threes doused the provisions and jumped into the current, ducking their heads repeatedly to fully soak themselves. The air was thick with smoke and the trees were bursting into flames, one after another.

"The wind is carrying the fire faster than anything can run." Juliet swept sodden locks from her face. "None of the hounds are gonna make it."

"Neither is Echo. The forest is going up like a tinderbox."

"This is my fault." Mike revved the truck to life. "Stay here. I'll get her."

As he roared out of the river, Alpha grabbed the tailgate and hauled himself into the back.

The vehicle roared up the bank and into the burning forest. The heat was searing and the air filled with the sounds of crackling grass and breaking branches.

"Cut the engine!" Alpha thumped on the cab roof. "I can't pinpoint over the din."

The truck stopped. To the left, they could hear a high-pitched screaming.

"God, that girl has a fine pair of lungs!" Alpha motioned to Mike. "She's over there."

The truck moved off again, its wheels kicking up sparks as they rolled over the burning undergrowth. Alpha slapped at the glowing embers drifting down onto his body.

Echo was in a tall conifer, several meters up. The bottom of the tree was already on fire. Mike pulled up next to it and kept the engine running.

"I can't climb down," the girl wailed.

"Jump." Alpha held out his arms. "I'll catch you."

"Are you *kidding*? I'm twenty feet up."

"I won't be able to stay here long," Mike yelled. "The water on the wheels is already evaporating. They'll melt soon!"

"Yeah, ok!" Alpha flinched as a burning branch landed next to the vehicle. "Jump, damn you!"

"I can't! I'm too high!"

"Do you *know* what that fire will do to your pretty face when it reaches you?"

Echo let out another wail. Alpha could hear Mike coughing as smoke poured into the cab. The boy began to roll up his window.

Worse, the leader knew Echo was right. He *would* try to catch her but the impact would certainly injure them both.

"Now!" he screamed, before his courage deserted him.

Echo closed her eyes.

A giant dog leapt over the tailgate and landed in the bed of the truck. Its fur was scorched and burns mottled the creature's legs. The hound drew back its lips to reveal vicious fangs. Alpha reached for his weapon.

The holster was empty. His gun had fallen out as he climbed into the truck.

"Wait! Stay there!" he hissed to Echo as he backed away, hands held uselessly in front of him.

"Please catch me, Alpha!" The girl hadn't heard him.

As the dog prepared to spring, Echo let go.

Eyes still closed, she cannonballed through the burning branches and landed on top of the creature. The dog gave an astonished grunt and crumpled to the truck bed. The girl bounced off its smoldering back and crashed into Alpha, slamming them both into the back of the cab. With a cry of pain, the leader grabbed Echo's pistol and emptied it into the hound. Then he pulled the girl towards him and began to feel her arms and legs for injury.

Echo opened her eyes and stared at the prone creature.

"Did I just jump from the top of a tree and land on a burning dog?" To Alpha's astonishment, she began to giggle hysterically. "Let's do that again!"

"Is she all right?" Mike's voice drifted out of the cab. "Can I go now?"

"By all means, hunter. She's great."

The leader started to laugh as well.

"Either she has post-traumatic stress or she's just discovered her inner daredevil."

-26-

The truck rumbled out of the forest and back into the river. The Threes surrounded the vehicle and pulled out the dead dog, letting the current carry it away like a huge wet rag.

"Hot, hot, hot!" Mike flung open the cab door and fell into the water.

"Is my face all right?" Still cackling, Echo patted her cheeks. "I got fur between my teeth!"

"You're all right. Apart from that big spot on your chin."

"Don't look at it, then!" The girl sat up, holding her side. "There's cream in my rucksack."

"I'm sure glad *someone's* enjoying themselves." Uniform waded towards the bank. The meadow scrub had burned away, leaving a sooty, charred wasteland, dotted with glowing motes. "Come on. We can use the residual heat to dry our clothes."

"Did he just use the word *residual*?" Tango sloshed after him. "He's not as much of a meathead as he looks."

"This meathead has ears, builder. And a big sword."

An hour later, the Threes huddled together in the ruined valley. Far off, to the east, the conflagration still raged and they could hear trees crashing to the ground.

"I guess setting up a community here is now firmly out of the question." Alpha wiped a streak of grime from his cheek. "Seems we have no option but to move on and look for more fertile land."

"I'm not sure there *is* any in this area." Mike raised his hand. "Or else the dogs would simply have migrated."

"Great." The leader pursed his lips. "Anyone got good news?"

"I saved four bottles of Coke," Tango said brightly.

"Better than nothing. Pass them round."

They chugged from the bottles, savoring the taste.

"I guess we have no choice but to look for the other Forts." Juliet smacked her lips. "Be nice if they had more of this stuff."

"They might know of a way we can get the Types out," Mike added.

"And proper weapons in case we come up against something worse than the dogs."

"Always looking on the bright side, Uniform. Huh?"

"Sunny kind of guy, Sir." The boy waded back into the river. "I'll refill the water bottles."

"I declare, I don't know what to do about *you* three." Alpha squinted at Sierra, Juliet and Mike. "You saved our bacon, that's true. But you also disobeyed a direct order."

"You can have the rifle," the boy volunteered.

"A bit late to be toadying, now. Keep it. I can't hunt and you know it." Alpha rubbed his sodden hair. "You'll have to be punished, but now isn't the time. I'll decide where and when. Do you agree?"

Mike nodded.

"Then let's get out of here while we still have light." The boy tossed the ignition keys to Echo. "You drive."

"I'm *injured*."

"You're bruised. And the driver's seat is the most comfortable."

"But I don't know how to operate a truck."

"You'll learn as you go along. It's what we're all gonna have to do."

The vehicle moved across the charred meadow, slowly but steadily, increasing in speed as Echo gained confidence.

Sierra waited until nobody was looking, then quietly emptied her bag of seeds over the side of the truck.

"No more farming for me," she muttered to herself.

Inside the cab, Alpha tapped Echo on the shoulder.

"At the end of the valley, veer right," he said. "After a few miles, you'll come to a highway. It'll be overgrown, of course, but this thing can handle most terrains, so you ought to be able to traverse it."

"How do you know it's *there*?" Echo stared at him.

"Look where you're going, girl." The leader kept his own eyes fixed on the horizon. "And don't *you* start questioning me. I picked you to drive cause you can actually obey orders."

"Not when it comes to wandering off." The girl looked ashamed. "You *told* me to stay with Tango."

"It's a miracle you weren't badly hurt."

"I don't know if you're relieved or annoyed."

"Both, I guess." Alpha let out a long sigh. "I didn't realize being the leader would be so *hard*."

"You're learning as you go along," Echo smiled. "It's what we're all gonna have to do."

"Nicely put." The boy grinned. "Oh. When you reach the road, try and look surprised. It'll be our little secret."

He winked at her.

"Now, let me out, so I can keep an eye on those other reprobates."

The Threes sat in the back of the truck, gazing dolefully as their wrecked paradise sped past. All except Mike.

He was studying Uniform, crouched in one corner, chin on his knee.

The boy had been between the feral dog and Alpha when it attacked. Mike understood why the hound had circumvented Uniform to get at the leader. Pack animals went for the weakest prey and their leader was lying on the ground.

That wasn't what puzzled him.

Alpha was facing the wrong way to witness what had happened. Juliet and Sierra were too preoccupied and Echo was in the forest. But Mike had seen it and was sure Tango must have too.

Despite being within striking distance, Uniform hadn't made the *slightest* attempt to save Alpha. Didn't raise his sword or draw his revolver.

Why not? What was the protector up to?

"I finally found my role." Juliet jolted Mike from his thoughts. She pulled a digital recorder from a package. "Saw this when we were looking for matches. It's solar-powered and still works."

"What are you going to do with it?"

"I'm taking Alpha at his word and recording the adventures of the new human race. I'll call it *The History of New Eden*."

"Cool." Tango patted her unruly hair. "Make me petite and blonde, like Echo."

"It's gonna be truthful. It *has* to be."

"What have you got so far?" Alpha asked.

Juliet spoke into the machine.

We are the Threes. And we are determined not to make the same mistakes as our ancestors. Mind you, we've been in New Eden one day and, so far, we've wiped out an entire species and destroyed all the habitable land we've encountered.

The leader frowned. Then he sat back and chuckled.

"Powerful beginning." He lay back on the truck bed and pulled the cap down over his face. "How we gonna top that?"

"Depends on what's waiting for us." Juliet tucked the recorder into her pocket.

And they headed through the carnage towards the unknown.

-27-

When I was a little girl, my mom used to take me on vacation to an isolated cabin in the woods. It was very beautiful but there was nobody else to play with and being alone in the middle of nowhere made me nervous. Who knew what dangers were out there?

New Eden is like that. Times one hundred.

The History of New Eden

They drove for several hours. Echo found an overgrown road and carefully followed it. After she had learned the rudiments of driving, Alpha let everyone else take a turn, much to their delight. Surprisingly, Tango proved the most adept, skirting the occasional fallen tree or rusted hulk without slowing down.

"Always been good at avoiding things." She spun the wheel and rocketed around a huge pothole. "Wheeeeeeeeeeeeeee!"

"Try to avoid crashing." Sierra gripped the dashboard so tightly her knuckles turned white. "And never say *wheeeeeee* again."

In the back, Uniform crawled over to Alpha. The others were lying on the bed of the truck, exhausted.

"Sun's on the left hand side of the vehicle, Sir," he whispered.

"What of it?"

"That means we're heading north, not south."

"A bit of information I'd thank you to keep to yourself."

"Ehm... I may have already mentioned it to the rest," Uniform said awkwardly. "Mike and Juliet would have figured it out anyhow."

The leader noticed the pair eyeing him warily.

"Do I have your loyalty, protector?"

"Of course. You're the Alpha."

"Then back me up when the time comes." He thumped the rear of the cab. "Stop here, Tango. Let's get out and build a fire. Give Mike a chance to hunt."

This time, the boy was able to kill a couple of rabbits. The Threes sat round the fire, tucking into the roasted carcasses.

"Meat at last," Alpha burped contentedly. "I declare, it's just as tasty as I hoped."

The others stayed silent, watching him.

"We circumvented the fire and this area is lusher," the leader continued. "We're definitely on the right track."

"We're going towards Canada." Mike threw the remains of his meal away. "The Forts are the other way."

"We have a lot of fuel in the drums but not enough to drive around forever," Alpha replied tersely. "Finding the Forts would be like looking for a needle in a haystack and we can already see that this direction is promising."

"What about Mike 32 and the other Types?" Juliet got out her recorder. "Do I record the fact that our leader decided to give up on them?"

"Say what you see fit," Alpha scowled. "Keeping you alive to do so will always be my priority."

"May I suggest a compromise?" Echo said diplomatically. "Why don't we make this area our base and let Uniform scout south in the truck? He might get lucky."

"I *am* an explorer as well as a protector," the boy agreed. "It was always meant to be part of any Uniform's role in New Eden."

"When there were 30 of you to protect the rest of the Types," Alpha said through gritted teeth. "You have to *trust* me, people."

"Trust is a two-way street," Mike retorted. "What are you hiding, Sir?"

"Nothing."

"I saw you take something from Harvey's truck." The boy wouldn't let up. "Seemed to scare you."

Uniform shot his leader a quizzical look.

"Look at this place." Alpha pointed to the green rolling hills stretching north. "We have a real chance of thriving here. Sure, we've got a vehicle now, but the simple fact remains. We don't have many options and this is the best one."

"Then hand over a share of the provisions and I'll be on my way." Juliet stood up. "I'll look for the Forts on foot."

"I'll be coming with you." Sierra got up as well.

"You can take your weapons and packs." The leader nodded to Uniform. "Those who stay will need the rest of the supplies."

"As you wish, Sir." The protector planted himself between the truck and the rest of the Threes, steady as a rock.

"So, you're only interested in keeping your people alive if they obey without question," Sierra grunted.

"You're not my people if you don't."

"He's the boss," Uniform added menacingly. "You ought to remember that."

"So be it." Sierra shouldered her rucksack. "Apologies for wanting to have a mind of my own. I wish y'all luck."

She turned her back and walked away.

Juliet grabbed her pack and followed.

"Don't be so silly." Tango tisked. "You won't make it on your own."

"They will if they have a hunter tagging along." Mike struggled to his feet and Juliet gave him a grateful smile.

The boy wondered if he was being used. Not that it mattered. He had made a promise to Mike 32 and had to honor it.

"Stop them, Uniform," Alpha commanded.

Mike paused, hand resting lightly on the butt of his revolver.

"Looks like I'd have to kill them in the process." Uniform didn't move. "Which won't help us none."

He rubbed his bristled head.

"Truth be known, we'd be in a pretty bad situation, ourselves, without a hunter and a farmer. I can bump off ginger top if you like."

"My hair's *flame*-colored," Juliet snapped. "How many times do I have to say it?"

The trio marched away.

"Aw, get back here, you spoiled brats." Alpha threw up his hands. "I'll *show* you why we can't go south."

-28-

The Threes squatted round their campfire. Alpha reached into his own pack and pulled out a square of paper. He unfolded and spread it out, while the others clustered round. Firelight flickered across the surface, so that the contours seemed to be moving.

"You forgot to look in Harvey's glove compartment, Jules," he said. "I found this map of the USA there."

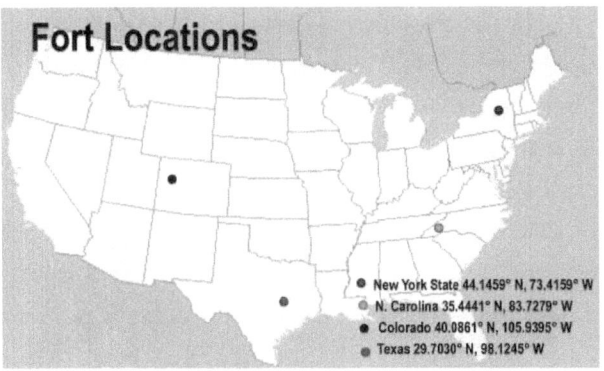

"The numbers are coordinates showing the exact locations of the Forts," he continued. "I'm guessing we have enough gas in the drums to reach the one in North Carolina and still make it back."

"So, how come we're going the other way?" Sierra spluttered. "Why would you *keep* this from us?"

"Turn the map over. Dr Stoddart wrote something on the other side before he died."

The teenagers almost tore the paper in their rush to see.

When I left Mrs Brown, I made my way to the control center. Everyone was dead but I could see they'd been trying to contact the other Forts to warn them about our predicament. The screens were still on so, for the first time, I was able to see their exact locations. I recorded them on this map.

It was obvious from the last few communications that we were not the only ones who had been sabotaged. The computer in Fort Texas malfunctioned too and all I got from the Colorado complex was an automated message asking for help. I could not contact Fort North Carolina at all.

But I fear they are the aggressor. North Carolina housed Central Command and was the only complex with master codes that could override the other Forts' systems. I can't understand why, but the attacks must have been launched from there.

This note is for any survivors. I must assume Forts Colorado and Texas are gone and Fort North Carolina is an enemy.

You are on your own.

"I couldn't bear to tell you what I'd found." Alpha's voice cracked. "I wanted to keep some spark of hope alive."

"I appreciate that, Sir," Mike said. "But we're not children."

"Actually, we are."

"He means it wasn't a burden you needed to bear alone," Echo smiled. "Now that you've told us, we understand."

Juliet looked *far* from understanding.

"So, we *have* to stay here," the leader sighed. "You see that, don't you? We've nowhere else to go."

"You're missing the most important thing," Mike tapped one of the scrawled lines. "Look what Dr Stoddart wrote, right here."

North Carolina housed Central Command and was the only complex with master codes that could override the other Forts' defenses.

"With a master code, we could open the blast doors open and set the Types free. According to Mike 32, they have enough firepower to stand a real chance getting past the mutants."

"But North Carolina is probably hostile."

"Don't be such a sad sack." Tango pinched the boy on the arm. "That note was written two hundred years ago. There's no telling how much the situation has changed."

"We'll never know unless we go look for ourselves." Juliet clasped her hands. Mike recognized the gesture as one she used when she desperately wanted something. "I couldn't live with that uncertainty."

"What are you proposing?"

"We drive to Fort North Carolina and secretly scope it out. If it's gone or still aggressive, that's an end to the matter. We retreat and start a new life here."

"You don't take no for an answer, eh Jules?"

"Gotta have *something* to record." The girl grinned. "Can't have every entry saying *Woke up. Hunted. Gathered crops. Went to sleep.*"

"Gonna be hard to do that, anyhow." Sierra's bit her lip. "I threw away my seeds."

"You did *what*?"

"I was in a bad mood."

"Lead us south, Sir." Uniform interrupted. "I only been in paradise two days and I'm bored stiff."

"You all feel the same way?" Alpha looked around.

One by one, the Threes nodded.

"And you'll obey orders this time?"

"Without question."

"Come back with me if it doesn't pan out?"

"You got it."

"I'm not a sentimental sort." The leader smiled. "But I appreciate you all rallying around each other. It's what I mean about hope."

"Yeah, you're a big softy at heart." Tango pinched him again.

"I guess I am." Alpha slapped her away. "But Uniform isn't. Next time someone disobeys a direct order, he'll beat them to a pulp."

"That I will, Sir."

Once the sun had gone down, Juliet excused herself. After a while, Mike went to check on her.

She was standing in an overgrown field, the full moon bathing her in pale luminescence. She drew her revolver and fired. The top of a nearby bush rattled, dropping a shower of monochrome petals. Juliet returned the gun to its holster. Drew again. More of the bush exploded. She holstered the weapon once more.

Mike approached her silently.

Juliet spun round and the gun seemed to leap into her hand.

"I think the plant is dead now." The boy put his arms up in mock surrender. "Nice shooting."

"Would be, if I wasn't trying to hit the tree next to it."

"Mind if I have a go?" He stood next to her. "Any time you're ready."

They drew together. Juliet was much faster but her missile whizzed past the sapling. The boy took his time, aimed and fired. A hole appeared in the tree.

"Fast is good, but not if you miss what you're trying to kill." The boy sighted down the barrel to show her how it was done. "Accuracy counts for more."

"I'll keep practicing until I can do both."

"Why so keen to be a gunfighter?"

"Alpha seems a nice guy but he's a weak leader," Juliet said. "I've disobeyed him twice and he still hasn't asserted himself."

"You ought to be grateful for that."

"His soft heart could get us killed. And he should have realized Fort North Carolina offers our best hope of survival."

She drew and fired again. This time, a hole appeared in the tree.

"What if the inhabitants are hostile?" Mike asked.

"That's why I'm learning to shoot."

The boy raised an eyebrow, remembering Mrs Brown's words.

Juliet won't let anything stand in the way of what she wants. She has no feelings or morals of any sort.

Once again, she had got exactly what she desired. They were, indeed, heading for North Carolina. Once more, Mike had helped the girl achieve her goal.

What if, someday, he decided not to?

"You keep practicing, then," the boy said nonchalantly.

"Maybe we *all* should."

The Journey South

One thorn of experience is worth a whole wilderness of warning.

James Lowell

-29-

We debated what to tell Fort North Carolina, in case it really is the enemy. Tango said the best lies stick closely to the truth and I agree. We'll say our own complex was overrun by mutants and we were the only people who escaped. Seven of us surely won't seem like much of a threat and that is *what happened, after all.*

We'll just not mention the other Types.

The History of New Eden

"Keep on this road, Echo, until you come to what used to be Interstate 87." Alpha had his feet on the dashboard, hands behind his head. "We can follow it south all the way to New York City. Maybe pick up extra tinned food when we get there. There'll be big stores in Albany too. It's the only sizable town in between."

"How do you know? You're not using the map."

"Grew up in the Big Apple," the boy said proudly. "Queens. Even at nine, I swore like a trooper. Guess Mrs Brown knocked that out of me with her insistence on good manners."

"Thank God you didn't pick up her Texan accent to boot," Echo smiled. "Uniform and Sierra did. They sound like they ought to have banjos strapped on their backs."

"Talking of manners, I'm forgetting mine." Alpha sat up straight. "Mrs Brown never used our real names, so I don't know yours."

"It's Ethel." The girl kept her eyes on the road. "I'll stick to Echo if you don't mind."

"What did your father do in the Fort, Ethel? I mean... Echo."

"He never took the time to tell me," the girl replied stonily. "In fact, he never spoke to me much at all."

She glanced at Alpha.

"And you?"

"I'm Harper Henderson III. My father was General Harper Henderson II, military commander in charge of keeping Fort New York State protected." Alpha stared at his knuckles. "That's pretty much all I know about him, apart from the fact that he failed spectacularly."

"*You've* kept everyone safe."

"Seems more by luck than judgment."

"I disagree. If you weren't up to the job, no amount of good fortune would have helped us."

"I thank you for that."

"Strikes me that none of us has much of a past. And what we do remember is too painful to dwell on." Echo steered round the remains of a rusted station wagon. "I, for one, would sorely like to start afresh."

"You're off to a good start," the leader grinned. "Haven't cried once all day."

"Yeah. Let me start by apologizing for being such a pathetic whiner. You risked your life to save me, so you have my complete support. And I give you my word that, from now on, I won't be shy about voicing that opinion."

"In that case, I want you to keep this safe." The boy pulled a small, sealed box from his rucksack and stuffed it into Echo's bag. "You're the medic, after all."

"What's in there?"

"A bunch of little vials. I found it in Dr Stoddart's glove compartment. I suspect it's WC-57 but I don't know for certain and I'm sure as hell not taking any to find out."

"I'll hang on to it." The girl rolled down the window and let the breeze ruffle her short blonde hair. "Just smell that fresh air!"

"You actually starting to *like* it out here?"

"I'm driving a truck through a forest. I killed a mutant hound with my butt. I'm losing weight and I've got a revolver strapped to my increasingly slim waist." The truck bounced over a log and Echo automatically reached out for Alpha's hand and squeezed. "For the first time, I'm thinking, what's not to like?"

The boy looked down in surprise.

"Don't you need both hands to drive?" But he didn't let go.

"Not unless we meet a vehicle coming the other way, Sir. And that's pretty unlikely."

"There's no need to call me *Sir*. Nor Harper, come to think of it."

The boy squeezed back.

"I'm just Alpha."

Echo let go of the leader and slammed on the brake.

"Lookee here!"

The truck stopped next to a brown and yellow sign. Its paint was peeling and plants curled round the supports, but they had no problem reading it.

Elizabethtown, Essex County
Population 1,160

"Population zero now," Alpha remarked drily.

They could hear a hubbub in the back of the truck. Sierra's hands appeared at the side of the open window frame, then her head.

"Civilization," She wiggled her eyebrows. "Can we take a look?"

"Don't see why not,"

"I'm gonna fall, anyhow." The girl began to slide out of view. "I'm leaning out the back like a junkyard dog."

She vanished with a squeal. There was a soft thud, followed by hysterical giggling.

"Guess you're not the only one who's feeling happier." Alpha winked at Echo. "Let's check the place out."

-30-

The houses were crumbling and the paint peeling. White picket fences leaned at crazy angles and telephone wires sagged until they almost touched the ground. The only objects to survive the ravages of time and the elements unchanged were plastic garden ornaments, flashes of bright color in the tangled brush of former gardens. A yellow children's slide rose from a honeysuckle bush, looking as if it had been played on only yesterday.

"This is about as creepy a place as you could imagine," Mike commented as the Threes got out and stretched.

"Don't get too far from the truck," Uniform cautioned.

"Why?" Tango laughed. "You think bears moved into the houses?"

"You never read Goldilocks?"

"I don't care. I'm bursting for the toilet." Sierra made for the nearest house. "This place will do. The door's open."

"Shout if you find a mummified body already sitting there."

"Eeeeugh. I'll go round the back." Sierra swerved away. "No peeking!"

"Watch out for poison ivy," Echo called. "I'm not spreading ointment on *anybody's* backside."

The others trooped off, casting a careful eye over the flora. When they returned, they opened some canned food and ate the contents.

"There's something not quite right about this place too." Mike kept looking around. "I just can't put my finger on it."

"Aw, not again," Juliet groaned. "Don't you ever turn off your danger radar?"

"Let's hope not." Alpha rubbed his sweating brow. "He was right last time and, anyhow, this place is too small for scavenging." He opened the cab door. "Let's get moving. You take the wheel, Sierra."

"But I'm the worst driver."

"Then you need practice." He tapped Mike on the shoulder as the boy was climbing into the back. "I finally thought of your punishment, hunter."

"What would that be?"

"You have to sit next to her," the leader beamed. "Best wear a seatbelt."

The landscape slowly changed. Forests of silver birch and pine gradually gave way to a sea of grass dotted with broken down farmhouses.

Sierra slowed as they reached the outskirts of Albany.

"Now, *there's* a sight," she breathed.

The town was big enough to have a couple of sky-scrapers, but they no longer scraped the sky. They had toppled in on themselves and looked like giant rotting teeth.

This time, there was silence from the back.

Sierra drove slowly. The highway was filled with cars but two centuries had reduced them to rusted blobs. Where they clogged the road entirely, she guided the truck over the tops, crushing them to ochre dust. Windows devoid of glass, peered at them from wilting, moss encrusted buildings and open doors were sinister squares, like the mouths of caves.

"And you thought *Elizabethtown* was creepy," Sierra grunted. "This place is giving me the heebie-jeebies."

She stopped in the town center.

"Have a look round if you want." She leaned back and pulled her cap over her eyes. "I'm sitting this one out."

Mike stuck his head through the open cab window.

"I don't think we should stop here, Sir," he yelled.

"Why not?" Alpha jumped down. "There's bound to be a Wal-Mart around somewheres."

"Something's still bugging me," the boy said. "This place doesn't feel right either."

"Can't we please get down?" Juliet complained. "It's getting mighty hot up here."

"Yeah, go on." The leader gave Mike a resigned shrug. "*I* can't see any sign of danger but be careful, anyways. Yell if you get into trouble."

The Threes jumped out and strolled up a wide thoroughfare lined with boutiques. Alpha lay back in the truck bed and shut his eyes, relishing a few minutes of peace.

Echo was passing a department store with Juliet, when a flash of blue caught her eye. She stopped and backtracked.

In the window was a shop dummy wearing a dress. It was a halter neck with white trim and a dainty lace frill at the bottom.

"I would look *so* fine in that."

"Not after a few days working in the fields, you wouldn't." Juliet took a quick glance and carried on. "I'm gonna see if I can find some tinned fruit. I'm sick of refried beans."

Echo wasn't listening. She could see her reflection in the glass and she positioned herself so that the dress was superimposed on her uniform.

"Perfect."

She patted her hair down and pushed open the door.

The shop was dusty and smelled faintly of mold. The girl made her way down the aisles until she came to the window display.

"I'm looking for something that will bring out the color of my eyes," she remarked to an imaginary assistant. "Why, thank you. They *are* pretty, aren't they?"

She stepped up and squinted at the price tag on the dress.

$450.00

"Hmmmmm, it's a bit steep," she said, stroking her chin. "Oh, no, it's not a problem, ma'am. Nothing is out of my price range these days. I'm with the Bank of Apocalypse."

She reached out and tried to remove the dress from the dummy. The 200-year-old fabric dissolved in her hands, scraps of desiccated cloth drifting down to the floor.

Echo blew a raspberry.

"Shoddy workmanship, all in all," she grunted. "I fear I shall be taking my custom elsewhere."

A shadow fell over the pavement outside and the girl froze.

A huge glistening snout slid into view, followed by a massive head. Echo's heart began to pound.

It was a bear.

-31-

The girl remained motionless. She had seen pictures of bears in the Division of Youth and vaguely remembered watching them on TV when she was little.

She hadn't realized they were quite that large. The creature in the street was almost the size of their truck.

The bear lazily turned its head and peered in the window. Motes of dust from the ruined dress circled the display, tickling Echo's nose, and she tried desperately not to sniff or sneeze. Instead, she remained stock-still, imitating the display dummies around her.

The beast put two giant paws on the window and the glass shivered ominously. The beast yawned lazily, revealing foot long, yellow fangs and a puff of breath fogged the glass. Echo felt she might faint.

It landed back on all fours and continued on its way.

The girl's legs gave way and she sank to the floor.

"No, ma'am, I'm fine," she whispered. "Just thinking I might prefer something in camouflage."

Then her head shot up.

Juliet and Mike had been in front of her and the bear was heading in that direction.

Echo got up and tapped her fingers together. Mike had a rifle and Juliet was smart. Surely they'd see the creature coming and hide? But what if they didn't? *She* hadn't spotted it until it was almost too late. What if they were in a store too? What if Mike had put down his rifle to carry supplies?

Her heart sank.

Too many *what-ifs* to let the bear carry on.

Echo raced back through the aisles and pulled open the door. The monster was ambling uphill in the middle of the street. There was no sign of Juliet of Mike.

The girl pulled out her gun. She had only ever shot at tin cans but this was a pretty easy target. She took careful aim, like Mike had shown her, then pulled the trigger.

There was a whoosh of air and the bear stopped. It sat up, felt its hairy rump with one paw and let out a low growl.

"Oh shit." Echo looked down at her weapon. "This thing is like a bee sting to that brute."

Nevertheless, she raised the gun and fired again.

The bear flinched and looked round. It spotted the teenager and gave an astonished roar.

Then it charged.

Echo let out a piercing shriek and darted back into the store, bolting between racks of clothes.

The bear crashed through the doorway without slowing, demolishing the brickwork on either side. It lumbered through the sales area, tongue lolling, sending up spouts of calico and nylon.

Echo looked around in panic. She grabbed a fire extinguisher from the wall and launched it through the store front window in a shower of sparkling shards. The rest of the glass collapsed like a melting glacier, as the girl jumped through the gap and raced downhill.

Seconds later, the bear squeezed its bulk out of the shop. With a satisfied grunt, it shook pieces of glass from its coat and came after Echo again.

As she sprinted back the way she had come, the truck rounded the corner at the bottom of the slope and rattled uphill. Sierra was driving and Alpha stood in the back, holding onto the cab roof.

The girl glanced back. The bear was gaining fast. The truck accelerated and Alpha fell backward with a curse, before regaining his footing.

Echo's legs were burning and her breath came in terrified spurts. All the same, she was aware the vehicle was heading straight for her and it wasn't slowing.

Sierra leaned out of the cab, gesturing wildly.

Get down, she mouthed over the revving engine. *Get DOWN!*

Echo felt a blast of hot, fetid air on her back. She threw herself forwards and landed on the cracked paving, face scraping along the concrete.

The truck rumbled right over her prone figure and slammed into the bear, almost sending Alpha over the top of the cab. He sank to his knees, winded, stars floating in front of his eyes.

The truck's wheels spun madly, burning rubber inches from Echo's shoulder. Heat from the drive shaft, directly above, wafted down and singed her hair. She pressed her cheek against the asphalt.

The creature slammed both paws on the hood of the vehicle. Its massive jaws were inches from the windscreen, lathering the Perspex with spittle.

Sierra kept her foot on the gas, but the enormous creature was matching the truck's power.

Slowly, it began to push the vehicle back until Echo's legs were visible.

Alpha recovered and began shooting. The bear swatted at the bullets in fury and the truck moved forwards a foot.

The overheated engine died.

The creature reared up on its hind legs and attempted to reach Alpha. One muscular leg scrabbled on the bumper as it tried to haul itself onto the hood. Sierra turned the key in the ignition and the engine spluttered and died again.

There was a sharp crack and the bear roared in pain. It slid back to the ground and turned to seek out the new assailant.

Mike was kneeling halfway up the hill, rifle pressed to his cheek.

The hunter fired again, but his efforts had no effect. The creature loped uphill towards him, face expressionless.

If the boy was panicking, he showed no sign. He calmly lined up another shot and his rifle recoiled.

The bear didn't slow down.

Sierra turned the key one last time and the truck burst into life. She slammed her foot on the gas.

The monster had almost reached Mike when the vehicle plowed into its hind quarters. It collapsed with a bellow and began to crawl towards the boy.

Alpha ran across the cab roof and leaped onto its shaggy neck.

He and Mike fired at the same time. One bullet hit the beast between the eyes. The other burrowed into the back of its skull.

The bear's eyes filmed over and it stopped breathing. Mike flopped backwards onto the road and let out a shuddering sigh of relief.

Alpha ran over to Echo's prone form.

"You all right?" he said, kneeling beside her. "This is getting to be a habit."

"I bet my hair's all frizzy now." The girl rolled onto her back and coughed, trying to clear gas fumes from her lungs.

"Albany better have a beauty salon."

-32-

Mike seems to have nerves of steel. I saw him take on that bear out in the open, when I was too scared to move from my hiding place.

I guess it's what he was trained for but it still took guts.

Mrs Brown did a good job training the Threes. They seem up to any challenge. Which only makes me feel even more useless. I'm just not like them.

Which is her fault. Why the hell did that woman dislike me so much?

The History of New Eden

"Bear tastes good!"

The teenagers sat around the campfire, eating hunks of sizzling meat.

"I'd like to make a small speech." Alpha stood up.

"About how you killed the monster using just a piece of string and a nail file?" Tango pulled a face at Uniform. "I just know this tale's going to get bigger with every telling."

"I would have helped if I'd been there," the protector huffed.

191

"Actually, I was gonna make a toast to Echo, Mike and Sierra. They all risked their lives to help each other. That's teamwork."

"You didn't exactly sit back and watch," Echo reminded him.

"Tango's right. By the third time I recount it, I'll have killed the beast with my bare hands." He grinned. "*Bare* hands. Geddit?"

"I don't want to be a party pooper," Juliet said. "But a bear shouldn't be that size, should it?"

They all looked at Mike.

"No." The boy looked at the huge carcass. "I understand the guard dogs being mutated. They were experimented on by the Fort. But how could *that* beast possibly be affected?"

Nobody had an answer.

The next day, they loaded the truck with all the canned goods they could find.

"Next stop, New York City," Alpha said. "It's only a couple of hours away."

He patted Mike on the shoulder.

"You were right. There *was* danger here. I don't know how you knew."

"I didn't." The boy took one last look at Albany. "It's something else bothering me about these towns. I just can't get a handle on it."

"I need something more concrete than your intuition, hunter. There's no way I'm passing up a visit to NYC. Wanna see Times Square again."

He leaned in and patted the dashboard.

"And a little plastic Statue of Liberty would look just dandy right here. Huh, Uniform?"

"Very tasteful, Sir."

Sierra tried to make conversation as she drove, but Mike was deep in thought. What was it about Elizabethtown and Albany that disturbed him so much?

Finally, he gave up. The suburbs of New York must be close. He would wait to see if the city gave him that same uneasy feeling.

"Mike?" Sierra ground to a halt. "Is there *supposed* to be a lake in our way?"

Ahead of her, Interstate 87 vanished into a huge body of water.

"A lake doesn't have waves." The boy pointed to white breakers rolling in from the distance.

"This has gotta be the Atlantic Ocean."

Alpha spread his map out on the ground.

"We lost, Sir?" Uniform asked.

"Nope." The boy traced the highway with his finger. "We're on the right road, no doubt about it. This Interstate is supposed to continue straight into the Big Apple."

He grimly folded the map.

"Seems like New York is gone."

Echo laid a hand gently on his shoulder.

"I'm sorry, Sir."

Alpha looked at Tango. She was hopping from foot to foot, casting hopeful glances at the sea.

"I recall you saying you loved the beach, builder."

"Oh, I do. I *really* do."

"Then go have a paddle." The leader smiled half-heartedly. "All of you may as well cool off with her."

"You coming too?"

"Presently. Don't go in over your waists, though." Alpha wagged a finger. "None of us can swim, remember? And leave your sword, Uniform. Can't have it floating away."

"Not an idiot, Sir. Despite all appearances."

The teenagers ran for the surf and waded in. Soon, they were splashing and yelling with delight. Only Echo remained, sitting next to Alpha.

"I guess we detour," the boy said, opening the map again. "Pick up Interstate 81 and follow it to North Carolina."

"Are you all right?"

"I'm fine." Alpha patted her knee.

"No, you're not."

"Aw, I hardly remember the place." The leader turned away so Echo couldn't see the tears in his eyes. "Look at how much fun those guys are having. Aren't you gonna dip a toe?"

"Salt water's bad for my skin." Echo scooped up a handful of sand and let it run through her fingers. "Besides, I don't wanna play over what's left of your home. You should have told the others."

"Why spoil things for them?" Alpha shrugged. "Mike seems to have calmed down, at least."

"I'm not so sure."

The boy was running up the beach, tunic in hand. He sank to his knees in front of them.

"I figured out what's wrong." he puffed. "Albany and Elizabethtown are still standing."

"*That's* what was bothering you?" The leader laughed grimly. "What did you expect? They'd just vanish?"

"In a word, yes. Nature should have annihilated them by now."

"I'm not sure what you're getting at." Alpha licked salt from his lips. "Both towns were filled with weeds and brush like you'd expect."

"Weeds that are a couple of feet high," Mike persisted. "After 200 years, plants should have totally enveloped the buildings. There ought to be full-sized trees in the streets."

"He has a point, Sir," Echo joined in. "The roads are overgrown, but shouldn't a couple of centuries of plants pushing through the tarmac have destroyed them completely?"

"I guess so." Alpha tried to make light of the situation. "Are you saying we have a horde of mystery gardeners clearing up the highway and the towns along his route?"

He gave a chuckle.

"If so, they're sure keeping themselves well hidden. As in dead."

"I don't know *what* to make of it." Mike pulled on his top.

"What the hell is stopping the remnants of civilization crumbling to dust?"

Goldilocks wakes up to find the Three bears watching her.

"What are you doing sleeping in my bed?" says baby bear.

"Never mind that," Goldilocks replies. "How did you manage to make porridge when you don't have thumbs?"

That's New Eden's first joke.

Mike told me about our baffling gardeners. After two years foraging around in Mrs Brown's data banks, I have a pretty good idea why the towns are still standing. But I can't tell the Threes, in case they turn back. And I need to find Fort North Carolina. I can't hunt or farm and don't want to. The Fort may still have technology and that's what I'm good at.

I want to belong somewhere.

The History of New Eden

The Threes decided to make camp near the sea. Beyond the fire, they could hear the crash of waves in the darkness and the night air had a brackish tang.

"Unlikely as it seems. we have to assume that someone or something is alive out here." Alpha passed round a can of beans. "That's why the highways are passable and the towns standing."

"Could be the survivors of Fort North Carolina." Sierra spooned some of the contents into her mouth. "But there's a couple of years plant growth on the roads, so they ain't coming around too often."

"Why clear places up, then not live in them?" Echo pondered. "Seems a waste of valuable time and energy."

Juliet stayed silent.

"It's all guesswork until we get more info," Uniform said. "We'll ask the Fort when we find it. If they're not trying to kill us, that is."

"Mike suggested we start practicing with the handguns," Alpha added. "Just in case."

"For once, I agree with him." Uniform laughed. "I'll teach everyone if you like."

"Juliet's been at it for two days already."

"Has she, now?" The boy placed the empty can on a rock. "All right, red. Let's see who can draw and hit this first."

"I don't want to embarrass you," Juliet smiled.

"If I was easily embarrassed, I wouldn't have this haircut." The boy rubbed his head, now turning to dark stubble. "Wanna try your luck as well, hunter?"

"Why not?"

Uniform took up a stance, legs apart. Juliet adopted a more relaxed pose, shaking her hands lightly. Mike elbowed his way in between them.

"Ready."

"Count down from three, Sir."

"All right." Alpha raised his arm. "Three... two... one... draw!"

The can leapt into the air. Juliet, Uniform and Mike looked round in amazement. None of them had even cleared leather.

"Oopsie." Tango blew imaginary smoke from her barrel. She had drawn from a sitting position without even aiming. "Did I puncture your egos along with the tin?"

"How did you *do* that?"

"Used to play the X-Box a lot." The girl shoved her gun back in its holster. "And Juliet's not the only one who's been practicing."

"You never cease to amaze me, builder," Alpha chuckled. "Seems the only thing you're *not* good at is building."

"Maybe I'm in the wrong job, boss."

"Well, you're not having *mine*." Uniform inspected the hole, dead center of the can. "But I'll graciously accept your guidance in this matter."

"Thank you, sweetie."

"Calling a Uniform sweetie?" Sierra whistled. "Good job you're fast as you are."

"Actually, I don't mind." The protector sat down again. "So long as Mike never addresses me that way."

"Farthest thing from my mind."

"I'll take first watch." Tango grabbed her blanket. "I'm sure you'll all sleep more soundly, knowing there's a real sharpshooter on guard."

She left with a giggle.

The girl was propped up against a fallen tree when a figure approached.

"Halt. Who goes there?" She pulled out her weapon. "What's the password and that kind of thing?"

"Eh... please don't shoot me?" Uniform emerged from the darkness. "I wondered if you might appreciate some company."

"I would. Don't like the dark much."

The boy sat down and twiddled his thumbs.

"I'm a plain speaker, as you probably surmised."

"And you want to know how I can shoot so well."

"Well... yes." The boy rubbed his head awkwardly. "Back in the Fort you didn't seem to know one end of a gun from the other."

"That's me, hun. I'll do anything to get a laugh."

"And the truth?"

"My father knew we lived in dangerous times. He taught me how to use firearms since I was knee high."

"Oh." The protector sat quietly for a while. "Do you miss him?"

"He was my dad. What do you think?"

"*My* father was an administrator in the Fort. He hated weapons." The boy looked lost. "Maybe you *aren't* the only one who's in the wrong job."

"I'll pretend I didn't hear that." Tango glanced sideways at Uniform. "You're the protector, whether you like it or not. We've all got weapons, but *you're* the one the Threes look to for security."

"You sound different from usual. Almost, eh… normal."

"I can do a handstand and titter like an idiot, if it's what you prefer."

"No," the boy said quickly. "But why the act? Don't you want the others to take you seriously?"

"That's Alpha's role and he's welcome to it. It's already changing him."

Uniform thought about that.

"When people think you're dumb, they let their guard down," Tango continued. "So, I watch and I listen. I notice things others don't."

"Like what?"

Tango shrugged.

"I saw you didn't try to protect your precious leader from that ferocious doggie back at our Fort."

"I didn't... eh…" Uniform began. "It's not…"

"Don't." Tango held a finger to his lips. "We all have our secrets."

The boy nodded solemnly.

They sat quietly for a while, looking at the moon.

"I'm really not one for small talk," Uniform said, eventually. "I like shouting."

"All you need is practice," Tango laughed. "If you pretend to be something long enough, you eventually become it."

"You really believe that?"

"Most certainly." The girl pulled the blanket around her shoulders. "That's why I act happy."

"Fair enough." Uniform reached round his back and presented her with a sunflower. "Anyhow, I picked this for you."

"Oh." Tango took the blossom and sniffed it. "I don't know what to say."

"That'll be a first." The boy got up and bowed stiffly. "I'll bid you goodnight, builder, before I make an even bigger fool of myself."

He began to walk off.

"Protector?"

"Yeah."

"You got a nice butt, know that?" Tango tucked the blossom into her hair. "Been watching it all day."

Uniform grinned from ear to ear.

-34-

I can't quite work Mike out. He's calm and confident but doesn't speak much. I'm sure he likes me, but he seems determined to keep his distance.

It's like he has some big secret eating away at him. Or maybe it's just because he's short.

The History of New Eden

Next morning, the Three's advance was more difficult. There were too many rusted hulks on the highway to risk plowing over them. Fortunately, the truck was designed for rough terrain, so they drove through the overgrown fields next to the road. Abandoned tractors and derelict villages crawled past while crows circled overhead like scraps of ash.

"We need to pull over," Mike told Alpha.

"We're making slow enough progress as it is."

The boy leaned over and whispered in the leader's ear. Alpha slammed a hand on the cab roof and the vehicle rumbled to a halt.

"We're gonna pretend to stretch our legs," he said to the others. "Stay by the truck and act normal."

"I'm not sure we know how, hun."

"Don't be flippant, Tango." Alpha lowered the tail-gate.

"Mike thinks we're being followed."

The Threes lounged by the vehicle sipping from their canteens and surreptitiously glancing at the surrounding hills.

"Fine place for an ambush," Uniform said. "It'd be safer to have this chit-chat while we travel."

"Would you consent to sit on my knee, Juliet?" Mike beckoned.

"*There's* an offer I wasn't expecting." The girl shuffled over and straddled him, the back of her head pressed against the boy's cheek. Her hair smelled good, despite days without being properly washed. Mike slid an arm round her waist.

"Cheeky!"

"I can't use these if we're in a moving truck." With his other hand, the boy slid a pair of binoculars from a nearby pack and raised them to his eyes. Juliet's crimson tresses were the perfect camouflage.

"Ever get the feeling you're being used?" the girl complained.

"There's something on top of that hill," Mike said quietly.

Juliet shut up.

"*Something* is a bit vague, hunter." Uniform resisted the temptation to turn and peer in the direction

Mike was looking. "Something like a tree? Or something with big teeth?"

"Too far to tell." The boy lowered the binoculars.
"But it's been that exact distance from us for a couple
of hours now."

"Is another bear tracking us? Do they travel in
pairs?"

"Sometimes. But if we killed its partner, it would
attack as soon as it caught up. It wouldn't be hanging
out on a hill, watching."

"Can we outrun it?"

"Not on this road," Alpha nodded at the rusting
hulks. "It's too congested."

The leader stood up and fastened the top on his canteen.

"As Uniform pointed out, this is a great place for an
ambush, especially now we're out of the truck. If that
thing was going to attack, I reckon it would be heading
for us right now."

"Maybe it's waiting for reinforcements." Uniform
got up and joined him.

"Never a silver lining to *your* black clouds, huh
Uniform." Alpha slapped the boy on the shoulder.
"You should carry a sign saying End of the World is
Nigh."

"Already happened, Sir."

"From now on, we pair up. Nobody goes anywhere
alone, even if it's just for a short distance." Alpha
glanced around. "I'll buddy Echo."

"S'cuse me mentioning it, but neither of you can shoot."

"We been practicing. Echo's getting pretty good."

"Aint I just?" The girl wrinkled her nose. "I hit a giant bear in the rear."

"In that case, I'll take Tango," Uniform laughed. "She could hold off an army on her own."

"Admit it, sweetie, you just love my company. Who wouldn't?"

"Mike, for one. He's still got his arm around Juliet."

"Sorry!" The boy let go.

"Shame. I was just getting comfortable." Juliet struggled up. "But you best partner Sierra, Mike."

"Why?"

"Yeah, don't do *me* any favors," the farmer scowled. "I can handle myself."

"I like my own space." Juliet threw her pack into the bed of the truck and climbed into the cab. "If I concentrate on driving, I won't have to listen to you lot wittering on."

She stuck her head out of the window and winked at the Threes.

"Get aboard, suckers."

"Interstate 81 will take us all the way to North Carolina." Alpha studied the map. "According to Dr Stoddart's coordinates, the Fort is near a Lake Fontana in the Great Smokey Mountain National Park. We turn off on the North Shore Road and it will take us right there."

"Any cities on the way we can explore?"

"Nope. A couple of largish towns, is all."

"Could be a blessing in disguise," Uniform said. "City's an even better place for an ambush than these hills."

"Is your *something* still following us, hunter?"

"Saw it about half an hour ago."

"Damned thing is like an itch I can't scratch," Uniform grunted.

"What if I got out and waited for it?" Tango suggested. "It's probably never seen a gun. I'll soon show it that stalking isn't polite."

"If it's never seen a gun, it won't be afraid of yours. Just stay put."

"Poor thing's ears must be burning, whatever it is." Mike lay down and tilted his face to the sun.

"Harrisburg is coming up soon. Biggest place on the route." Alpha consulted the map. "I wish we could stop and look around. I'm dying for another bottle of Coke."

The truck suddenly accelerated. The Threes were catapulted across the vehicle bed and Echo's head slammed against the tailgate.

"What are you playing at, Jules?" She gingerly touched the rising bump. "Give us some warning before you do that."

"Behind us!" Juliet's arm shot out of the cab, thumb pointing behind her. "Good job I checked in the mirror."

The teenagers peered over the back.

"Oh, crud!"

Another bear was lumbering down the hillside towards them.

The last one had been big. This one was *enormous*, at least twice the size of the vehicle.

"It's a mountain on legs!" Alpha slammed his hand on the top of the cab. "Speed up, Jules!"

The truck careened wildly around abandoned cars and the Threes were thrown from side to side. The bear bounded after them, slowly gaining.

"Why is it so determined to catch us up?" Echo moaned.

"I don't think we killed its partner!" Mike grabbed his rifle.

"We killed its *cub*."

-35-

Juliet was afraid to go faster. Rusted cars loomed and receded as she wound her way through them. The vehicle was capable of outrunning any animal, no matter how large, but she knew that hitting an obstacle would doom them all. Sweat broke out on her forehead as she wrenched the wheel left and right.

In the back, Mike tried vainly to get a bead on the pursuing creature, but he was being flung from side to side.

The bear was still gaining ground.

"Tell Juliet to stop, Sir," he yelled. "It's the only chance we've got. If I can just get a head shot…"

"There's a dust storm ahead." Sierra peered over the roof of the cab. "We can hide in that."

The Threes could see a swirling gray cloud in the distance.

"What do we do, Sir?" Uniform urged. "Sir?"

But Alpha was staring over the side of the truck in amazement. The others followed his gaze, mouths dropping open.

"Is anything *else* gonna join this shindig!"

A horseman had appeared over the rise and was galloping alongside them. Long black hair streaked behind him and his bronzed body glistened in the sun. He was shouting something but his words were whipped away by the wind.

"Who the hell is he? Everyone's supposed to be dead!"

The rider gestured wildly with one sinewy arm, commanding them to leave the road. The bear was a mere fifty yards behind.

"We'll make introductions later." Alpha leaned over and yelled into the cab. "Head for that dust cloud, Juliet! It's thick as soup!"

But the girl veered off and headed in the direction the horseman was pointing.

"Follow damned orders, for once, will you?" Alpha screamed.

Either Juliet was ignoring him or couldn't hear, for she plowed through the long grass and over a dip. Before them stood a small brick homestead. The rider gestured towards it, then wheeled his mount and galloped away.

"What's red doing?" Uniform cursed. "The bear could take that place apart with one swipe!"

"The dust cloud is only a few hundred yards away!" Echo cried. "Why doesn't she go that way?"

The Threes pounded on the roof of the cab in frustration, but Juliet kept driving. She slewed to a halt outside the front door and leaped out.

"Get inside!" she shouted. "It's not a dust cloud. It's a glittermist!"

"A *what*?"

"It's more deadly than the bear!" The girl hauled open the door of the house. "Trust me! Grab any bottles of water you can. They'll save your life."

The Threes hesitated. Both the bear and the cloud were the same distance away, heading towards them from different directions.

"Do as Jules says." Alpha darted into the house. "She obviously has information we don't."

The interior of the house was dark and musty, dust layering the furniture. On the wall was a picture of a smiling family in a cracked frame. Juliet pushed the door shut.

"Thank God the windows are still intact." She ran to a dresser, pulled open a drawer and began removing tattered sheets and clothes. "Block up every hole you can find. The chimney. The gap under the door. Any air vents or cracks in the glass."

"Do it." Alpha dragged a rotting mattress from the bedroom and upended it against the fireplace. "What are we up against, Juliet?"

"Have you forgotten the bear?" Echo reminded them. "*It's* not going to bother coming down the damned chimney."

"The bear will be dead in a few seconds." Juliet snatched the picture from the wall and slammed it into a broken windowpane. "If any glitterbugs get in, crush them immediately. They feed on anything living."

"I'll have questions about how you knew that later."
Uniform ran around the room, shutting doors to the
other parts of the house.

A shadow loomed up outside and the bear's head
crashed through one of the windows, taking the entire
casing with it. Uniform spun instinctively and shoved
his sword into the creature's snout. The bear tried to
back out but the shaggy mane prevented it retreating. It
opened its maw and bellowed in agony.

"Oh, God." Echo bit her knuckle. "The dust cloud
is *eating* it!"

The creature's hind quarters were surrounded by a
sparkling aurora. As the teenagers watched in horror,
the fur, then skin, began to peel from its body.

Sierra turned away, retching as the beast was de-
voured alive. Mike and Alpha pushed desperately at the
shaggy head, now the only part of the bear still intact.
Tiny silver bugs began crawling through the fur, deci-
mating the flesh. The bloody skull dropped into the
room. Echo and Sierra slammed a table into the gap,
then leaned against it.

A dozen metallic bugs skittered round the edges and
scurried down the wall. Uniform and Juliet began
stamping on them.

"Something's biting me!" Echo shrieked, scrab-
bling at the back of her neck. Uniform pulled off the
tiny creature, dropped it and crushed it underfoot.

More bugs began to edge around the table. Juliet grabbed a bottle of water and poured it over the wood. The creatures gave an evil fizz and dropped to the floor.

"Pour water on every gap," she shouted. "These things are robotic. It'll short circuit them."

The others grabbed bottles and canteens, spraying water everywhere, while Echo and Sierra kept the table pinned against the window. The tiny objects crackled and popped each time they made it through a hole.

The attack stopped as quickly as it had begun. The teenagers watched through the opposite window as the cloud drifted back onto the highway and moved north.

"What about the truck?" Alpha gasped. "Is the tuck all right?"

"It's plastic, so it's safe." Juliet sank to the floor. "These things only eat living material."

"I would *very* much like an explanation, Juliet." The leader folded his arms. "What did we just encounter and how did you know about it?"

"I came across the term *glittermist* in Mrs Brown's data banks." The girl rubbed at a small hole in her leg where she had been bitten. "Didn't ever believe we'd encounter one."

"What is it?"

"Nano technology," she said miserably. "The plague wasn't all the Forts released."

"The Forts caused this?"

"They knew the future colonists of New Eden would need all the help they could get. So, they used their new technology to assist them." She picked up a tiny burned out sliver of silver. "These are nanobots with an internal GPS system. The Forts released them and gave them a defined route."

"Explain."

"They were programmed to patrol the highways between Forts, eating cellular material. They'd demolish any plants on the highways and adjoining towns. That way, the colonists would have lines of communication and places to live when they expanded. Problem is, animals and humans are living cellular material too."

"And you decided not to *tell* us about this."

"They're not supposed to still *be* here," the girl objected. "When the first colonists awoke, the Forts were meant to send out an electromagnetic pulse that would destroy the nanobots, leaving the way clear to use the roads and towns again."

She closed her eyes.

"Which, of *course*, never happened because of the sabotage." She let out a sigh. "I didn't put two and two together until I saw the cloud."

Mike stared at her.

Juliet will not let anything stand in the way of what she wants.

Alpha was looking at her as well.

"I won't forget this," he said quietly.

"Excuse me, but ain't we *all* forgetting something?" Sierra interrupted. "There was a guy on a *horse* out there. You think he got eaten too?"

"He's obviously more clued up about glitterbugs than we are." Uniform was staring out the window.

"Guy's right outside our front door."

36

I've made an enemy in Alpha. This is the third time I've disobeyed him and he sees me as a troublemaker who doesn't respect his authority. The misfit in his little band.

Tough. I don't deny he's smart and brave, but he's also arrogant and insecure. He thinks it's his right *to be the leader, even though he doubts he's up to the task. In my book, you have the right to control your* own *destiny. Anything else you have to fight for.*

I like Alpha well enough. But, someday, that fight may just come his way.

The History of New Eden

The horse was a sweat flecked Percheron, coal black, with heavily muscled forelocks. The teenager astride it was even more impressive - long, braided hair, dark as his steed and bare arms and legs tanned by the sun. Wound round his loins and draped over one scarred shoulder was a length of thick cloth, held in place by a silver clasp. A leather shield was fastened to his saddle and a knife protruded from one boot.

His left hand clasped the animal's reins. His right carried a spear decorated with feathers.

"He's gotta be from Forth North Carolina," Sierra whispered.

"Yeah." Sierra cautiously opened the front door. "Only, he looks like he should be *attacking* a fort."

"There *is* a touch of Sitting Bull about this fine gentleman." Alpha agreed. "Then again, it's been 200 years. The descendants have obviously gone native."

"Maybe a bit *too* native," Echo shuddered.

"Mike, you keep us covered." Alpha walked slowly out into the ruined farmyard. "The rest of you, don't touch your weapons."

The mounted warrior regarded them impassively.

"Uniform?" Alpha raised his hands, palms outwards, to show he wasn't holding a gun. "With me."

"By your side, Sir."

The pair approached the stranger. The horse whinnied nervously but a kick from its rider silenced the animal.

"We... are... friends." Alpha carefully took the revolver from its holster and dropped it on the ground. "We mean no harm."

"Sure that's wise, Sir?"

"No. But I'm counting on Mike plugging him before he launches that pig sticker at me."

The leader tapped his chest.

"My name is Alpha. *Alpha*." He indicated the Threes. "I am the chief of this tribe. This is Uniform. *Uniform*."

Alpha jerked a thumb at his companion.

"Lose the weapon, protector. We don't wanna scare him."

"He sure don't *look* scared." Uniform unbuckled his gun belt and let it fall. "There might be more of them, you know."

"There aren't," Mike said from the window. "I'd have seen them."

"What is *your* name?" Alpha pointed to the warrior. "You. Name."

"Ask him what the horse is called," Tango shouted through the window. "Maybe he'd let me ride it!"

"Not the time or place, builder," Uniform cautioned, trying to keep a smile off his face.

"My name is Snoopy Dog." The boy raised a hand in greeting. "Ye need no longer fear the cloud that eats. It is following the wind north."

He looked at them quizzically.

"Were ye sent by the Great Father tae scout these lands?"

Alpha and Uniform looked at each other.

"Eh. Not exactly."

"And yet, ye travel in a covered wagon. Withoot a cover."

"What the hell is he talking about?" Uniform hissed.

"Beats me." Alpha kept his hands up and took another few steps. "We are from a land far, far away. We have traveled many miles to find the Fort you speak of."

"Do ye come in peace?"

"Depends on the reception we get." Uniform looked longingly at his weapon lying in the mud.

"Can you take us to *your* leader, Snoopy Dog?" Alpha asked. "We wish to parlay. We bring gifts."

"Don't know that tinned beans count as gifts," Juliet advised.

"Maybe he'd like a ginger squaw." Tango shot back.

"Flame-haired!"

"You numpties are as clueless as ye look." The stranger shook his head in disbelief. "Snoopy Dog? You *fell* for that?"

"I *like* Snoopy Dog," Tango yelled. "Don't tell me your real name is boring."

"Naw, it's a fine yin, lass." The boy thumped his chest. "I'm called Rob Roy McGregor."

"Rob Roy will do!" Tango whooped. "Hello, Rob Roy!"

"Hi, crazy bird." The boy waved back. "How's it goin?"

"I thought..." Alpha said uncertainly. "You look..."

"Like Sitting Bull. Aye, I heard." Rob Roy narrowed his eyes. "Must have left mah suit and tie back in the wigwam."

"My sincerest apologies. We meant no offense."

"Then tell guy wi the rifle tae relax." Rob Roy thrust his spear into the ground. "He right. I'm on mah own."

"You... eh... seem to have a Scottish accent." Mike shouldered his weapon and sauntered out. "How is that possible?"

"All in good time, pal," the rider said impassively. "First of all, ye need tae tell me exactly who ye are and what ye want wi the Fort."

37

Rob Roy explained that encountering a glittermist was a rare occurrence because they are susceptible to water. Most have been caught out and destroyed by sudden showers over the last two centuries.

He's surprised by the fact that we didn't know this. I reckon he's in for a few more surprises.

The History of New Eden

The Threes made camp while Rob Roy sat on his steed and watched. Tango approached the horse, eyes like saucers.

"You can stroke him," the boy said. "Just dinnae get near his teeth."

"What's his name?" Tango nervously tickled the horse's ear. "He's gorgeous."

"Big Nose."

"You're joking!"

"He's got a big nose," the boy shrugged. "Seemed appropriate, eh?"

"Big Nose!" The girl squealed, hugging the surprised beast's muzzle. "I love you!"

"Why don't you dismount and join us?" Juliet waved him over. "We have food and water."

"No offense, doll, but we jist met. I'd like tae hear your story first."

"The whole thing?"

"It's no like I have tae rush back hame an put the cat oot."

"As it happens, I'm the official historian for our group." Juliet glanced at Alpha. "Your permission, Sir?"

"Nice of you to ask, for once," the leader replied acidly. "He risked his life to save us. I reckon we owe him the truth."

So, Juliet told the horseman their story.

Rob Roy listened until the girl had finished. Tango was still glued to his horse.

"I believe ye," he said. "That sorry tale's too naff tae be made up. Besides, I was told legends of a complex in the north when I was a wee lad. Now I ken why nobody ever came fae that direction."

He scratched his lip.

"But the place yir looking for isnae called Fort North Carolina. It's Fort Virginia and always has bin."

"Virginia's *the* next state." Juliet looked at the other Threes, puzzled. "Harvey wouldn't get a detail like that wrong, would he?"

"Well, whatever you call the place, it attacked you once before. I dinnae think you'll find the inhabitants any friendlier this time roond."

"Will you speak for us?" Alpha asked. "They're your people and you can see we're no threat."

"Me?" Rob Roy laughed sarcastically. "*I'm* no fae any Fort."

The Threes looked at him in astonishment.

"You *must* be. Everyone else was killed by the plague."

"I'm sure that was the intention." The teenager smiled. "But some folk survived. A certain Type, ye might say."

"Tall, dark and handsome ones?" Sierra queried.

"That jist me, toots." Rob Roy grinned. "As it happened, anyone who had a serious genetic defect was immune tae the Le Mans bug."

"You mean…"

"They caught the disease but it didnae kill them. Instead, their deformity became… hereditary. I'm nae doctor, so I cannae tell ye why."

"I imagine the Bug triggered some internal defense mechanism in the survivors," Echo said. "It meant their children would also be immune if the plague ever came back.

"I suppose the disease didnae clock us as being human. An opinion that the Fort happens tae share, by the way."

The boy gave a bark of laughter, devoid of any humor.

"Ironic, isn't it? The poor souls least suited tae surviving an apocalypse were the only yins left alive when it passed."

His expression hardened.

"The citizens of Fort Virginia call us Dregs. We call *them* Wholesomes." He spat on the ground again. "May they aw rot in hell."

"I sense you don't exactly live in harmony," Juliet noted.

"My people farm the land as they have for generations. Difficult enough, but we scrape a living. Then the Wholesomes come and steal half of everything."

"Excuse us for one second, Rob Roy." Alpha beckoned to the others and the Threes huddled round.

"Do we believe him?"

"Of course," Tango enthused. "He calls his pet Big Nose and talks funny."

"Don't mean he's being truthful," Uniform warned.

"Does in my book, honey."

"There you go, then," the boy sighed. "He's practically a saint."

"Saint or not, he's all we got." Alpha dispersed them with a wave. "And he did save us from the glittermist."

"So did I," Juliet grumped.

"I'll give you a medal later," Alpha replied scornfully. "In the meantime, let's show this guy some hospitality before he takes off."

"Are you hungry?" Echo called out to Rob Roy.

"I could eat a horse, blondie."

"Don't listen to him, Big Nose!" Tango squealed.

"Why don't you dismount and share our food?" Alpha opened a packet of dried fruit. "We can discuss what to do next."

Rob Roy hesitated.

"We're not sure about each other. That's evident," the leader cajoled. "But if we were truly hostile, Mike would have shot you."

"Fair enough." The teenager pulled his steed's mane. "Doon you."

The horse knelt and Rob Roy slid off.

"This might take a wee bit of time."

He hobbled towards the fire, grunting with effort. Now that the boy was on the ground, the Threes could see his feet pointed inward, making it almost impossible for him to walk properly.

Sierra moved to help him.

"Thanks, hen." He waved her away. "I can manage."

With a supreme effort, Rob Roy tottered to the fire and collapsed.

"Bit slow getting around when I'm no on Big Nose," he gasped. "Guess I'm at yir mercy, now. But if you're cannibals, I warn ye, I'm tough."

"Here." Alpha passed the boy a bottle of water. "Why don't you tell us *your* story."

-38-

The boy took a swig and settled back.

"After the plague, the survivors tried to start again," he began. "For years, they struggled on wee smallholdings across the country. Many died. But they managed against aw the odds. And, of course, they bred. But a hereditary deformity means just that. None of them were... normal. Then the first Wholesomes came, wi trucks and guns. They rounded everyone up and moved them tae a set of valleys in the midwest. Built a barrier tae keep everyone in. Enslaved them."

He hung his head.

"It's been that way ever since."

"We might be from a Fort but *our* intentions are honorable." Echo rubbed her injured neck. "We're just lost and looking for a home."

"I can take ye tae mah village." The boy relaxed. "Let ye see the situation for yourself and gie ye a chance to rest properly. Besides, ye need me tae show you a way through the barrier that keeps us all contained."

"How come *you're* out here on the loose?"

"I refuse tae be some dirt digger and the Fort cannae catch me." The youth gave a smile. "They call me The Horseman. I'm a pure outlaw."

"We'd be happy to accompany you, horseman."

"Pleased tae hear it. Ye can hide the wagon there, an all."

"Is that really necessary?" Alpha asked.

"You cannae be rolling across the landscape in *that* big contraption." Rob Roy eyed the vehicle enviously. "Naebody has set eyes on transport wi fuel in generations. Those thieving Wholesomes will nick it like a shot, along wi your guns. The weapons they have left are falling apart or scavenged."

"All right." Alpha slapped his knees. "We'll go to the village with you. Besides, I reckon Tango would knife me in her sleep if she didn't get a chance to sit on a horse at some point."

"Wouldn't wait till you were asleep, babe."

"Let's offski, then." Rob Roy whistled for his steed and beckoned to Tango. "You want a backie, hen? You seem awfy fond of the cuddie."

"Could you repeat that?"

"What? Do ye no understand English?"

"Not when *you're* speaking it."

Big Nose lay down and Rob Roy pulled himself onto the broad back. The horse stood and he was, once more, a dignified warrior.

"I'll try puttin it mair simply." He reached out his hand. "You seem very taken by my horse, young lady. Would you perhaps like to ride behind me?"

"More than life itself!" Tango glanced at Uniform. "Is that OK?"

"I ain't the boss of you."

"I know. You're jealous." The girl swung herself onto Big Nose and blew the protector a kiss. "But thanks for saying yes in such a sweet way."

"I'll keep her safe, big man." Rob Roy winked. "Dinnae get your knickers in a twist."

He dug his heels into the horse's flanks and moved off, Tango whooping with glee behind him.

"We're treading a thin line here." Mike took Alpha aside as Rob Roy cantered away. "I'm all for staying hidden until we've gathered more Intel. But we'll have to make contact with Fort North Carolina, eventually."

"Fort Virginia."

"Whatever. It's the only way of getting the codes that will let us back into our own complex and save the Types."

"If this guy's telling the truth, the 'Wholesomes' might not be too obliging."

"I count marching in and demanding the codes at gunpoint as contact," Uniform grunted.

"Nice to see you being positive for a change."

"Won't last, Sir."

Uniform climbed into the cab.

"I'll drive."

"What's with the whole Scottish shtick?" Tango asked as Big Nose trotted along in front of the vehicle. "It's a sexy accent, but there must be more to it."

"After the plague, there was nae electricity or TV or computers, an too few survivors tae even consider getting that stuff up an running again." The boy urged his horse through a small stream. "But it didnae seem right, just tae let the past slide intae oblivion. Aw those different cultures and customs gone forever, eh?"

"So you decided to preserve them the best way you could."

"Aye. Oor toon is built roond the old county library, so we hae plenty tae read. In fact, it's *aw* we hae. So, when they turn nine, everyone in the village picks a country, subject or person they like and memorizes everything they can aboot it. That way, the subject comes alive again for a wee while."

He patted his chest.

"I represent Scotland. Though I did get maist of mah info fae reading the works of Sir Walter Scott an *Trainspotting*."

"And, if you pretend to be something long enough, you eventually become it."

"That's totally right." Rob Roy glanced admiringly over his shoulder. "You're a smart lass."

"I knew it." Tango smiled contentedly. "I just *knew* it."

-39-

We came here to contact Fort North Carolina, but we're tagging along with a guy who hates the place and can't even get the name right. Then we're gonna stay with people who claim to be enslaved by them. That doesn't make sense to me.

And I don't trust Rob Roy. We've offered him no proof that our own story is true. For all he knows, we are just as bad as any other Wholesomes. Yet he seems happy to take a bunch of armed strangers right into his village. Hmmmmmm.

I'm gonna stick close to him. He has something up his sleeve. Well... he would if he had sleeves.

The History of New Eden

Late afternoon, the Threes reached the barrier. It was a huge tangle of barbed wire several feet high.

"Can we get through that?" Echo studied the fence in alarm. "I don't want to rip my tunic. I wouldn't look good in animal skins."

"Ye'd look great in a potato sack, blondie," Rob Roy grinned.

"Why, thank you. Still not going through the barbed wire."

"I've already cut it, though ye cannae tell." The boy unlooped a rope from his saddle and lashed it round a length of cable. "It's mah personal escape route."

"How do you know where to find the break?" Sierra studied the near-invisible breaches. "The scenery's the same for miles."

"It's got mah name on it." Rob Roy proudly pointed to a yellowing scrap of paper hung on the wire.

WANTED

DEAD OR ALIVE
Rob Roy McGregor: AKA The Horseman
Anyone sheltering the fugitive will be killed.

"Fort put it oot," he said proudly. "Ignore the *will be killed* bit. I'm sure it's just a typo."

He tied the rope to the truck's bumper. Uniform reversed, pulling a section out.

"Drive through, put it back and naebody will be any the wiser."

"Take a good look and memorize exactly where we are, Uniform," Alpha whispered. "I want to be sure we can find the way out, if we need to."

"Human compass, Sir."

Then they kept going.

It was evening by the time Rob Roy stopped.

"Hame sweet hame, lads and lassies. We call oor toon Library, fur obvious reasons."

They were looking down into a wide valley. Below them was a large village built over the ruins of a pre-plague town. It comprised of wooden and adobe huts with a few larger stone dwellings, including what must have once been the town library, a red brick building with a bell tower. There were corrals full of cattle, a large barn and freshly harvested fields. The Threes could see people milling about.

"Where are their horses?" Tango tugged at the boy's shoulder.

"We're no allowed any, an have tae trade wi the other villages in carts pulled by oxen."

Tango's face fell.

"But I hae a wee herd hidden in the hills that I rounded up an broke maself." The boy patted her cheek. "I'll let ye see them later."

He held up his spear and waved it.

"Leave the truck here. They're a nervous bunch, this lot. If it gets any nearer, they'll scatter."

Uniform leaned out of the cab window.

"I strongly caution against that, Sir."

"Me too," Juliet agreed. "There are enough people down there to easily overwhelm us."

"Hah! You havnae met *that* bunch of jessies!" Rob Roy laughed. "They're scared of their ain shadows. Keep the guns if it makes ye feel better, though."

He helped Tango down.

"There. Now ye can shoot me in the back if I'm leading ye intae a trap."

"Leave the truck," Alpha commanded. "Take the keys."

They walked down the hill beside Rob Roy's horse. Villagers stopped and stared up at them. Some ran into their homes. Others hobbled behind, helped by their neighbors.

"You're causing quite a stooshie," Rob Roy remarked.

A lone figure left the township and strode towards them. There was something strange about its outline.

"Charlotte-Emily!" The boy called out. "I got guests!"

"How very pleasant for us!" A female voice drifted up. "We are always delighted to receive unexpected guests."

"That's the Bronte Sisters," Rob Roy explained. "They talk funny but dinnae hold that against them. They make a fine pumpkin ravioli."

The figure drew closer and the Threes shrank back, stunned.

It was a girl. Or, rather, two girls. They were joined at the waist, with two sets of arms and one pair of legs encased in pink bloomers. They carried a set of crutches.

Charlotte-Emily stopped, appalled.

"Bless my soul. Are those *Wholesomes*? If not, why do they wear such peculiar attire?"

The Threes suddenly realized how unusual they looked in their matching green outfits.

"Calm doon, toots." Rob Roy tried to allay his companion's fears. "They're fae the legendary Fort in the north!"

"Excuse our rudeness." The girl's faces clouded. "But have you lost your senses, Master Rob? Bringing outsiders straight to our front door?"

"Sorry, pal." The boy turned to Alpha. "Charlotte-Emily can be a bit thrawn."

"We've got one of those, too." The leader waggled his fingers at Uniform, who was rubbing his butt and scowling.

"*What*? I'm sore after sitting on that seat for hours."

"See?"

Rob Roy slid off his horse and the newcomer handed him the crutches.

"I'll make the introductions," he grinned. "This is Charlotte-Emily. Charlotte is on the left. Emily right. I believe their sort were once called conjoined twins."

"Which of these fellows is the leader of their company?" Emily asked.

"Him." Rob Roy pushed Alpha forwards. "Dinnae worry, boss. C-E winnae bite."

"What a fine specimen of male virility!" Emily whistled. "Permit me to bat my eyelids."

"Please retain a sense of decorum, sister." Charlotte glared at her. "Even if the gentleman's chin looks like the prow of a sailing vessel."

"You are simply jealous because he obviously favors me."

"Say something before they start punching each other," Rob Roy whispered. "It's painful tae watch."

The leader recovered quickly. He handed his pistol to Rob Roy and bowed gallantly.

"An absolute pleasure to make your acquaintance, ladies. Eh... Whose hand would I actually be shaking?"

"We prefer to embrace." The girls enfolded Alpha in their arms. "It's not really the 19th century, after all. We're both extremely emancipated?"

"Stop it, you two. I ken what you're up tae." Rob Roy pulled Alpha away. "They're frisking ye for hidden weapons."

"Your Highland hospitality is legendary." Charlotte-Emily put four hands on her hips. "You would surely bring home a killer bear if it looked at you with a hungry eye."

"Aye. And you'd skin and eat it."

"I was meaning to ask about bears," Juliet interrupted. "We met one and it was as big as our truck."

"Eh?" Rob Roy scratched his head. "That's their normal size, ginger."

"Don't call me ginger. Ever."

"Wow." Sierra warily approached Charlotte-Emily. "You're the same color as me."

"Indeed. Often we are made compare with exotic beauties."

"I was beginning to think I was the only black person left on the planet."

"Most delightful it is to meet with a kindred spirit." Charlotte-Emily reached out a hand and led the girl down the hill. "Do please relate to us your travails in getting here. If we find the story amusing, we may even let you live."

"Those scamps," Rob Roy chuckled. "You got tae love em."

Seeing that Charlotte-Emily was unharmed, the villagers cautiously emerged from their dwellings. They were wary at first but reassured by Rob Roy's presence. They seemed to hold him in high regard.

A few were blind. Their companions led them forwards so they could feel the teenager's faces.

"That tickles!" Tango giggled.

An elderly man approached them. He wore a battered top hat and his heavily lined face was framed by a wispy gray beard.

"This is the Mayor." Rob Roy said, facing the man. "These are my friends, President Lincoln."

"Welcome to Library." The man shook Alpha's hand warmly. "You are welcome to share what little repast we have."

"Christ," Uniform muttered. "Is there anyone here who isn't a nutter?"

"Shhhh." Tango elbowed him. "Show a bit of tact, for once."

"It's an honor to meet you, Mayor." The leader bowed again.

"You have tae keep your head up, so he can lip read," Rob Roy said. "President Lincoln is deaf."

"Allow me, Sir." Mike tapped the man on the arm.

Thank you for your hospitality, he signed. *You have no idea how pleased we are to meet other human beings.*

"I didn't know you could do that!" Alpha's jaw dropped.

"Not a skill I ever thought I'd need again."

A huge, toothless grin split the President's haggard face.

"Tonight, we shall celebrate!" he shouted. "We have new members!"

"He knows we're not staying." Alpha looked perturbed. "Doesn't he?"

"Ach, jist play along for now." Rob Roy turned his face away from the Mayor so the man couldn't tell what he was saying.

"At least you'll get a party oot of it."

-40-

The villagers seem like nice people. But they're not our *people.*

On the other hand, they're trapped in their own little world and made the best of it, like the Types once did. But, surely, they long for something more?

Perhaps not. Could be you don't know how much freedom means until you taste it. Like poor old Mike 32.

Never mind. We'll be moving on soon.

The History of New Eden

That night, the villagers built a huge fire and roasted a steer. Many of them were dressed as characters or places from books they had read. An ancient Egyptian walked past, pushing a toga-clad gent in a wooden wheelchair.

"Seems like a heap of effort to go to." Uniform regarded a clown with stumps for arms. "How does she put *makeup* on?"

"Don't think they have a lot of scope for fun here." Tango gave the circus performer a cheery wave. "What would *you* dress as if you had a choice?"

"Wolverine from the X-Men." Uniform didn't hesitate. "I'd look good with sideboards."

"A super-strong mutant? Might have guessed."

"Too late." He pointed to a fat, middle-aged man in a tight yellow costume and mask. "There's already one sitting over there."

The villagers brought out a couple of patched up fiddles and two women began to play.

"That's a lovely tune," Sierra nudged Charlotte-Emily. "What's it called?"

"*Bad Romance*. It is extremely old and nobody can quite recall who penned it." Emily got to her feet. "Let us partake in a waltz, sister."

"Nothing would please me more," Charlotte agreed. "After two glasses of fine homemade sherry, I am ready to cut a rug."

Those who couldn't walk drummed on their knees while the rest danced. The blind were guided by other participants, moving in rhythm with their partner's bodies. People laughed and chatted, handing round platters of steak.

Mike sat on an oak barrel, watching the festivities. Charlotte-Emily whirled Sierra round and round, using all four arms to stop her spinning into the crowd. Tango and Uniform were bouncing about with each other, the firelight flickering over their faces. Mike had never seen the protector smile so much. With his hair long and his face softer, he was almost handsome.

Alpha and Echo were deep in discussion with the President, talking about Fort Virginia, no doubt.

Juliet was with Rob Roy, as she had been since they got here. Mike hated to admit it, but he was jealous of the attention she was paying him.

As if on cue, the highlander hobbled over, Juliet supporting him. The boy was carrying a bottle.

"Found this wee beauty under a counter in the Williamsburg Target," he said happily, handing Mike a plastic cup. "The drink, no the lassie. It's a 200-year-old whisky!"

The hunter sipped tentatively, then coughed and spluttered as the heat spread through his body.

"Aye. Tastes like a badger's bum." Rob Roy knocked back his own drink. "Maybe it's meant tae. Maybe it's gone aff. Who can remember?"

"Don't care." Mike held out his cup for a refill. "The last party I was at, I played Pin the Tail on the Donkey."

"You stuck pins in a donkey, ye wee monster?" Rob Roy looked shocked. "I thought the *other* Wholesomes were uncivilized."

"It's not like it sounds."

"Why don't you ask the pretty lassie tae dance?" Rob Roy tutted. "You cannae sit on a barrel wi your face tripping ye all night. No in the middle of a fine shindig like this."

"I don't know how." Mike blushed. "I'd look stupid."

"Stupid, is it?" The boy put his arm around Juliet. "I'd *love* tae whoop it up wi a bonny gal like this, but I'd fall over, even withoot the whisky. How daft would *that* look?"

Mike went even redder.

"May I, Juliet?" he asked tentatively.

"Sure thing."

The boy led her into the melee. He shuffled around awkwardly for a while, swinging his arms.

"Told you I couldn't dance."

"Then we'll do what they do." Juliet reached out and pulled him close. "Just follow my lead."

They moved in time to the music, pressed together. The girl leaned her head on Mike's shoulder and watched the villagers stumbling around, laughing and singing.

Ra Ra ah ah ah
Roma roma ma
Gaga ooh la la
Want your bad romance

"I have to say," she whispered. "This is a *very* surreal moment."

Uniform spotted them and stopped leaping around. He took Tango's hands and they, too, began to sway, looking into each other's eyes. In the corner, Alpha put his arm round Echo.

Mike glanced at Rob Roy. The boy raised his glass to them and smiled wistfully.

"I want this to be my home!" Sierra panted as she spun past. "Charlotte-Emily says Rob Roy hasn't got a girlfriend and he's *fine*!"

Mike hugged Juliet tightly until the song ended.

"Thank you. That was nice."

The girl leaned forwards and pressed her lips to his. The boy's heart leapt.

"That's my first kiss ever, hunter." Juliet skipped back, fanning her face. "I'm glad it was you."

With a shy chuckle, she ran back to Rob Roy and accepted another cup of whisky.

Mike touched his lips. He wanted to jump for joy but Mrs Brown's words kept echoing in his head.

Juliet can laugh, make jokes and cry. But it's all an act. She has no feelings or morals of any kind.

He marched over.

"Can I have another drink?"

"Knock yourself oot, wee man." The boy burped. "This bunch are usually so miserable they could turn milk sour. Never seen so much food, neither. We should hae visitors mair often."

The party went on for hours. When Mike finally climbed, exhausted, into the straw bed provided for him, his head was groggy. He wanted time alone to cherish Juliet's kiss. Remember it. Believe it really meant something.

But he was asleep within seconds.

The next day the real Wholesomes arrived.

-41-

Mike woke up to find Charlotte-Emily shaking him.

"An advance party from the Fort has arrived," Emily whispered, clasping a hand over his mouth. "Rob Roy spotted them early, so Alpha rode off to hide your truck. However, I fear this presents us with a truly awkward situation."

"It would behoove you to get dressed and make yourself scarce," Charlotte added. "Pray, do not show your face, no matter what transpires. Those unsociable gentlemen will surely retire once they have what they came for."

Mike pulled on his clothes and peered through a chink in the curtains, watching Charlotte-Emily make her way towards the intruders.

A mounted group occupied the middle of the town square, horses pawing up clouds of dust. They carried old rifles and handguns strapped to their waists. Their black uniforms were similar to those of the Threes but dirty, patched and stained. Each face had the pinched look of someone used to hardship and violence.

A burly man with a handlebar mustache stood up in his saddle.

"It's tithing time, Dregs," he shouted. "This is your official warning."

The villagers emerged, blinking from their homes. They looked at the ground, hands behind their back, like guilty children.

"We will count the cattle, measure crop acreage and the water in your well before moving on to the next village. Then you will load provisions onto your ox-wagons and deliver them to the Fort."

A flash of alarm crossed President Lincoln's face. He moved forwards, but Charlotte-Emily cut him off.

"We have already made the required lists, Superior." She curtsied daintily. Mike noted that her speech patterns had suddenly changed to match those of the intruders. "You have had a hard ride and must be hungry and thirsty."

The man paused.

"Pumpkin ravioli?" he asked hopefully.

"Of course. We also prepared meat for you the previous evening." Charlotte-Emily pointed to the barn. "If you wish to rest your horses then, presently, we shall bring all you can eat."

"I have my orders," the man said uncertainly.

"Indeed. As you do every year. And we have never lied about our quota, is that not so?"

"Because you would not dare, Dreg." a rat-faced youth sneered.

"We would not. There is nowhere to hide our live-stock, water and crops that you could not easily find, as you surely know."

"This is true." The lead Wholesome pulled on his mustache.

"Then it is our pleasure to offer you much-needed rest and sustenance. We know your time is precious."

"Do not presume to guess what is precious to me." Mustache curled his lip. "*Your* life certainly is not."

"Understood, good sirs." Charlotte-Emily curtsied again. "We simply wish to spare you half a day of counting when you could spend idle hours relaxing in the shade." She glanced at the barn again. "We can heat baths with our forge."

"An offer I will grudgingly accept." The leader made to dismount. Then he stopped and pointed.

"What is *that*?"

"Pardon?" Charlotte followed the direction of his finger with her eyes. "It's... eh... the ground."

"Those are hoof prints." The man pulled a switch from under his saddle. "You are not permitted steeds."

Charlotte-Emily looked lost.

"The Horseman was here, wasn't he?" The man's face darkened. "The one you call Rob Roy."

Charlotte-Emily stayed silent. Mike, peering round the curtains, could see her shoulders tighten.

"Answer me!"

"We cannot catch him," Emily pleaded. "He rides a horse, as you do. Preventing this is beyond the ability of people who are feeble or infirm."

"Liar!" The man lashed out with his switch and a cut opened on Charlotte's cheek. "You feed him. You give him shelter!"

"Not true, Superior." Charlotte-Emily staggered back, shielding both faces with her arms. "He is a nefarious outlaw and takes what he wishes."

"Tell me where The Horseman is!" The man lashed out again and again. "Tell me… or I will… beat you until… you are a pile of blood… and mangled flesh."

With each phrase, he struck the helpless girl. She sank to her knees, crying.

"Please!" President Lincoln ran towards them, hands raised. "She is telling the truth."

"Silence!" Rat Face spurred his horse forwards, knocking the man over.

"Tell me where The Horseman… *is*." Mustache continued to hit the sobbing girl.

"Oi, tubby!" A voice called. "Lift that stick once more and I'll take it from you, then ram it where the sun don't shine."

The Wholesome's eyes bulged.

"Who *dares* speak that way to a Superior?"

"I do." Mike stood in the doorway. "Now, beat it, before I slap that hairy lip into the next state."

The man went purple.

"Bring that upstart to me," he commanded. "I will drag him behind my horse until he begs to die."

"He does not look mutated like the others," Rat Face said cautiously. "He has a uniform and a gun."

"Do as I say!" The leader looked as if he would strike his second in command instead. "You are afraid of one Dreg?"

"Two Dregs." Alpha materialized in another doorway.

"Three." Echo was right behind him.

"Four." Tango moved out from a tall woodpile, waggling her fingers in greeting.

"Five," Sierra shouted from the roof of the barn.

"Six." Juliet stood up behind the rim of the well.

"Seven," Uniform yelled from a window, Mike's rifle aimed at the riders.

"You know what?" he said thoughtfully. "I'm sure I saw this in a Western once."

"Seven youths." The leader grinned, revealing rotten teeth. "There are *twenty* of us. And you will get no assistance from these cringing peasants."

"Don't need help." Tango tipped her cap leisurely over one eye. "I could bring you all down myself."

"Finally! We encounter resistance." The Wholesome held his belly and laughed loudly. "And a chance to kill some of you scum, at last."

"Maybe we should leave and get reinforcements," Rat Face said nervously.

"Reinforcements?" Alpha shook his head. "Now we *really* can't let you leave."

"Leave? We'll *never* leave."

"Got that right," the teenager smiled.

With a roar, Mustache dropped the switch and reached for his gun.

Tango drew first, fanning the hammer of her revolver so quickly her hand was merely a blur. Four Wholesomes toppled from their horses.

The villagers scattered, fleeing back into their dwellings.

Mike dropped to one knee, took careful aim, and fired with deadly accuracy. Alpha and Echo retreated back into the doorway, shooting from the hip. Sierra and Juliet flung themselves down and began pouring bullets into the melee.

The horses reared in panic, throwing more riders. Seeing the tide turning, Alpha and Echo burst from the cabin again, running towards the enemy, blasting as they went.

The fat commander raised his pistol and fired. Alpha spun backwards with a cry and landed in the dust, clutching his chest. Echo screamed and knelt by him, trying to staunch the flow of blood. Rat Face yanked his horse round and galloped away, leaving his companions dead between their mounts' milling feet.

Charlotte-Emily reached back, jerked two hidden knives from her belt and plunged them into Mustache's leg.

As he screamed in pain, the other two bloody arms reached up and pulled him from his horse.

"Eight." She thrust the blades into his chest.

Echo, Juliet and Tango dragged Alpha into the nearest cabin, leaving a trail of blood in their wake. Uniform sprinted from cover and threw Mike his rifle.

"The ugly one's getting away!"

"Sierra?" The boy looked at the top of the barn. "How did you get up there?"

"Round the back!"

Mike raced behind the barn, found a rickety wooden ladder and climbed to the roof. A receding trail of dust revealed Rat Face's location.

The boy raised the rifle to his cheek. Closed one eye. Summoned all of his concentration. Squeezed the trigger.

The Wholesome raised his arms and fell backwards, almost in slow motion. The horse kept galloping, dragging his bouncing body over the horizon.

"You *are* the man." Sierra threw her arms around the boy's neck.

Mike held her tightly, suppressing a sob.

"What's wrong?" The girl studied his face. "What's happened?"

"Alpha's been shot."

"Oh, no." The girl turned and ran for the ladder.

Mike waited until she was out of sight. Then he opened the breech of his rifle and looked inside.

A single bullet was missing, the one that had killed Rat Face. Uniform hadn't fired a shot.

Mike slammed the breech closed. Once again, when Alpha's life was in mortal danger, the protector hadn't lifted a finger to help him.

-42-

Now the cat is out of the bag and halfway up a tree. We have to get out of here, but Alpha is fatally wounded. I don't know what the others will do if he dies.

Gotta admit, though. I really did enjoy killing those creeps.

The History of New Eden

When Mike entered the house, his leader was lying on a straw mattress, slicked with gore.

"He's dying," Uniform raged. "Alpha's dying!"

"We have to get the bullet out!" Echo held a rag over the hole in the boy's chest. "Where's my damned medical kit?"

"Got it." Tango dashed in and laid the bag beside her.

"Sorry, babe. But I have to do this."

Echo slid her fingers into the wound. The boy writhed and moaned through gritted teeth as she fished around and pulled out the bullet.

"We have heated the knife, as you requested." Charlotte-Emily rushed to the leader's side.

"Give it here." Echo didn't hesitate. She pushed the blade onto Alpha's wound and he screamed in agony as the flesh sizzled. The girl held a gauze pad against the scorched skin.

"Jules, keep this in place."

The other Threes stood round, wringing their hands, as their leader lapsed into unconsciousness.

Echo began to cry.

"That was an old fashioned gun and the bullet was rusty," she rummaged around in her kit. "It'll infect him. Kill him."

"Don't you have antibiotics?"

"I don't think they'll work after all this time. They must have an expiry date and it's sure as hell not two hundred years."

Echo pulled out the box Alpha had given her from the kit. Several plastic ampoules with needle points spilled out. Echo grabbed one and stuck it into Alpha's neck.

"What did you just give him?" Mike goggled.

"Who cares?" Echo swallowed hard. "I don't have anything else."

"Echo?" Juliet repeated. "What did you give Alpha?"

"A serum he found in Dr Stoddart's truck." Tears flowed down the girl's cheeks. "I think it might be WC-57."

"You don't know what that will do to him!"

"He'd die otherwise." She kissed the boy's cheek. "It's only a tiny amount."

Her face hardened.

"Get out. All of you. He needs to rest."

Rob Roy was sitting on his horse on the edge of the village square. Charlotte-Emily headed straight for him, but Mike got there first.

"I heard Alpha got hurt." Rob Roy seemed genuinely sorry. "Is he...?"

Mike grabbed the boy's plaid and pulled him from the horse. Rob Roy landed with a cry and the hunter planted a foot on his chest. Charlotte-Emily reached for her knives and found herself staring down the barrel of the boy's gun.

The villagers and the Threes looked on in amazement.

"You know the Wholesomes were due to arrive, didn't you? You were *expecting* them."

"They were not due for another two days," Lincoln protested.

"This guy hasn't evaded them for so long without knowing their every move." He pushed with his boot and Rob Roy grunted in pain. "Yet he was dumb enough to leave hoof prints in plain sight? I don't buy it."

"A canny observation," Rob Roy acknowledged through gritted teeth.

"You set us up. Hoped we'd defend the village from that advance party." Mike removed his foot and allowed the highlander to sit up. "After this, we can never approach the Fort and get the codes we need to free *our* friends."

"They would most certainly have been doomed had you tried," Emily said defiantly. "Once you ventured into the enemy's lair, I fear you would never have come out."

"What have you pair *done*?" Lincoln rounded on Rob Roy and Charlotte-Emily. "The Fort will seek retribution on our village for this outrage."

"Then the sorry band who reside here will *have* to fight!" Charlotte rallied. "With Rob Roy's help and the strangers, we can *beat* the Wholesomes. Can you not appreciate the logic in that?"

"You told me the Fort has an army." Mike groaned. "We can't defeat that sort of force. Now our leader is dying because of your treachery."

"That was never meant tae happen." Rob Roy apologized. "We didnae expect ye tae be quite sae... *bold* in yer approach."

"All of you, in here!" Echo bellowed. "*Now*!"

Mike turned and raced into the cabin with the other Threes.

Alpha was propped against the wall, his chest bandaged.

"That was some fight," he coughed. "We kicked their asses, huh?"

"Well, *you* look uncommonly sprightly for someone on death's door," Juliet frowned. "You do *know* a bullet was just pulled out of your chest?"

"Stings a bit," the boy admitted. "But I'm great. In fact, I feel like a new man."

He grinned wolfishly.

"I'm just very, *very* hungry."

Fort Virginia

A traitor is everyone who does not agree with me.

King George III of Britain

-43-

Rob Roy betrayed our trust. And Alpha has been changed by the serum. Nobody seems to want to talk about it. What's wrong with them? Have they forgotten the monster we saw back at Fort New York State? I want to ask Mike but there still seems to be a barrier between us. It's like he doesn't trust me.

I feel more alone than I ever have.

The History of New Eden

That night, Library's Town Council summoned the Threes to a meeting. The villagers thronged round the walls of the largest barn, sat in the rafters or peered through the windows. Their mood was very different from the evening before.

"We have discussed today's events." President Lincoln wrung his hands miserably. "Rob Roy, we have sheltered and fed you whenever we could, despite the Fort placing a price on your head."

"I am indebted tae ye."

"Your actions speak otherwise." The old man said sadly. "We have no choice but to banish you and Charlotte-Emily from our community."

The outcasts looked stunned.

263

"Strangers." President Lincoln regarded the Threes. "What you did was brave and noble."

"Why, thank you." Tango curtsied.

"But the opposite of what we wished."

"Oh."

"When their advance party do not return, the Fort will send a far larger force," Lincoln explained. "One we have no chance of defeating."

He took a deep breath.

"You, too, must leave."

"When we are struck at without reason, we should strike back again." Charlotte-Emily burst out. "So hard as to teach the person who struck us never to do it again. You must defend yourselves, or they will surely demand a price in blood."

"They will punish the village, yes," Lincoln admitted. "But they are not stupid. They will leave enough of us to farm and raise cattle for them, as we always have."

"Y'all should come with us," Sierra advised. "The land here was bad to begin with but now it's exhausted. Up north is far more fertile."

"You'd have a good life there," Echo agreed. "And we could use the extra hands."

"We have four." Charlotte-Emily held them all up. "And fervently wish to be a part of your glorious enterprise."

"I hae horses hidden in a hillside pasture." Rob Roy said. "I'll freely give them tae ye, President Lincoln."

"How many animals, boy?"

"Eighteen."

"We have a population of almost two hundred, many of them disabled in some way." The Mayor tapped his useless ears. "Even if we made it, the Fort would simply track us. They cannot allow an uprising to go unpunished, lest other villages follow our example."

He sat down wearily.

"Do you think I wish to sit around waiting so see if my neck will be stretched? I assure you I do not. But there is no other course open to us."

Alpha rubbed his eyes, deep in thought. Finally, he stood.

"Sure there is," he said. "You could fight back, like Rob Roy and Charlotte-Emily want."

There was a horrified murmuring among the villagers and one or two barks of derisive laughter.

"That is a foolish and haughty suggestion, boy."

"Our weapons are superior to the Fort's advance party - and they won't need theirs anymore," Alpha continued, undeterred. "Rob Roy told me he's been scavenging guns and fixing them up for years."

"Hoped I'd get tae use them agin the Fort, someday," the boy agreed. "Seems like that time has come."

"Are you not listening?" Lincoln roared. "You beat a small force because you took them by surprise. The Fort will send an *army*."

"So? We got right on our side." Tango was lounging on a bale of straw. "If you put our names together it spells *J.U.S.T.A.C.E.*"

"Justice is spelled with an *I*," Lincoln growled.

"Give me some wiggle room, will you?" The girl sat up. "I'm saying that, if we show the other villages we're willing to fight, they might rise up too. They'll overthrow the Fort and everyone will live happily ever after."

"Bit optimistic, builder." Uniform cautioned. "The odds are well and truly against us."

"I'm not a coward," Juliet joined in. "But I didn't sign up for a suicide mission."

"You should have thought of that before insisting on coming here," Alpha replied bluntly. "We caused this mess and we're going to fix it."

He looked down at his blood-stained bandage.

"Besides, they shot me."

"Enough of this nonsense." President Lincoln knocked a hammer on a barrel. "The meeting is over."

"Can you not see we are already on our knees?" Charlotte-Emily exploded. "Every year, there are fewer crops. Fewer fruit on the trees. If we keep handing over half of what we toil for, we shall end up starving. We must either flee this unhappy place or make a stand."

"I have spoken." Lincoln sat down. "We will endure. We always have."

"Wait!" A youth inched forwards, waving a bat in front of him. "My name is Joe DiMaggio and I represent baseball."

He hesitated.

"I... I'll join with you."

"But you're blind!" Juliet goggled.

"Then I'll fight at night." The boy laughed. "Thanks for pointing it out, though."

"Nice." Mike elbowed the mortified girl.

"G'day." A man in an iron mask shoved himself to the front. "I'm Ned Kelly, the Australian outlaw. You may count on me. I'm the blacksmith and can make swords and spearheads."

"Welcome aboard." Alpha looked startled. "No need to wear *that*, though."

"You haven't seen my face, mate."

"I'm Al Capone." A one-armed boy pushed in behind him. "If yous mugs is determined to take over this joint, I wanna piece of the action. Capisce?"

"Totally stoked, dudes." A youth with baggy jeans and long hair flipped up a skateboard and expertly caught it. "*So* psyched to ollie round those douchebags."

"Sure, you can't leave the Oirish out of a barney." A girl raised her withered hand. "Grace O'Malley, Pirate Queen, at your service. Oim itching to do harm to dose oppressors."

She indicated a silent boy standing next to her.

"So's me pal, Oscar Wilde. Only he can't speak."

"Jim Bowie." A boy scratched his ruined cheek with a huge knife. "I'm the Alamo and I'll make a last stand. Seems kinda appropriate."

"That's just great!" Juliet buried her face in her hands. "An expert on getting massacred. Now all we need is General Custer."

"Over here!"

"I don't *believe* this."

One by one, more teenagers came forward, along with a handful of men and women. Eventually, thirty or more stood with the Threes.

"Looks like your rebellion is happening, Mayor." Alpha began shaking the new recruit's hands. "Whether you like it or not."

"We will be slaughtered." President Lincoln insisted.

"So what?" Rob Roy hobbled over to the Threes. "Whit you hae now isnae living. It's just surviving."

"How long before the Fort misses the advance party?" Alpha asked Charlotte-Emily. "Then sends forces to avenge them?"

"Those ruffians still had several villages further out to inspect." The girls did a mental calculation. "We would surmise a week, give or take a day."

"They'll not be expecting much of a fight, I'll bet." Alpha grinned. "If we work fast, we can build up defenses."

"Can you really offer serious resistance?" For the first time, a glimmer of hope sparked in Lincoln's eyes.

"I will not order my people to make a doomed action because of some child's misplaced bravado."

"Less of the child, old man. You'll address me as Sir from this point on."

"I shall do *what*?"

"My father was General Harper Henderson III, commanding officer of Fort New York State." Alpha stuck out his injured chest. "He was defeated and killed by your enemies because he was caught unawares. I will *not* make the same mistake."

Lincoln stared at him for a long time.

"Very well," he said finally. "We will fight."

"And you'll win." Alpha sat back down.

"Now, can I *please* have something else to eat? I'm still famished."

-44-

For the first time, I'm afraid of Alpha. He looks at me the way a wolf eyes a lamb and I can't tell what he's thinking. Maybe it's just my imagination. Maybe being on my own for two years has made me misread people.

Or, maybe, Alpha isn't really a person anymore.

The History of New Eden

Two hours later, Rob Roy returned, leading a string of ponies laden with old rifles and handguns.

"Oh boyohboyohboy!" Tango latched onto the nearest animal. "This one's mine. I'm gonna call him James, after my grandmother."

"That lassie is beyond weird."

"You have no idea." Uniform warily approached one of the animals. "Can you teach us to ride in such a short time?"

"Enough tae get around, big man." Rob Roy looked around. "A lot of activity goin on, eh?"

"We're building fortifications. And me and Alpha are working on some cool ideas."

"I wouldnae broadcast them," Rob Roy cautioned. "Nothing goes on here withoot the Fort kenning aboot it eventually."

"You saying they have an inside man?"

"That's mah suspicion, though I cannae prove it."

"Oh, great." Uniform threw up his hands. "As if this fight wasn't one-sided enough. I better go tell Alpha."

"You no gonnae pick oot a horsie first?"

One of the creatures nudged Uniform's shoulder and the boy ducked involuntarily.

"Too busy." He backed away, keeping his eyes on the beast.

"Och, these nags wouldnae hurt a fly," Rob Roy laughed. "You're just a scaredy-cat!"

Uniform stopped.

"What did you call me?"

"Nae offense, pal." The boy was taken aback. "Loads of people are fairt of thon big beasties."

"Apologize," Uniform said menacingly.

"I dinnae apologize when I'm right, big man."

"Say *sorry*." The boy's fingers twitched above the handle of his gun.

"Winnae." Rob Roy clutched his spear. "And it makes nae odds tae me if ye hae the advantage."

"Let's take a walk, sweetie." Tango grabbed the protector's arm and marched him over to the well.

"Time for a heart to heart." She sat him down and rubbed her palms together. "You won't shoot *me* for being honest, will you?"

"Don't be stupid," Uniform sulked.

"I'll come right out with it then." She crouched next to him and whispered in his ear. "You're terrified of fighting, aren't you?"

"What? No!" Uniform stammered. "I'm... No!"

"That's why you didn't try to save Alpha from the mutant dog. And it's the reason you never fired a shot when we were battling the advance party."

"How do you know *that*?"

"Rifle makes a different noise from a handgun. I didn't hear it go off until Mike used it." Tango glanced at the hunter, helping build a brick wall by the barn. "He hasn't said anything. He doesn't know *what* to say."

"But he suspects."

"He's confused. He told me you took on the other Uniforms back in Fort New York State without a problem."

"That was easy." The boy looked away. "They were bullies just like me. All talk and no action. I was never in any real danger."

Tears sparkled in his eyes.

"I want to be brave, like you. I thought I *would* be when the time came."

When the words finally emerged, it seemed like they were torn from Uniform's throat.

"I'm a coward, Tango." He began to cry. "You must hate me."

"Hate you?" The girl reached out and brushed the tears away. "Why would I? You're the bravest person I ever met."

"What?" the boy sniffed.

"Uniform. A real coward doesn't hide on the battle-field."

"Fat lot of good I'll be."

"You'll give the Fort someone nice and big to shoot at, baby." She squeezed the boy's hand. "Someone that's not me."

"A little aid here, people," Mike shouted. "Don't be sunning yourselves all day."

"None of us can help how we feel. I know that more than anyone." Tango waved at her horse, who continued to munch grass, oblivious to her affections. "If I was scared as you, I'd jump on James and you wouldn't see me for dust."

"Nah. You wouldn't leave your friends in the lurch." The boy sniffed loudly and straightened his shoulders. "So, neither can I."

He kissed her cheek and got up to help Mike.

"Aw, Uniform," Tango whispered to herself as the boy walked away.

"I really wish you hadn't said that."

-45-

I have a big choice to make. I wish I could talk to someone.

I wish I could talk to Mike.

I wish Mike would talk to me.

The History of New Eden

Alpha had turned one hut into a War Room. Echo sat with him behind a large table, scribbling notes with chalk on a stone slate. People came and went, receiving orders and passing on messages. Rob Roy lounged in a chair, relishing his role as official adviser.

"You desired information on the Fort?" President Lincoln entered, holding a roll of paper.

"Know thine enemy, Mayor." Alpha drew up a seat for the old man. "What can you tell me?"

"Only stories passed down through the generations." Lincoln sat, his joints popping loudly. "The first Wholesomes made their presence known five years after the plague. They were most astonished to find survivors and none too pleased about it being our ancestors."

"Didnae want a bunch of mutants mucking up their nice New Eden," Rob Roy grunted.

"I presume they intended to farm, at first. But why go to that effort when they could live off what we produced?" Lincoln laughed bitterly. "So, they brought us all to the valleys, fenced the whole area and took away our horses."

He grunted.

"Ironic, is it not? I am Abraham Lincoln, yet I am a slave."

"How far does the barrier stretch?"

"Hundreds of miles."

"I don't get it." Echo scribbled on her slate. "If the Fort had put that much effort into agriculture, they could have easily fed themselves. It's what they were *instructed* to do, when they came out of suspended animation."

She looked up, puzzled.

"Why the hell didn't they try?"

"Someone obviously gave them a new set of orders." Tango tugged her lip. "Someone they were too afraid to disobey."

"But that leader would have died decades ago."

"True." Tango lapsed into thoughtful silence.

"The Wholesomes have a strange way of thinking, which we have never comprehended." Lincoln handed Alpha the roll. "This poster was written by them. They insist one be pinned up in every village. Ours is in the library."

He sniffed.

"My own works are relegated to a shelf at the back."

Alpha unfurled the paper and read the handwritten proclamation.

CITIZENS OF NEW EDEN

The Lord passed Judgment on those who Turned Away from Him and He Ended their Domination on His Earth.

Then the Godless Forts were Destroyed and their Sinful Experiments ended.

The Chosen Ones have returned to Begin a new Human Race.

We will protect you, despite your Curse, for the Lord has spared you to Serve Us.

Rejoice! Produce! Pray! In heaven, you will be Forgiven and made whole again.

Underneath was a crudely drawn symbol. A cross with VC emblazoned on it in red.

"Fond of capital letters, aren't they?" Alpha handed the poster to Tango. "I feel like I'm being shouted at by some beardy guy on a soapbox."

"Our real curse was no having fancy weapons." Rob Roy pointed an imaginary pistol. "Or trucks. Or an impenetrable Fort."

"I have not seen them with vehicles or modern guns since I was a young boy." Lincoln reminded him. "I presume the centuries have taken their toll on their fuel and weaponry."

"There ye go, then. Anither point in oor favor."

"Yet we have far less," President Lincoln reminded him. "Their control over us is absolute."

"*Was* absolute." Alpha leaned across and consulted Echo's tablet. "Point two. Do we know the enemy's strength?"

"No." Lincoln shook his head. "When we transport our supplies to the Fort, we are made to stop a mile away, then wait for our oxen and carts to be returned."

"Which could mean the Wholesomes don't want you to see how badly their resources are depleted." Alpha nodded happily. "Can we increase *our* force?"

"Jim Bowie and Al Capone have ridden tae the nearest townships," Rob Roy said. "Some of the younger and more able inhabitants are making thir way here on foot. Perhaps forty of them?"

"How sweet." Tango looked up from the poster. "They've run away to join the Library."

"Very droll, hen. The other villages are too distant fur anyone tae get here in time."

"Better than nothing." Echo made another tick.

"I have a question." Tango put up her hand. "According to your legends, did the people from Fort Virginia ever call it anything else?"

"Like what?"

"Like Fort North Carolina. It *is* in what used to be North Carolina."

"Not to my knowledge." Lincoln shook his head. "Besides, these boundaries are meaningless now."

"And do you know what this is?" She pointed to the symbol at the bottom of the poster.

"It's the Fort's emblem but I do not know what the letters pertain to." The Mayor took back the sheet of paper and quickly rolled it up again, as if he couldn't bear to look at it. "The Wholesomes... eh... *discourage* questions."

"Thank you, President Lincoln."

"I have a question myself," the old man said. "Why are you teaching all the villagers to shoot when we only have enough guns for a fraction of the population?"

"We'll get more," Alpha said casually.

"From *where*?"

"The bodies of our foes."

Lincoln raised a shaggy eyebrow.

"For what it's worth, I am impressed with you youngsters." He rose and shuffled to the door. "I still think we're doomed."

"Thanks for the vote of confidence." Alpha gave him a thumbs up. "Rejoice, produce, pray!"

With a snort, Lincoln made his way out.

"That's what Uniform will be like when he's old," Echo giggled. She looked at the stone slate. "Point Three. How would any mole pass on information to the Fort? There's no radio here."

"There's nae radio anywhere," Rob Roy said. "But I hae a theory."

The boy explained. Every so often, a Wholesome from the Fort rode the length of the barrier, checking it was still secure. In his opinion, a mole in each village could easily leave a message to be picked up by the man at some assigned point.

"When's the next rider due?"

"No for a month or so."

"It'll be too late by then." Alpha thought for a moment. "Just in case, we'll make it a rule that everyone stays near the village. Anyhow, building up the barricades should be our priority."

"What if he makes a run for it?" Echo asked. "Any mole would be desperate to report a rebellion to the Fort, even if it meant blowing his cover."

Alpha smiled broadly.

"That's *exactly* what I'm hoping."

-46-

Someone has stolen my recorder! I had to write this entry on a scrap of paper I found in the library.

We go out of our way to help you people and this is how you repay us?

I am pinning this note on the barn door in the hope that someone will return it.

I won't hold my breath.

The History of New Eden

Over the next few days, the villagers toiled like slaves. They were used to hard work and nobody complained. But they were quiet and subdued. For two hundred years, they had thought their plight impossible. In a way, they were as afraid of hope as they were of failure.

Tango drew up plans for the building of defensive walls and trenches and Al Capone and Jim Bowie organized work teams. Ned Kelly toiled at the village forge, fashioning armor and weapons. Sierra took the truck and dragged back swathes of barbed wire from the Fort's barrier. Mike taught the villagers how to set traps and fire the guns. Uniform, equipped with a shiny new sword, showed them the best way to wield scythes

282 · A Town Called Library

and axes, while Charlotte-Emily fashioned homemade spears and demonstrated how to throw them. Echo rounded up those too infirm to be any real help in fighting and put them to work cooking for the rest.

Rob Roy was put in charge of the cavalry, leading those who couldn't walk on mounted maneuvers.

Juliet looked lost.

Alpha was a powerhouse. Despite his wound, he was everywhere. Cajoling. Reassuring. Commanding.

And eating.

There was no more revelry at night. Everyone collapsed on their straw beds and caught what sleep they could before getting up at dawn. Then, the Threes, the town council and the young rebel leaders would hold a meeting to set that day's tasks.

Afterwards, a core group retreated to the War Room to discuss strategy.

"Which direction will the Fort's forces come from?" Alpha asked.

"They'll sweep in fae the west on horseback, along the valley floor." Rob Roy replied. "The hills would gie them a better vantage but they're pockmarked wi rabbit burrows an gopher holes. Too many horses would break thir legs."

"Excellent news." Alpha consulted his trusty map. "Tango? I want you to teach Charlotte-Emily how to drive."

"That oughtta be a sight, hun, considering she has four arms."

"She'll take the truck to this hill, ten miles west and keep lookout."

"We would do well to have Florence Nightingale accompany us," Charlotte suggested. "She is deaf but has eyes sharp as any hawk."

"Along with a tongue that never stops wagging," Emily groaned. "I shall be forced to wear a muffler."

"Deal with it. Tango will ride out every couple of days to bring food and water."

"On my very own horse!"

"Meanwhile, Rob Roy will get as close to the Fort as he can. When their forces move out to attack, he'll ride ahead and alert Charlotte-Emily and she'll high tail it back here and tell us. That way, we'll have plenty warning before the Wholesomes arrive."

"What if the truck won't start or the enemy capture it?" Juliet objected. "That's our only means of escape."

"It's worth taking the chance."

"No, it's not! You can't just toss aside your responsibilities cause a bigger group to lead has come along."

"Our role was to start a new human race, remember?" The leader countered. "Since it turns out there's one here already, it's our *job* to help."

"It's not my job," Juliet sulked. "I was never given a role."

"I suppose cheerleading's out of the question?"

"What's *happened* to you, Alpha?" The girl shouted. "It's like you're possessed. You're supposed to protect *us*, not toady up to some guy who double-crossed you once and is most likely willing to do it again!"

"Ca, canny, ginger." Rob Roy objected. "I'm trying tae help."

"Really? Then tell us how many soldiers the Fort has."

"They're not allowed near it," Echo reminded her.

"I'll bet *he's* been there." Juliet indicated the high-lander. "You saying you *never* got curious, horseman? Never risked taking a proper peek at your adversary?"

The boy wriggled uncomfortably in his chair.

"Aye, aw right." He looked at the ceiling. "I may hae had a wee shooftie once or twice, fae the hills."

"Every piece of knowledge we have about the enemy is invaluable," Uniform scolded. "Even if it's not something we want to hear."

"Ach, it's nae biggie." The boy waved his hand dismissively. "I didnae exactly hae time tae count, but there couldnae be much mair than 2,000 fighting men."

"Two… thousand!" Juliet almost fell over. "They outnumber the villagers more than ten to one."

Her dismay was mirrored on the other's faces.

"What did ye expect?" The boy was unrepentant. "That they'd saunter over wi a dozen men and challenge us tae a game of charades?"

"Sir, we cann*ot* beat those odds, no matter how many walls we build."

"We've got more than walls." Alpha seemed completely unfazed. "Tango, can you construct a couple of wooden catapults?"

"I can. And they *will* work."

"You're all insane!" Juliet kicked out at a passing rooster in fury. It leapt, squawking into the air, leaving a flurry of feathers. "Two thousand men and you're gonna fire rocks at them? I refuse to be part of this insanity!"

She turned and marched out of the room.

"Did I say anything about rocks?" Alpha flexed his shoulder. Despite the severity of his wound, it had almost healed.

"I'll see if she's ok." Mike made to leave.

"No. Give her time to cool off." The leader stopped him. "She'll come back when she smells breakfast. I sure would."

-47-

I have a big decision to make. Do I want to belong so badly that I'd die for it?

Or do I want to survive?

The History of New Eden

The others tucked in, but Mike left his eggs and grits untouched, glancing every now at the door.

Juliet didn't return.

After they had eaten, the Threes emerged from the War Room to find the girl strapping a blanket on her steed.

"What are you doing?" Mike gasped.

"I'm leaving. Heading north to see if there's a community somewhere the Fort missed." The girl turned to Rob Roy. "Will you let me have the horse? None of you really need mounts, since you're determined to dig in here and get yourselves killed."

"Help yirself. I cannae force ye tae stay and ye wouldnae survive without it."

"Is anyone coming with me?"

Uniform took a step forward. He glanced at Tango and stopped.

"It's my role to protect the Threes," he said sadly. "That's what I aim to do."

"Sierra?" Juliet pleaded. "You're not dumb. Not too fond of taking orders, neither."

"I'm fond of these people." The girl looked round at the nervous villagers. "You're on your own this time, girl."

"Mike?" Wide eyes fastened desperately on the boy. "Maybe we could start a life together in the north. You won't let me go alone, huh? Not *you*, of all people."

The boy shook his head miserably.

"Fine. I'll go on my own."

Mike's heart slid into a deep, dark pit.

He knew what he had to do. Knew he would never recover from it.

"You can't let Juliet go, Sir." He unslung his rifle. "She'll die if she heads north without proper supplies and she knows it. She'll head for the Fort and switch sides."

"*Mike!*" Juliet's lip trembled. "How could you *say* such a thing?"

"I can understand her leaving, hunter," Alpha said. "But she'd never do something like *that*."

The boy felt sick. Yet, he had no choice.

"You never wonder why Mrs Brown kept her in suspended animation for so long?"

"We weren't exactly on speaking terms when I left."

"It's because she won't let anything stand in the way of what she wants. She has no feelings or morals of any sort."

The boy knew the words off by heart. He'd gone over them in his head often enough.

"She's a psychopath, just like her father, Willard Chain. The man who designed and unleashed the Le Mans bug."

The Threes stared at the girl in disbelief.

"No," Sierra breathed. "No. No."

Alpha lurched forwards and struck Juliet with a force that stunned the others. She collided with the horse, blood spurting from her nose. The leader raised his hand again, but Uniform caught it.

"Quit it, Sir." He forced the boy's arm back, though it took all the strength he possessed. "Lock her up by all means, but I won't allow this."

"Do not *dare* defy me, protector!" Alpha spat.

Uniform recoiled. There was something in the boy's stare that seemed barely human.

Seeing her chance, Juliet vaulted onto the steed and spurred it into a gallop. Uniform and Echo ran towards their own mounts, Rob Roy hobbling behind. But the horses were still unsaddled and locked in the corral.

With a guttural cry, Alpha raced after the girl, loping in a way his companions had never seen a human run.

"Oh, my God." Sierra gasped. "He's catching her."

"That's impossible!"

But Alpha was, indeed, gaining on Juliet. His lips were pulled back over bared teeth in a feral snarl and his eyes bulged demonically. The girl glanced over her shoulder and gave a cry of fear.

She dug her heels into the animal's flanks and the horse accelerated.

Alpha launched himself into the air like some predatory beast, his fingers curled into talons. He missed the horse's rump by inches and one hoof caught him in the side. The leader crashed to the ground, tumbling over and over in the dirt.

Mike lifted his rifle and sighted.

"Oh, please stop," he sobbed. "Please stop."

But Juliet kept going.

As he pulled the trigger, Tango slammed the rifle up. The bullet whistled harmlessly into the air and the fleeing girl vanished over a low hill.

"Tango!" he cursed. "I was aiming for the horse!"

"I know, honey. I call that one Billy Bob and you can't shoot him."

"We'll go after her." Uniform vaulted the corral rail and hoisted a saddle onto his mount.

"Leave it be." Alpha rose and dusted himself down. "We're better off without her."

He seemed completely unharmed by a lashing hoof that should have broken his ribs.

"This changes nothing."

"I think it does, Sir."

"I've asked you to trust me before and you wouldn't oblige." The leader gave a sinister sneer. "Now you'll damned well obey me."

He glared at them.

"Stop staring and get working."

"I wouldnae argue wi someone like that," Rob Roy whispered. "He's pure mental."

The remaining Threes were inclined to agree.

Mike sat on his bunk, eyes red-rimmed. Mrs Brown had been right all along. Juliet had betrayed them.

Betrayed *him*.

But what hurt most was the simple fact that she was gone.

The door creaked open and Uniform edged in, carrying a plate.

"I reheated breakfast." He placed a pile of shriveled eggs in front of the boy. "Gotta keep your strength up."

"Still not hungry."

"I know you cared about Juliet." The protector sat down. "If Tango did something like that, it would kill me."

"She wouldn't."

"Maybe Jules *has* gone north."

"Don't bet on it."

"People change. Tango has. Echo too. Even I'm different." Uniform picked up a burned yolk and looked at it suspiciously. "Though I'll never be much of a cook."

"It's the difference in Alpha that's worrying me." Mike finally looked up. "I firmly believe he would have killed Juliet if he'd caught her."

"Yeah. I thought he was gonna bite my head off this morning." Uniform shivered at the memory. "Literally."

"It was brave of you to stand up to him like that."

"Really?" The boy looked surprised. "Thanks."

"You think he's losing it? Going power-mad?"

"I'd rather not broach the subject with him now I've experienced his newfound strength. He could tear my arms off and beat me up with them."

"Apart from Alpha, you're the only one the villagers will follow." Mike looked Uniform in the eye. "If he's out of control, you're the obvious choice to take over."

"I will *not* be party to mutiny, hunter." The boy held his stare. "My whole life, I been trained to follow his lead."

"We're not Types anymore," Mike said evenly. "The only thing you have to follow is your own conscience."

There was a whinny from outside and the sound of thundering hooves.

"What *now*?"

The boys ran outside to find Alpha leaning casually against the woodpile.

"Well, well," he said. "Grace O Malley just took off in an *awful* hurry."

"Eh? Why?"

"I imagine it's because she's the Fort's mole." The leader smiled. "Juliet's obviously headed to warn them. Wouldn't go well for poor old Grace, if she sat around here while an outsider risked life and limb to tell her bosses about this uprising."

He gave a toothy grin.

"So, now the traitors are gone, we can start working on my *real* plan."

The sun beat down on Juliet as she rode across the unforgiving landscape, her jaw throbbing with each crash of the horse's hooves. She gingerly touched her face where Alpha had hit it and found the skin swollen and tender. Worse, she only had a vague idea where the Fort was.

The girl heard galloping behind her and pulled a pistol from her saddlebag.

"Don't shoot," Grace O Malley shouted. "Oim on your side."

"How did you find me?"

"Horses leave tracks." The girl drew alongside. "Are you lost? Oi'll guide you to the Fort."

"Why would you?" Juliet wearily put away her gun. "And how do *you* know where it is?"

"Sure, oi can find me way home, can't I?"

"Home?" The word sounded meaningless out here in the wilderness. "But you're a Dreg."

"I am *not!*" Grace retorted, her Irish accent suddenly vanishing. "I was born whole, but the Fort did this, so I could join Library and report back." She held up the withered hand. "I pretended to be a refugee from the north and Library took me in."

"A high price to pay."

"I'll be well rewarded for my sacrifice."

"So, you're the traitor."

"No more than you," the girl bristled. "It was my duty and, anyhow, surely it's my own choice which side I support."

"Why did nobody else come after me?"

"Alpha wouldn't permit it. He thinks he's fooled you, somehow." Grace tapped her nose. "He's wily, that one. I suspect he's hiding something, but I've no idea what it is."

"I do." Juliet touched her bruised face again. "He talks to Echo at night and the walls of the huts are thin."

-48-

Alpha gathered the Threes in the War Room.

"I've asked Uniform to present our strategies," he said. "You have the floor, protector."

Uniform outlined his defensive tactics, using a stick to draw diagrams on the dusty ground. He finished and waited expectantly.

"Jeez," Sierra said. "That's pretty remarkable,"

"I sense a *but*."

"But still not nearly enough to defeat an army of 2,000."

"That's true." Uniform leaned his stick against the wall. "You haven't told us what your secret plan is, Sir. You do have one, don't you?"

"Of course."

"Ain't it time you spilled the beans then?" Sierra prompted.

"I apologize for keeping my cards so close to my chest," the leader told them. "But I can't be sure every mole is gone from Library."

"None of *us* are traitors!"

"I would have said the same about Juliet till yesterday."

"Then we got a problem." Uniform looked outside. "Some of the villagers are muttering they've made a big mistake. They saw Juliet take off and now they want to leave as well."

"They can't. We need every fighter we've got."

"I don't see how we can stop them. It's their town."

"Put the word out. Anyone trying to escape will be shot."

"Sir!" Sierra couldn't keep the shock from her voice. "We're supposed to be trying to save these people."

"That's what I'm doing," Alpha snapped. "The Fort is coming, whether Library likes it or not. We lose any more men and *nobody* here will survive."

"Gonna make us pretty unpopular, Sir," Uniform said uncertainly. "I'll be sleeping with one eye open from now on."

"I've a solution to that." Alpha removed his bandages. The wound in his chest was now simply a scar.

"You'll each take one of the vials in Echo's medical kit. Believe me, it will make you far more alert. Plus, faster and stronger than you could have thought possible."

The group looked at him in horror.

"What? You'll need that advantage to get through what's coming."

"I won't take it." Tango backed away. "I've seen what it's done to you."

"I almost caught a galloping horse, if that's what you mean."

"I mean, you're not the Alpha I know." The girl wouldn't look at him. "You're not nice anymore."

"That's got nothing whatsoever to do with any drug." The leader's eyes glittered. "We are at war, builder. Being *nice* is a luxury I can no longer afford."

There was a commotion outside and President Lincoln burst in.

"Books are being removed from the library," he shouted. "And bales of wheat from the barn!"

Through the open doorway, they could see Ned Kelly, Charlotte-Emily and Al Capone staggering across the square, arms filled with heavy tomes.

"They're acting on my orders," Alpha said calmly. "We've run out of material to build walls."

"We need the wheat to feed ourselves!" the Mayor pleaded. "And the books are the heart of this town!"

"If the Wholesomes win, there will *be* no town. Didn't you understand that when you agreed to fight?"

"But the books…" Lincoln was on the verge of tears. "They are ours!"

"And this is the best way to use them."

"You're… you're… *savages*!" the Mayor cried. "Even the Wholesomes left our most precious possessions."

"Your life should be the most valuable thing you have. That seems to have been beaten out of you."

"Do not destroy our books, Sir." The man got down on his knees. "Look. I am begging you."

The Threes turned away, ashamed.

"I'm sorry, but this has to be done." Alpha nodded to Sierra.

"Come on, Mr President." Sierra gently helped the man to his feet. "The villagers can pick their favorite story and keep it." She shot Alpha a filthy look. "*Can't* they, Sir?"

"By all means."

Mike joined Sierra in escorting the protesting man from the War Room. As soon as they were outside, Lincoln grabbed the boy by the arm.

"Do not let him do this, young fellow. *Please*."

"Don't worry. I'm gonna have a word with our esteemed leader right now."

Mike strode back indoors.

"This has gone far enough," he fumed. "Order the library put back."

"The books and wheat are part of my secret plan."

"Crap." Mike slammed the door behind him. "I don't think you *have* a proper strategy. You've taken on more than you can handle and now you're clutching at straws. *That's* why you want us to take the serum."

"Hold on, Mike." Uniform laid a hand on the boy's arm. "He's just distraught, Sir. He doesn't mean it."

"I mean it, all right." Mike shook him off.

"Don't use that tone of voice with me, hunter," Alpha said softly. "I know you're hurting because of Juliet, but there's a limit to what I'll allow."

"Me too." Mike's hand rested lightly on the butt of his revolver. "I won't let you become a dictator."

"You're treading on thin ice," the leader warned. "Don't push it."

Echo shook her head imperceptibly, warning the boy to back off.

Mike faltered. Then he took a deep breath and drew his shoulders back.

"In my opinion, you've become too erratic to remain in charge," he said bluntly. "It pains me to do this, Sir, but I'm relieving you of command."

-49-

"Protector." Alpha motioned to the teenager. "Put Mike under arrest. I don't have time for this nonsense."

Uniform drew his pistol. But he pointed it at Echo.

"I know you have your weapon out under the table," he warned. "Don't even think of using it."

"You *betraying* me, Uniform?" Alpha couldn't hide his astonishment.

"I'm against cheating, Sir."

"Unbuckle your gun belt and let it drop," Mike said. "You're confined to your quarters and Uniform will take over our forces."

The leader's eye twitched.

"Don't be *stupid*, Mike." Tango got in front of the boy. "With his new abilities, he's twice as fast as you."

"You should listen to her," Alpha snarled. "You *really* should."

"Go to your hut, Sir." Mike moved the girl away. "Don't make this any more unpleasant than it has to be."

"You little... *upstart*!" The leader rose, sliding the heavy table to one side as if it weighed nothing. Echo dropped her weapon and grabbed the medical kit before it slid off.

"Please stay calm," she pleaded.

"Back down, hunter." Alpha's fingers flexed above his revolver, a vein pulsing in his neck. "This is a battle you can't possibly win."

"Hasn't stopped *you* trying." Mike hunched, ready to draw. "It's the only thing left about you I respect."

Tango swung the rifle hesitantly towards Alpha, then back at Mike. Finally, she slid on the safety catch and pointed it at the ceiling.

"Not my fight," she said dolefully. "I won't shoot either of you. You're my friends."

Alpha clenched his fists, jaw working from side to side. Then he took a deep breath and slowly sat down.

"Neither will I," he said miserably. "But you're wrong about me, hunter."

He slid the gun from his holster and let it drop to the ground.

"If y'all think I'm such a terrible commander then, by all means, let Uniform take over. Allow any villagers to leave if that's what they want. They'll be hunted down and annihilated. Return the books. The Wholesomes will burn them along with the village. Don't take the serum. Fetch the truck and save yourselves instead. Do what the *hell* you like."

He kicked the pistol away.

"I promised to defend this village and I won't desert those still willing to fight. If you have a change of heart, right here is where you'll find me."

Mike stared at him, then lowered trembling hands to his sides.

"No need," he said, voice shaking with relief. "Uniform and I don't want your job."

"Are you saying this was a *test*?" Alpha blinked.

"Whether you admit it or not, that serum *has* changed you," the boy insisted. "I just needed to be sure the person I admired was still underneath."

"Enough to *die* for it?"

"I was hoping you'd shoot me in the arm."

"You're a reckless one, hunter." Alpha guffawed. "And all credit to you, Uniform, for doing what you thought was right."

"Got that notion from you, Sir."

"I honestly *do* have a plan," the leader relented. "I'm not telling anyone until the last minute, though. Just in case."

"I guess I trust you." Mike sat down before his legs gave way. "But do you *really* need the books?"

"I want you all to think about something," Alpha sighed. "What happens to the villagers if, by some miracle, we *do* win?"

"They rebuild their lives without any threat from the Fort."

"They can't." Sierra stood in the open doorway. "The land here is exhausted. In a couple of years, nothing will grow at all."

"Then they go north, where the soil is better."

"They've no way to shift thousands of books," Echo said. "Yet, they'd never leave without them."

"So, the library has to go." Alpha finished. "Do you agree, hunter?"

Mike rubbed his temple.

"Do you *agree*?"

"Yes, Sir. I'll inform President Lincoln."

He held out his hand.

"And you can give me the serum, Echo. Next time I have to face a man down, I'd like to be surer of success."

"I'm next," Uniform said. "Can't let this nut job be faster than me."

"I always will, protector. Serum or not."

One by one, they lined up. Except for Tango.

"I'm still not sure," she said. "I'm due for a delivery of food and water to Charlotte-Emily. Can I take that time to think?"

"Of course," Alpha replied solemnly. "Don't want to be accused of being a dictator."

"The rest of you can go back to work." Echo took the vial from her bag and gave it to Mike. "You'll find hard labor is a bit easier once you've taken this stuff."

She lifted the table with one outstretched arm.

"I ought to know."

Mike toiled all day without tiring. The boy found he could move rocks he would never have attempted to shift before. His eyesight and hearing seemed sharper as well. The only drawback was being much hungrier than before. The sun rose higher in the sky, bathing the village in a hazy glow. He turned his face upwards, soaking in the heat.

For the first time since Juliet left, he smiled.

"Sierra picked up a handful of pebbles and launched one. The missile soared right over the barn.

"It's a shame we couldn't give all the villagers WC-57." She watched the pebble vanish into the blue. "But Echo says there are only a couple of vials left."

She hurled another stone.

"I never wanted to be a farmer," she said. "But I still don't understand why Fort Virginia didn't set up an agricultural community of their own."

She dropped the stones and looked at him quizzically.

"They must have had livestock, seeds and replicators to multiply them. Why the hell didn't they use those resources rather than enslave the survivors of the plague?"

"Good question."

-50-

Al Capone cornered Alpha at the edge of the coral. The boy had his shirt off and Charlotte-Emily watched appreciatively as he hefted rocks onto the top of a wall.

"What's with da hole in the northern defenses, boss? It's making me nervous." Capone was blunt as always. "You got dis place locked up tighter dan a nun's bedroom, but you left a gap at one end, big enough to drive a truck through."

"That's precisely what it's for." The boy didn't pause. "To drive a truck through."

"You talking bout a getaway vehicle?" The boy narrowed his eyes. "Gonna turn yellow and leave us in the lurch, if da fight don't go your way?"

"Call me a coward again and you'll find yourself in a concrete overcoat at the bottom of the river." Alpha had spent enough time with the villagers to begin picking up their individual lingoes. "I got no intention of going anywhere, but I can't let our vehicle fall into enemy hands. It's too valuable to them."

"I see da sense in that." Capone scratched his skinny neck. "Yous won't mind if I'm da guy behind the wheel?"

"Echo will drive." Alpha lifted another stone and slammed it on top of the wall.

"An da rest of us will all be pushing up daisies."

"*She* won't."

"So, you're stuck on da cute dame. Who wouldn't be?" Capone tapped the boy's heart. "But a weak point in our defenses sure makes me jumpy."

"All part of the plan." Alpha wiped sweat from his brawny chest. He seemed broader than he had a few days ago. "No Wholesomes will get through. I guarantee it."

Capone eyed the leader's rippling muscles.

"If you say so," he grunted. "But I see blondie coasting past an *dis* mug is hitching a ride."

The Threes ate supper together in Alpha's cabin. All were ravenous.

"Go easy on the meat, will y'all?" Sierra snapped. "The villagers have little enough to spare, especially since we took away their crops."

"In a few days, they'll either be rid of the Fort or dead," Uniform was standing by the door, peering out. "May as well tuck in."

"Bluntly put as always, protector."

"But correct, Sir."

"No." Alpha pushed away his plate. "I can get used to hunger. Distribute the food to the villagers. They need it more than us. Get Tango to help you."

"Ehm… Tango's not here." Uniform sounded worried. "She should have been back a while ago, but her horse aint in the corral."

"Go check her quarters. The builder's so fond of that critter, she probably has it tucked up in bed."

"Will do."

He appeared a few minutes later, face white.

"Her stuff is gone," he cried. "Blankets, backpack. Even the flower I gave her."

"Echo." Alpha slowly put down his meal. "Check the medical kit. Tango seemed awful concerned about that serum."

The girl rummaged through her bag.

"It's missing."

"She wouldn't steal it." Uniform stammered. "Look again."

Echo tipped the bag up and the contents fell out.

"The last two vials are definitely gone."

"I have to find her." The protector turned to leave. "Something's happened."

"We'll send Rob Roy out to Charlotte-Emily. See if Tango showed up at the truck." Alpha said. "He's the fastest rider and he knows the way. You don't."

"What if she's injured?"

"He'll find her en route and bring her back." Alpha wiped his mouth. "In the meantime, tell the villagers we sent Tango on a special mission. Another defection would put the wind right up their sails."

"She's not a traitor…" Uniform began to object.

"Time will tell, protector."

"May I be excused?" The boy asked dejectedly. "I need some time to myself."

"Take as long as you want. Just don't leave the village. That's an order."

"Understood, Sir." Uniform turned and left, almost running.

"He gave her a flower?" Sierra mused. "Who knew that mutt had a heart to break?"

"It had better mend fast." Alpha began clearing the meal again. "What the hell is Tango playing at?"

Rob Roy returned at dusk, exhausted from his ride.

"Charlotte-Emily saw Tango," he said miserably as the Threes helped him from his horse.

"Told you so." Uniform breathed a sigh of relief. "Where is she?"

"She didnae go near the truck. She rode past, along the valley floor, going hell fur leather."

The rider accepted a canteen.

"I dinnae ken whit tae say, big man. She was heading fur the Fort."

"I don't…" The protector looked around uncomprehendingly. "She wouldn't…"

"We'll have to make do without her." Alpha gently touched Uniform's shoulder. "I'm sorry, my friend."

"I better get some rest." The boy straightened his shoulders. "Suddenly, I got an army I wanna kill."

-51-

Juliet and Grace stopped at the edge of the plain. In front of them was a large shanty town, overhung with a pall of smoke from chimneys and cooking fires. There were huts made of corrugated iron, sod and debris round the outskirts and, nearer the middle, two wooden rows of rickety clapboard shops marked out the town's main street. Huge blast doors were set into the hillside above the sprawl, identical to the ones in New York State. The whole area was surrounded by a defensive wall.

"I'll live in the Fort now instead of that cesspit, and won't that be mighty fine?" Grace sighed contentedly. "Worth all I've given up."

"What's that?" The girl pointed to a large iron cross on a nearby hill.

"It is dedicated to Willard Chain. The man who created the Le Mans bug?"

"Oh, I'm familiar with the name," Juliet said. "Quite an impressive monument."

"It's not a monument." Grace crossed himself. "It's a reminder of the evil Godless men can do. No one ever goes near it."

She began to move off.

"Shall we go down? I could do with a decent meal."

"If I wanted to mingle with a dirty rabble, I'd have stayed back at the village." Juliet patted dust from her tunic. "Ride right through and head for the Fort itself."

She spurred her horse forwards.

"Let's see what kind of welcome we get."

They got through the barrier easily enough, when Grace announced who she was. As they approached the blast doors, they slowly opened. The townspeople stopped and stared as a group of men marched out to meet the pair in two perfectly regimented ranks.

"State your business," one of them snapped.

Before Grace could speak, Juliet rose up in her saddle.

"I'm from Fort New York State," she called. "And I seek sanctuary."

They were led down several corridors and Juliet carefully took in her surroundings. Some of the lights were out and the air filters gave off an unhealthy hum. Time had not been any kinder to the machinery here than in her own Fort.

"Where are we going?" she asked.

"To meet our leaders in the Star Chamber."

The Star Chamber was a large room with an imposing wooden table set in the middle. Guards in dark blue uniforms stood to attention on either side of the door. On one wall was the logo of a cross and underneath the words.

Rejoice! Produce! Pray!

Opposite, the Stars and Stripes hung limply from a flagpole, robbed of any wind necessary to make it fly.

Four men and one woman sat around the table, wearing black robes. At the head was the eldest, shaven headed with little round glasses. He looked like a mild-mannered accountant.

"I am Commander Reynolds." He picked up a clip-board and pointed. "Your name, please."

"Juliet."

"Full name."

"Juliet 3."

"And I'm Grace," the girl added. "Grace O Malley, as you probably know."

Reynolds ignored her.

"You claim to be from Fort New York State, Juliet."

"I do."

"You have quite an imagination."

"I don't."

"Why are you here?"

"The village called Library is organizing a rebellion," Juliet said. "I came to warn you."

"Have *you* any defects?"

"Told I got a bit of a temper."

The man didn't laugh.

"I mean, are you Wholesome?"

"Yeah. I'm a regular angel."

"There are indications that what you say may be true." Reynolds still sounded skeptical. "You were scanned and found to be pure."

"And I'm Wholesome, of course." Grace hid the withered hand behind her back. "Don't you recall sending me out?"

"Your loyalty is noted," the man replied curtly. "Do you vouch for this stranger?"

"I saw her struck to the ground by her own leader. He would have killed her if she hadn't fled."

"Was he a Dreg?"

"No, Commander. But he was definitely a mutant of some sort. He had superhuman strength and speed."

"Hmmm." The man turned back to Juliet. "Why would you offer to aid us?"

"I want to live here. I'm good with technology. I'd be an asset."

"You wouldn't happen to have a bite to eat, perhaps?" Grace's stomach gave an empty growl. "I'm powerfully hungry after that journey and food in Library is scarce."

"Find decent lodgings in town for Grace O Malley," Reynolds said icily. "She has our thanks."

"But I deserve to stay in here." Grace held up her twisted hand. "For, didn't I let you do *this*?"

Reynolds looked at the deformed limb with naked disgust.

"Take her away and bring the other prisoner in."

The sentries led the girl, still protesting, into the corridor.

They returned accompanied by Tango.

52

"Hi, honey!" She gave the astonished girl a hug. "I just spent twenty minutes trying to explain to some flunkey where I come from."

She finally acknowledged the others.

"Hey there, guys."

"What are you *doing* here?" Juliet rounded on her companion.

"Same as you, babe." Tango smiled. "Didn't fancy ending up with a bullet in my head, defending a lost cause."

"You left Uniform? I thought you liked him."

"He's sweet, but we aren't married. Besides, he'll run for the hills are soon as the first shots are fired."

"Quiet," Reynolds snapped. "I'll ask the questions here. Show some respect for your elders."

"Elders? *We're* two hundred years old. Give or take a decade."

"According to your story, yes." Reynolds looked at his notes. "However, it might be a ruse so you could size the Fort up." The commander observed them over his spectacles. "For all I know, you're double agents sent by Library."

318 · A Town Called Library

"How are we supposed to report back to them?" Juliet snapped. "Smoke signals?"

"More impertinence." The woman spoke for the first time. Her hair was frizzy and gray, heaped in an unfeasibly large coil on her head. "You are not making a good first impression."

"Neither are you, grandma," Tango replied. "While you sit here, young people from the other villages are arriving at Library in droves. You're facing a full-scale rebellion, chiefs."

"And we will stamp it out." Another man spoke up. "They are only Dregs."

"Library has fortified itself," Juliet butted in. "You'll take heavy losses unless you do something drastic."

"Like what?"

"You must have *some* replicators that work. Why haven't you cloned more fighting men? Or given the ones you've got WC-57?"

"She *is* a spy," the woman said. "She asks too many questions."

"I didn't swap sides to end up on the losing team."

"Replicating living things is a sin." The gray-haired woman adjusted her black cloak. "As is changing a human being by artificial means. Only God should have that power."

"Is that why you attacked the other Forts two centuries ago?" Juliet raised an eyebrow. "Because they intended to genetically alter their populations?"

"Yes. Our people have managed to live rich lives without such blasphemy."

"I'm not sure I count living in a dingy sandbox as rich living."

"I wasn't too keen on changing into a monster myself," Juliet said. "Our companions from New York State have no such qualms and it will make them formidable adversaries."

The Star Chamber regarded the girls suspiciously, weighing up this new information.

"May I ask a question?" Tango tapped two fingers together. "Why is this place called Fort Virginia when it's actually in North Carolina? And why does your logo say VC on it?"

"Odd time to bring *that* up, Tango." Juliet looked at her companion quizzically.

"Indeed," Reynolds added. "Why should it concern you?"

"Save your breath. I already guessed the reason."

"Enough!" Reynolds slammed his hand on the table. "Explain yourself."

"All right." Tango pushed back her chair and stood up. "My name is Bethany Chain and my father was Willard Chain, creator of the Forts and the Le Mans bug."

"What?" Juliet swiveled around in her seat.

"Guess I should have mentioned it sooner, honey."

"This is preposterous!" Reynolds spluttered. "You have sealed your fate with such a sacrilegious lie."

"My mother was *Virginia* Chain, who I'm guessing is the real power in this Fort. Otherwise, it wouldn't have changed names." Tango winked at a camera set high up on the wall. "Wanna back me up, mom? I'm pretty sure you're listening."

I always prayed you survived. A disembodied voice floated out from the speaker on the roof. **Turning up after 200 years, however, has exceeded my wildest expectations. The Lord truly works in mysterious ways.**

"Born survivor, ma."

The Star Chamber almost fell off their seats.

"Mrs Chain?" Reynolds stammered. "This is your *daughter*?"

It is, commander. The computer said evenly. **Prepare the best quarters for these girls and see they are bathed and fed. After that, I will talk with them alone.**

"Meeting the boss. That's more like it." Tango winked at them.

"You lot can go back to pretending you actually have a role to play."

53

The girls reclined on plush velvet chairs. They were clean, perfumed and eating from a bowl of fruit.

"I don't get it. Why did Mrs Brown tell Mike *I* was Willard Chain's daughter?" Juliet glowered at her companion. "And how come you didn't bother to set him straight, back at Library. He tried to shoot me."

"He would have missed on purpose, hun. He's got a crush on you."

"Answer the question."

"My father had a lot of enemies." Tango popped a grape into her mouth. "For all his flaws, he cared deeply about his family. He knew I was a way for others to get to him and was determined to keep me out of harm. Everything about me was a closely guarded secret, even the fact that I existed. No info. No pictures."

"Which is where I came in?"

"When he sent us to safety, he swapped your identity with mine. Including our entrance tests to get into the Fort."

"Why me?"

"You're pretty and intelligent, like a Chain should be. The perfect cover." Tango reached for another grape. "Me? I was told to act the idiot, so nobody would suspect I was the offspring of a couple of geniuses. I guess I got into the habit."

She laughed bitterly.

"If you pretend to be something long enough, you eventually become it." Tango picked another apple from the bowl. "I presume mom's the one who sabotaged the other Forts. That wasn't something I wanted to share."

"Which would be easy if she was integrated into the computer here, just like Mrs Brown."

You are an astute young lady. The computerized voice filled the room. **My husband made a good choice. The question is, can I trust either of you?**

"I'm your daughter," Tango said. "Surely, that should count for something."

Your mother died a long time ago. I'm simply a machine and can show no favoritism.

"Whatever you say, ma." Tango lay back in her seat. "Why don't you use some logic then? Why *are* we here?"

You could be spies for Library, as Reynold's suggested.

"What if we are? They're a bunch of mutants dressed in weird costumes." Tango stretched. "If you don't trust us, go ahead and kill your only daughter, in case I tell the villages what they already know. You have overwhelming forces and they don't stand a chance."

"*Not* the best opening ploy I ever heard," Juliet cautioned.

It's honest and forthright. You impress me, Bethany.

"The name's Tango."

Then, I see no harm in telling the truth.

"I'm all ears," Tango giggled. "Not in a mutant way, though."

All right. Get comfortable.

"Already am." Tango passed the fruit bowl to Juliet. "Care for a Kumquat?"

"Shhhhhhh. I'm listening Mrs Chain."

Tango's father, Willard, was obsessed with finding a serum to 'improve' the human race. I hated what he was doing, but he insisted it was really to save me. I had cancer, you see.

"I'm sorry."

No need. I had made peace with my Lord, Jesus Christ. I was perfectly prepared to meet my maker and told Willard so. But he wouldn't hear of it. He railed against what he thought was an unfair deity. Against my wishes, he injected me with his 'miracle' drug. Experimented on his own wife!

"He was trying to help you, ma."

That's as may be, but the cancer was too far advanced to cure. Willard tried strain after strain of his drug, and I was too weak to protest. Then, he stumbled on a version that could cause a devastating plague.

Despite that, I still loved him. But he began to talk of starting again. Of creating a stronger human race. He would do a better job than God, he boasted.

The voice let out a heartfelt sigh.

Such blasphemy, Bethany.

"He was an arrogant man, mother, as we both know."

When my death became inevitable, he had me scanned and integrated into the computer that ran Fort North Carolina. He made me a beast and then a machine.

"He didn't want to lose you, ma."

He lost me long before he released the Le Mans bug. Willard's intention was to have the Forts' survivors take his sinful serum but I knew they would lose their souls in the process. Man was made in God's image, and that is not to be tampered with.

The girls listened with rapt attention.

What was I to do? My own daughter was in Fort New York State. Yet I couldn't let humanity become a race of monsters, so I sabotaged the other Forts.

"Course not, mother. I understand."

When the inhabitants of this complex came out of suspended animation, they had no memories, so I could bend them to my will. I forbade them to use the serum, replicate living things or plant genetically modified seeds.

"Which would make colonizing New Eden pretty difficult," Juliet whistled.

Indeed. But God provided, as I knew He would. We found small pockets of mutants living in smallholdings across the USA. Our people brought them back to the Midwest and gave them tools so they could farm for us.

"And took half of what they produced, ma."

We had no choice. We could not farm ourselves, even if we had wished to.

"Why?"

Mrs Chain sighed regretfully.

Because of the beasts.

54

When the first generation came out of suspended animation, Mrs Chain continued. I had them load all our supplies of WC-57 into trucks and dispose of them. Alas, they had no memory of what it could do. An oversight on my part.

Guilt tinged her voice.

Rather than drive it far away, they poured it into Lake Fontana.

"The bear," Juliet said quietly. "That's why it was so huge."

Yes. Wildlife had multiplied while we slumbered. They drank from the water and were changed. Became giant, vicious killers.

Juliet closed her eyes.

We built a great barrier to keep them out, at huge cost to our own recourses. Now, our men spend every waking hour they have to keep it intact. The villages think it is to keep them in, but it's really to keep the creatures out.

"Why don't you tell them so? Why make them hate you?"

My objective is fear, not hate, the voice said simply. We do not have enough food for our growing population and we cannot drink from the lake for fear of being changed. **The virus is still dormant inside the Dregs and the animals sense this, so will not touch them. They only attack Wholesomes.**

Mrs Chain sighed again.

Despite their deformities, the Dregs don't need us. We need *them*. They cannot know the advantage they have.

"If you had bred with the villagers, surely your own children would have been immune."

And become mutants themselves? I will not turn my subjects into abominations. I'd rather they died.

Mrs Chain sounded defeated.

However, the Fort is breaking down and I am running out of power. I fear I will be gone soon.

"Don't say that, ma." Tango pleaded. "I just found you."

"Sounds like you're between a rock and a hard place," Juliet said. "Not a lot of choices, huh?"

We could migrate to the far north, where the land is better and animals fewer. But without us to keep them subjugated, so would the Dregs.

"You have numbers on your side. They surely can't be that much of a threat."

The combined population of the villages is over 10,000. We have ruled by division but, if we fled, they would band together and come after us. Besides, we have no seeds and my people have long forgotten how to farm.

"Then you have a big problem," Tango said. "Alpha's not suicidal. When your forces finally triumph over the town, he intends to escape with the Threes in a truck."

Why would a handful of children on the loose be a problem?

"Fort New York is full of WC-57. If they bring it back and start distributing it among the villages, *you'll* be facing a force you can't defeat. Alpha's the kind of leader who could unite *all* the Dregs.

This is vital information, daughter. Thank you.

Juliet stared at her. Tango was making this part up but the girl didn't know why. She stayed silent.

It seems the situation is graver than I feared.

"I have a solution, ma," Tango said. "Split your forces in two and I'll lead half of them to Fort New York State. Then I can destroy the serum before Alpha gets there."

Why would you need so many men?

"There are clones inside, armed with modern weapons. They'll put up fierce resistance but would be no match for a whole army. And it gets better."

How so?

"As well as guns, the Fort has trucks, supplies and fuel." Tango blew on her knuckles. "With those, you could go so far away, the Dregs would never follow."

That is a fine plan.

"I can only see one problem. A section of the Fort is controlled by a rogue computer named Mrs Brown.

That's where the clones have retreated and she will try to keep you out."

No matter. I shall give Commander Reynolds the override codes. If you led him safely to the Fort, however, it would prove your loyalty.

"I can certainly do that."

You two would help destroy clones of yourselves? The woman sounded doubtful.

"I'm one of a kind," Juliet shrugged. "They never replicated me."

"I'm rather maladjusted myself, ma. New Eden would be better off without more Tangos running around, doncha think?"

Yes. One of you is enough.

"I'll help too," Juliet said. "Alpha is clever. You will lose many men overcoming Library and that will give the other villages heart."

You have a solution?

"Alpha has left a gap in his northern defenses as an escape route," Juliet said. "Divide your forces, as Tango suggested. I will lead the other half and show them where the weak point is. Library will easily fall when attacked from inside as well as out."

"Once I've destroyed the serum and defeated the inhabitants of Fort New York State, Alpha will have nowhere to run." Tango continued. "With guns, supplies and Library so easily overcome, the Dregs will never dare follow you north."

She shrugged.

"Your people will just have to learn how to farm. Can't be worse than the life they have now."

That is breathtaking in its ingenuity. Mrs Chain made no attempt to hide her admiration.

"If we defeat Library and Fort New York State," Tango said, "We'll have proved ourselves worthy of a substantial reward, don't you think?"

What would that be?

"You're dying, ma. Even if you weren't, you couldn't come with us." Tango took another bite of her apple. "Who better to appoint a successor than your own kid?"

Oh, very clever, Bethany.

"If we give your people a new lease of life, I will rule once you are gone." Tango wiped juice from her chin. "Juliet will be my second in command."

Commander Reynolds won't like it.

"Commander Reynolds will be my problem. Unless you're particularly fond of him."

I am not.

Mrs Chain gave an almost human laugh.

You *are* your father's daughter, Bethany.

"It's Tango, ma. But yes, I am." The girl gave a thin smile. "Don't hold it against me."

She stood up and wiped her hands.

"Now, let's go to war."

Part 8

The Battle for Library

It is not the strongest of the species that survives, nor the most intelligent that survives. It is the one that is the most adaptable to change.

Charles Darwin

55-

Tango and Juliet stood outside the blast doors. Two armies were waiting in the morning haze, horses impatiently stamping their hooves.

We're loading up with provisions, Mrs Chain said. **Your forces should be ready within the hour.**

"In that case, I'm going to visit my father's monument."

That's off-limits, child.

"Not to me," Tango climbed onto her horse. "He may have been a monster but he was still my dad."

Why the urgency? It'll be here when you get back.

"It won't." The girl motioned for Juliet to mount. "Order it pulled down by the time I return. From now on, *my* Wholesomes only look to the future."

I see. Will you instruct them to forget me also?

"Yes."

If I had feelings to hurt, I'd be pretty annoyed.

"If *I* had feelings to hurt, I'd still be mad that you tried to kill me when I was thirteen years old."

Tango galloped off, Juliet close behind.

The girls dismounted in front of the iron cross. It was black and rusted, weeds growing from the cracks. There was no inscription.

Tango knelt down in front of it, head bowed.

Juliet stood a few feet behind, holding her breath. Quietly, she drew her pistol and pointed it at her companion's back. She slowly cocked the hammer, trying to be as quiet as possible. The action still made an audible click.

"I'm sorry it had to end this way, Tango," she said softly. "Library isn't my concern, but I can't let you kill the Types."

"How will you explain my death to mother?" Tango didn't turn round.

"I'll say Rob Roy was on one of those hills, watching us. That he shot you with Mike's sniper rifle."

"Then you take over from me as leader. Very ambitious."

"Your father destroyed the world. The Wholesomes are screwed up enough without another psychopath in charge."

"My father was a decent man, despite what ma claims." The girl said softly. "He may have discovered the plague, but he would never have unleashed it on the world."

"Then who did?" Juliet kept her weapon trained on the girl.

"Mom, of course. Dad was completely crazy about her. He never could see what a nasty piece of work she was."

"The plague broke out in Germany right after he flew there."

"Yeah, think about that. My father was trying to persuade the world's top scientists to adopt his idea of building Forts and using WC-57. He wouldn't want them dead."

"But your mother would."

"Exactly. I bet she ordered some fanatic to swap one of his WC-57 samples for the Le Mans bug. When he opened them for a demonstration..."

She puffed out her cheeks.

"Poof! So long, Godless world."

"So, you got the psychotic streak from your mom and not your dad." Juliet tightened her finger on the trigger. "How does that change anything?"

"Ma is lying to us. She has no intention of sending her people north." Tango pushed both hands into the earth. "If we come back with guns and trucks, she'll order me killed, wipe out the villages and expect God to provide in some other way. *Nobody* messes with my mother and gets away with it."

She pulled two small vials, wrapped in plastic, from the ground.

"I intend to stop her. That's why I hid these here, on the way in."

"Are those Echo's last vials of WC-57?" Juliet hesitated.

"Stole them." The girl said blithely. "One's for you. It'll give us a small advantage when we turn against the Fort."

"Eh? You reckon I'd switch sides *again*?"

"How dumb do you think I am." Tango smiled. "I know *you're* Alpha's secret weapon."

She pushed a syringe into her arm.

"Oooh. That tingles!"

"How did you figure it out?" Juliet finally lowered her gun.

"Cause his plan was *my* idea, silly. We're working together." Tango held out the serum. "Here. Take this."

"Why didn't you tell me before?" Juliet accepted the vial. "I could have *killed* you just then."

"With ma listening to every word back at the Fort? I had to get you alone and I hoped you wouldn't shoot a pal."

"So, what's all this nonsense about Fort New York State still having banks of serum? It was used to flood the suspended animation tanks."

"Ma took the bait, didn't she?" Tango grinned. "Reynolds will be carrying the override codes for Fort New York. All I have to do is get them from him."

"You really are something." Juliet plunged the vial's point into her leg and a fierce heat spread through her body. She waited until the accompanying dizziness subsided.

"So, what's *your* strategy? How are you going to stop the Types being massacred?"

"Haven't actually thought that far ahead, sweetie. But trust me. I won't let them be harmed."

She buried the empty containers again.

"Anyhow, we're off to a good start. You're leading half the men against the village than would have normally gone. It'll give Alpha a fighting chance."

"Why are you doing this? I thought psychopaths didn't have any feelings?"

"We do. Just not enough to get in the way of what we want." Tango patted the earth back into place and stood up. "Besides, if you…"

"…Pretend to be something long enough you eventually become it," Juliet finished.

"Always look on the bright side, I say." The girl scrubbed dirt from her knees. "Right, we've given Rob Roy plenty of time to see us. He really is up on one of those hills."

She pinched her friend's cheek.

"Let's not disappoint him."

Juliet threw her arms around her friend's neck.

"Goodbye, Tango," she whispered. "I hope you make it."

"I got no intention of dying!" Tango hugged her back. "But I do have a message for Uniform."

"So long as it isn't rude."

"Tell him… I hope he can forgive me."

"I will."

They got back on the horses and rode back to their respective forces.

"Let's go, chaps," Tango called. "Last one to Fort New York State is a big, fat stinker."

She blew a kiss to Juliet and moved off. The girl wheeled her own horse and headed east at the head of her own army.

It was only as she approached the valleys that she began to think about Tango's message.

Tell him... I hope he can forgive me.

But Tango had been trying to help the Threes all along. She hadn't *done* anything that needed forgiveness.

The girl bit her lip.

Unless she hadn't done it *yet*.

56

Charlotte-Emily roared into Library. Alpha waved her north and she drove through the defensive gap, parking the truck in the barn.

The villagers thronged after her.

"Rob Roy shall be arriving presently," she said breathlessly. "He witnessed two columns of soldiers leaving the Fort. One is currently heading this way." She scratched her heads. "However, he claims the other is going *north*. We are somewhat perplexed, we must admit."

"Fantastic." Alpha grinned. "That means they'll attack us at half strength."

"Yes!" President Lincoln clapped his hands. Then he turned to the boy. "You do not seem surprised."

"All part of the plan, Mayor."

"That is not the most astonishing revelation!" Charlotte-Emily lowered her voice. "We must urgently discuss a peculiar turn of events. At the head of each army…"

"Shhhhhhhhhh. Enough now." Alpha waved her into silence. "War Room, please. You, President Lincoln, Capone, Bowie and the Threes only. Or else we'll be sitting on each other's laps."

"Report, Charlotte-Emily." Alpha sat on the table and crossed his legs.

"The Wholesomes shall not reach us until nightfall and we presume they will camp at the end of the valley until morning. Only a fool would attack in the dark after a full day's ride."

"A shame, but I agree."

"Sir." Charlotte-Emily couldn't contain herself any longer. "Something is truly amiss. Tango is in front of the army going north and Juliet is leading the one coming this way. We declare, we do not know what to make of it!"

Everyone began talking at once. Alpha leaned back and gave a satisfied smile.

"Exactly as I hoped."

The hubbub stopped.

"*What*?"

"Jules is a double agent." The leader paused to let his words sink in. "I made it look like she defected and I tried to kill her so the mole would leave and back up her story. It was all an act. She's one of us."

"But she's a psychopath!" Mike's head was whirling. "She's Willard Chain's daughter."

Alpha ran a hand wearily through his hair.

"*Tango* is Willard Chain's daughter," he corrected. "He swapped her identity with Juliet to keep his kid safe."

Mike and Uniform stared at each other.

"How do you know that?"

"Tango told me. Much as I'd like to take credit, the whole plan is hers, not mine." Alpha jumped off the table. "She's divided the Fort's forces, as she promised."

Uniform stepped forward and punched him in the mouth. The boy landed on his back with a grunt.

"That's the second time you've knocked down an Alpha." Mike helped the leader to his feet. "It's getting to be a habit."

"Thank you, hunter," Alpha said.

Mike hit him even harder. The leader sprawled across the table, blood spurting from his nose.

"Me next." Sierra cracked her knuckles.

"Stop it!" Echo threw herself over Alpha. "He couldn't tell you the truth and neither could Juliet or Tango! None of you are actors. Your surprise had to be genuine for his plan to work."

Mike and Uniform considered this.

"We couldn't be sure there wasn't another traitor, could we?" She cradled the leader's head. "At one point, half the villagers were so afraid, they'd happily have deserted and warned the Fort of our plans, just to be spared."

"Anyone else want to take a pop at me?" Alpha sat up. "Or can we please move on?"

"Sorry, Sir." Uniform apologized. "Got a little emotional."

"Not as sorry as me." Mike had turned bright red.

"I'm sure Juliet will understand why you spilled the beans on her. Your intentions were good, even if you had the facts wrong."

"Sheesh," Capone snorted derisively. "You really don't know dames, boss."

"So, what's the rest of Tango's plan?" Uniform was still scowling. "Why is she going north?"

"To save the Types."

"How exactly is she gonna achieve that?"

"I don't rightly know." For the first time, Alpha looked uncertain. "She's a quick thinker, though."

"You trusted a psychopath!" Sierra raised her hands to the heavens.

"The alternative was losing *this* battle for certain." Alpha turned to Uniform. "You know her best. Don't *you* trust her?"

The protector swallowed hard. The others could almost see his mind churning.

Eventually, he spoke.

"I do, Sir."

"Post watches and get some sleep. We've made our bed and we must lie in it."

Alpha gave a salute and unthinkingly, the others returned it.

"Tomorrow, we'll either be victorious or dead."

Well past midnight, Rob Roy stole into camp, rags wrapped around his horse's hooves to deaden their sound. Ned Kelly opened the north gate and let him in.

"Helluva ride, mate." He helped the boy down.

"You're no jokin. Ah had tae go right round the Wholesomes in the dark."

"Go get some shut-eye. I'll tend to Big Nose." Kelly led the exhausted horse away. "Glad you made it back."

"Never a doubt aboot that." Rob Roy hobbled towards the barn. "I wouldnae miss this barney for aw the tea in China."

Juliet's journey east had also been a lonely one. The Wholesome commander, Colonel Damares, was none too pleased at finding himself in joint command with a sixteen-year-old girl.

"Just remember what happened to Joan of Arc," he said acidly.

"She's probably at Library waiting for us."

Damares didn't get the joke.

"I won't presume to tell you your job," Juliet continued. "You proceed any way you see fit. But I'm taking your hundred best fighters, with the deadliest weapons, and leading them around the north of the village. Once you have the enemy occupied, I'll guide them through that gap in their defenses and right into the heart of Library. Then all resistance should crumble."

She tilted her head at the commander.

"That seem like a good strategy to you?"

"I guess."

Damares seemed mollified, but he didn't speak to her again for the rest of the journey.

Now the pair surveyed Library from a safe distance, their army strung out across the valley in two long lines. The morning sun glittered on their swords and rifles and clouds of steam rose from the horses' muzzles.

"New walls and fences. Ditches. Even hedges. Your old friends have been busy." The Colonel lowered his binoculars. "I don't see any gap, though."

"Damn. They must have taken down the neon sign saying *in here if you want to win*." Juliet checked her pistol. "What's your plan of attack?"

"Gallop straight up the plain and roll right over them."

"I imagine that's what they're hoping for."

"So what? They're Dregs." Damares' lip curled. "Don't worry. I'll give them a chance to surrender."

"Good luck with that. Where are my men?"

"The Centron on the left." The Colonel pointed to one large group of riders. "They're the finest I've got and awaiting your instructions."

"Give me time to get into position before you charge," she warned. "I'll look pretty dumb if you win without my help. Can't let *you* take all the credit."

She rode off, knowing that, now, it was exactly what he *would* do.

57

Two mounted men ringed the commander, one carrying a white flag.

"We're ready to go," the leader said. "What are your terms for the villagers?"

"Unconditional surrender." Damares put his hands behind his back. "If they come out with their hands up, we will let them live."

"That's very generous."

"I'm lying, you fool. Once they have laid down their weapons, I'll order the attack."

"Yessir." The man saluted and led his troop into Library.

Two minutes later, the party rode out again. The commander waited impatiently while they cantered towards him. As the group approached, he squinted at them uncertainly. The black uniforms seemed to hang looser than they should and the cap peaks were pulled too far down over their faces.

"They're not our men!" he shouted.

The riders wheeled to a halt, drew back their arms and let fly. Three had defective legs and their arm muscles had acquired added strength as compensation. The other two were Mike and Alpha, whose missiles went so high they disappeared from sight.

The Molotov cocktails sailed over Damares' head and he flung himself to the ground. Behind him came the whump of ignited gas, followed by terrified whinnying and men screaming.

Rob Roy held up two fingers.

"Haw! Right *up* ye, yah big bunch of tubes!" He peeled away from the main group and headed into the hills, skirting the rabbit warrens he knew so well.

The other riders turned and galloped back into Library before the enemy could collect themselves.

"They have desecrated a flag of truce," the Colonel roared, ignoring the irony of his own treachery. "When we take the village, I want every man, woman and child put to death!"

His forces bellowed their approval.

Back in Library, Alpha leapt from his horse. The emissaries lay dead in the town square.

"That should make them throw caution to the wind," he said. "Get the catapults."

A dozen villagers wheeled two clumsy wooden towers out of the barn, using harnessed horses to pull them.

"Load em up and be careful!" the leader shouted. "Don't want our first fatalities to be self-inflicted."

Two Hessian sacks, tied at the top with rope, were hoisted into the catapults' cups. The bags slowly writhed, as if filled with jelly.

"When Sierra and I give the signal, launch." Alpha nodded to the girl. "Any time, farmer."

In unison, they sliced through the ropes keeping the sacks closed.

Two axes descended on the catapults' rigging and the bags rocketed over the barricades. As they flew through the air, they opened, and dozens of rattlesnakes were released in a giant wriggling fan.

They landed among the Wholesome army. Horses reared up, throwing their riders, then fled, some dragging their masters along behind.

A cheer went up from Library.

"Enough! We'll not remain here and be a sitting target." Damares raised his hand. "Charge!"

The massive army surged forwards.

On the northern hill, Juliet saw them begin to move.

"Idiots," she muttered to the nearest men. "We're not nearly in position."

The first line of defense was a high hedge. Behind it, the townspeople stood next to wooden boxes. The line held rifles, bows and every handgun they had managed to scrape together.

"Don't anyone move till I give the signal," Uniform yelled from the end of the row. "They got one more surprise coming."

For a week, the farmers had dug small holes in regimented rows all along the valley. The Wholesomes reached the burrows and horses began to fall as their legs sank into the tiny pits. More riders toppled over the heads of their mounts and were trampled by the herd behind.

And still they came.

"Up on the crates," Uniform commanded. Half the villagers stood on the makeshift ramparts so they could see over the hedge.

"Look to your front." The boy strode up and down the rank. "Mark your target when he comes."

The Wholesome army bore down on them, spittle flying from the horses' bobbing heads.

"First rank, fire!"

The villagers let loose a deadly salvo, then stepped down to reload. The other half immediately took their place.

"Second rank, fire!"

They switched again.

"First rank, fire!"

And again.

"Second rank, fire!"

But the Wholesomes, carried by their own momentum, were now a mere twenty feet from the barrier.

"Retreat!" Uniform pulled reluctant warriors from their positions. For the first time in their lives, the villagers were in control and obviously relished the feeling.

"Fall back, damn you! Stick to the plan!"

The villagers scuttled away. The Wholesomes reached the barrier and urged their horses over the top.

But they hadn't encountered mere hedges. They galloped straight into rolls of barbed wire, pulled from the perimeter fence and now draped with foliage.

The first line was ripped apart by the barbs and the charge floundered to a halt.

"Fire at will!" Uniform roared.

The villagers let loose volley after volley into the jagged hedge.

The Wholesome army turned and took flight.

"We moidered dose chumps!" Al Capone did a little dance. "Run back to your mamas, ya goons!"

"It's not over. They're just regrouping." Alpha got up on the barricade. "Casualties, Sierra?"

"We lost two."

"I mean *them*."

The girl did a quick count.

"About 300, I'd say."

"They still outnumber us 4 to 1." The leader gave a thin smile. "Better odds, but now we've lost the element of surprise."

He raised his hand.

"Threes to the War Room!"

58

"What's the enemy's next move?" Alpha sat down and crossed his arms. "Uniform?"

"Juliet is going to move against us from the north, but we don't have to worry about that *if* she's really on our side."

"Oh. That reminds me." The leader snapped his fingers. "Make sure everyone has orders not to shoot her."

"Yeah." Mike raised an eyebrow. "Please don't forget that bit."

"The foray from the west was a disaster for the Wholesomes, Sir," Uniform said. "They must realize they'll never get past the barbed wire."

"So?"

"If I was their leader, I'd wait for Juliet to be in place in the north, then attack from south and east simultaneously. A three sided front."

"On horseback or foot?"

"They're cavalry. Speed is what they prefer." Uniform tapped his chin thoughtfully. "I reckon they'll stay mounted."

"How long before the next wave?"

"It'll take them a good half hour to regroup and move."

"Good. Send out every able body to collect guns from the bodies while their forces are still in disarray. Then move all the weapons to the south wall. Mike? You get on top of the library tower with your telescopic rifle. Pick off anyone who looks to be in charge."

"Got it covered, Sir. Any more Molotovs?"

"A couple, but we've used up all the fuel we can spare. We need what's left for the truck so we can head out after this and help Tango."

"What about the east wall?" Echo said. "You can't leave that unarmed."

"I believe we have a representative from The Old Testament waiting outside." Alpha looked through the open doorway. "Could you fetch him?"

Echo escorted a stooped man with a walking stick into the War Room.

"He *is* old." She regarded him dubiously.

"Solomon, at your service," the man said in a papery voice, glancing resentfully at the girl. "I shall try not to expire while I am talking."

"Time to test out your idea." Alpha shook his hand. "I sure hope it works."

"It did against the Egyptians."

"Eh... That's probably a legend."

"As will you be, for trying the same trick."

"So long as it's not a legendary defeat." Alpha tugged Echo's arm. "Take half our troops. Follow him and do what he says."

"No need to weaken the south wall." The old man had a twinkle in his eye. "You have fifty in Library who cannot fight because they are blind or find it difficult to walk. We can use them."

"Are you sure?"

"Do not be like the Wholesomes and assume we are useless. Your success depends on being open-minded."

"Very wise, Solomon." Alpha nodded. "Move everyone who can't fight normally to the east wall. This gentleman will tell them what to do. You got about 20 minutes, so get cracking."

"Verily. I shall proceed with as much haste as my old bones can manage."

Juliet reached her position on top of the northern hills.

"When Damares attacks again, we'll go in," she told her second in command. "Stay right behind me and I'll lead you to the heart of Library. The villagers will be so busy fighting off the main force, we'll meet with little resistance."

"Good. I want to kill as many of those ignorant scum as I can."

"Oh yes." Juliet gave the man an innocent smile.

"A lot of ignorant scum will die today."

"Here they come!" Mike shouted from the bell tower. "Positions, everyone."

Damares cavalry had split into two columns and circled the village. They lined up, south and east, heat rising from their flanks. Juliet watched from her lofty vantage point.

"We go in at a canter, not a gallop. If there *are* any booby traps, I want to spot them before it's too late." She raised her hand. "Forwaaaaaaaaaaards!"

Her column started down the hill as the rest of the Wholesomes charged.

Damares' eastern cavalry were closest. They thundered towards the low wall at full speed, the commander grinning in triumph.

When they were fifty feet away, Solomon's defenders stood up.

Each held something shiny. Old mirrors. Scraps of polished metal. Shards of glass with the backs covered in pitch. Ned Kelly took center stage, armor shining like some Grail Knight.

Light from the blazing sun bounced off the reflective surfaces, straight into the cavalry's eyes.

There was pandemonium. Horses reared up or crashed into each other, and the charge ground to a halt as the steeds twisted their heads left and right to escape the glare.

"I hear thunder." Damares peered through splayed fingers, still trying to get his mount under control. "What devilry is this?"

Library's herd of longhorn cattle suddenly crested a rise and stampeded towards the cavalry's flank. They were herded by Rob Roy and a dozen other riders, firing guns in the air. Great horned heads thrashed from side to side, eyes rolling in panic, and a terrified lowing filled the valley.

They, too, were blinded by the glare and crashed headlong into Damares' troops.

Horses and men were sliced apart by the vicious horns as the herd tore the mounted force apart. The survivors wheeled and fled in panic the way they had come.

"Job done, lads." Rob Roy twirled a finger above his head and led his own small band back into Library.

The attack on the southern side was faring no better. Every armed and able-bodied villager was waiting behind the barriers. The Wholesome charge faltered under a remorseless hail of bullets, arrows and spears. Some riders began to pull back.

"Press on!" the Lieutenant in charge screamed, waving his pistol from the safety of the rear. "I will kill any man who retreats!"

The words choked in his throat. He sat up straight in his horse, holding his chest, then slid from the saddle.

"Gotcha." In the bell tower, Mike lowered his rifle and gave a satisfied smile.

The cavalry scattered.

Juliet reached the northern gate. She closed her eyes, trusting her horse not to falter and it sailed over the low obstruction, followed by the rest of her troops.

They were in.

The few villagers in the area fled in alarm as the column trotted between two rows of houses, heading for the town square. Juliet noted with satisfaction that all the adjoining alleyways were sealed off with bales of wheat.

"What are we riding on?" The second in command looked down at the spongy layers of paper beneath them. "These are books!"

"What's that smell?" Another shouted. "It's foul."

"Must be the Dregs!" A third jeered.

"It's gasoline," Juliet muttered, covering her mouth to avoid the fumes rising from the trampled volumes. "Before your time, I guess."

Suddenly, the paper carpet ended. The girl pulled up, raising a hand to halt her companions.

"Why have we stopped?" The second in command protested. "We're almost there."

"This is as far as you go, boys."

Sierra and Echo leapt from opposite rooftops and landed effortlessly between Juliet and her followers. Each held a Molotov Cocktail.

"This is our favorite method for getting rid of rabid dogs."

They threw the homemade bombs down on the paper, then launched themselves through an open window.

A wall of fire sprang up, spreading rapidly up the paper trail. With a cry of terror, the column turned and tried to outrun the flames.

None of them made it.

Juliet continued into the town square to applause from the villagers. Mike waved to her sheepishly from the tower of the library.

"Yeah." Juliet raised her middle finger at him. "*Now* you trust me."

"By our calculations, the Wholesomes have lost well over half their force." Alpha had gathered everyone in the barn. "Our casualties are twelve killed and six wounded."

"We've taken enough horses and weapons from their dead that every villager is armed and mobile," Uniform added.

"I would never have believed it." President Lincoln clasped his hands in gratitude. "They must leave us in peace now!"

"Not an option for them." Juliet was sitting on a pile of hay, Sierra's arm around her. "If they lose, the villages will definitely rise against them. They've nowhere else to go."

"Into the Fort, surely?"

"Mrs Chain won't allow failure. I've met her."

"They'll come on foot this time, firing as they go." Alpha scratched a graze on his arm that was already beginning to heal. "They're better trained than we are and still have almost double our numbers."

"What will we do?" Lincoln asked dolefully.

"Keep killing them. I want this place awash with blood."

"Takes a long time to get down from that tower." Mike stumbled into the barn and looked wildly around. He spotted Juliet and stopped.

"You have something to say?" The girl folded her arms.

"I thought... Mrs Brown said..." Mike rubbed sweating palms on his grubby tunic. "Tango... She..."

"Coherently, please." Juliet stood up and marched towards him.

"I should have trusted you." Mike closed his eyes. "Go on. Hit me."

"There's been a lot of that going on," Alpha remarked.

"If you thought I was a psychopath, why didn't you tell the others sooner?"

"I figured you deserved a chance." The boy screwed up his face, waiting.

"Then I'd be churlish not to offer you the same courtesy," Juliet leaned forward and kissed his cheek.

Mike opened one eye in astonishment.

"But you ever hide something like that from me again?" The girl punched him in the shoulder. "You'll *see* a psychopath, I promise you that."

59

"We've nabbed enough horses so the whole village could make a run for it," Uniform said. "Might be our best option."

The core group were back in the War Room.

"Most of them hae nae experience riding," Rob Roy replied. "We'd be sitting ducks if the enemy gave chase."

"We could attack," Sierra suggested. "The Wholesomes must be pretty demoralized. It might tip them over the edge."

"They'd hae tae be mair than demoralized for that tae work," the boy insisted. "They'd hae tae be unconscious."

"Then we dig in," Alpha said. "That way, we have cover, at least."

"Yous mugs oughtta make a move." Al Capone lifted his canteen in salute. "You've done all you can. Grab the truck and go help your friend, Tango."

"Yeah. Get outta Dodge. We'll carry on from here," Jim Bowie sliced the air with his knife. "If we take the rest of the Wholesome army with us, at least the other villages will be free."

"I guess that makes sense." Alpha nodded. "Echo. Load the truck. You can drive."

"We are truly regretful to see you depart, my fine friends," Charlotte-Emily winked. "This place will be exceedingly dull without you."

"This place will be massacred without me." The leader put hands on hips. "The other Threes can go, but I'll be staying to see this through, like I promised."

"And me." Echo took up the same stance. "I leave and Charlotte-Emily will be making moves on you in a hot minute. Not having that."

"I'm staying put too." Sierra said. "*Nobody* runs me outta town."

"I got a book stashed on top of the tower I'm not finished." Mike shrugged. "It's called *Where's Waldo* and I haven't found him yet."

"Give it to me when you're done." Juliet nudged him. "We can start a reading club."

The Threes looked at Uniform.

"I'll stay," the boy said quietly. "I'd want Tango to be proud of me."

"They'll come from every direction again, though the fire will protect the north entrance." Alpha stood up. "Charlotte-Emily, Al, Jim and Rob Roy. Divide the villagers into three groups and man the perimeters. Put the children and the wounded in the Library cellar. Keep the twenty most able men back to reinforce any breaches. We'll support them when the Wholesomes break through."

"My very own Alamo." Jim Bowie clapped his hands. "Never thought I'd get to say that."

"Ain't you da fortunate one?" Capone helped the boy to his feet. "Shame it ain't St Valentine's Day. I feel all left out."

The Dregs saluted and left.

"We don't stand a chance, do we?" Uniform waited until they were gone.

"Succinctly put, protector. But probably accurate."

"Man of few words, Sir."

"We'll have to trust that Tango can save the Types and defeat the Fort on her own. Then again, she's always been full of surprises."

Alpha regarded his companions.

"May I add, it has been the greatest privilege of my life to know you," he said humbly. "If the Types turn out to be half the people you've become, I'll consider the human race saved."

He grinned.

"I didn't even practice *that* speech."

"If Tango were here," Uniform remarked wistfully. "She'd insist on a group hug."

"I got no problem with that."

The Threes put their arms around each other and touched heads.

Nobody spoke.

-60-

At one o'clock, the enemy attacked for the last time. As predicted, they came on foot, shooting as they approached. Library returned fire.

The Wholesome losses were heavy, but the foe was unstoppable. Juliet had been right. Losing was not an option for them.

The villagers fell back as the enemy swarmed over the barriers. In the library tower, Mike fired and reloaded and fired until he was out of bullets. Then he ran down the stairs and into the town square.

The villagers had retreated into their houses and were protecting them stoically. He drew his pistol and crouched behind the well next to Juliet.

"Wanna make a wish?" The girl was fanning the hammer as fast as she could.

"Sure. I wish I was somewhere else."

Damares entered the square, leading a group of twenty or more. Sierra came screaming out of an alley, reached out a hand, and tore open the commander's throat. Then she was gone again, bounding over a six-foot-high barrier. Rob Roy galloped past in the opposite direction, reins between his teeth and a gun in each hand, firing as he went.

But the Wholesomes finally sensed victory. They screamed defiance and doubled their efforts.

Alpha and Echo were leaping from rooftop to rooftop, pouring volleys down into the melee. Echo was hit in the head, mid-jump, and plunged to the ground with a sickening crunch. The leader landed beside her, teeth bared, howling in rage.

He stood firm as more Wholesomes poured into the square. He was shot in the shoulder, then the hip. Still, he wouldn't stop fighting.

Uniform crouched in an alleyway, frozen against the wall, too afraid to move. Next to him, the skateboarder was sprawled, lifeless over his board.

Ned Kelly staggered into the passageway, blood dripping from under his helmet.

"Been nailed with a lucky shot, mate." he wheezed. "Damn."

He fell, face down, and lay still.

Uniform dropped his gun and began to cry.

Charlotte-Emily and Al Capone stumbled towards the well, carrying Jim Bowie.

"Get indoors, you idiots!" Mike stood up and waved them away. "Head for the library."

A bullet caught him in the stomach and he collapsed next to Juliet, blood seeping through his fingers.

"Changed my wish," he coughed, blood dribbling from his mouth. "Wish I hadn't stood up."

His eyelids slowly closed.

"Mike! No!" Juliet picked the boy up and sprinted for the library. She was hit in the leg and sprawled head first, dropping him in the dust.

Sierra landed in the square, crimson from head to foot. She looked around in desperation, not knowing who to help first. Alpha had been shot again and was lying in the dirt next to Echo, feebly trying to crawl towards her. Mike was motionless beside the well, Juliet shielding his body with her own.

She spotted a figure cautiously emerging from the alley and recognized the gait immediately.

"Help us, Uniform! For God's sake!"

The protector broke into a shambling run. His body was encased in Ned Kelly's armor and the iron helmet wobbled on his head. He had abandoned the pistol and carried only his sword.

"Get everyone inside," he cried in a muffled voice.

Then he headed straight for the largest group of Wholesomes.

A hail of bullets bounced off his protective covering as he waded into the throng. His sword flashed in the sun, moving so rapidly that it resembled a whirling propeller. Within seconds, the group lay in pieces. Uniform turned and plodded towards the next cluster, deflecting bullets with the blade. But his movements were slower and there was no doubt he had been wounded.

Sierra seized her chance. She grabbed Alpha and Echo in each hand and carried them into the library.

When she emerged to get Mike and Juliet, Uniform had dispatched a second batch of Wholesomes and was limping towards a third.

"Oh, please stop, protector," she pleaded, dragging her companions to safety. "They're cutting you to pieces."

When she came out again, Uniform was on his knees, weakly clutching his sword. A dozen Wholesomes stood in a ring around the boy, firing at him as he tried to rise.

"I'm coming, Uniform!" Sierra curled her hands into claws and tensed, ready to make a dash into the circle, determined to take as many as she could with her.

Something rushed past her.

Something huge.

A Wholesome looked round and gave a strangled cry.

It was the last sound he ever made. Enormous jaws clamped on his torso and crunched it in two.

The other attackers shrank back in terror.

It was a wolf.

But this creature was the size of a car. It lashed out with one gigantic paw, lifting two men into the air. They smashed into the nearest wall and slid to the ground.

Three more creatures bounded into the square, fur bristling on their backs. The Wholesomes shrieked in terror and retreated, chased by the snarling monstrosities.

"Grab Uniform!" Juliet was in the library doorway, using the frame to support herself. "The wolves' senses are super heightened, like ours. They must have smelled the blood from miles away and came through the gap we made in the barrier."

Sierra threw Uniform over her shoulder and sprinted back into the building, as another fanged monstrosity appeared at the west end of the square. Juliet slammed the heavy wooden door after her.

"What about the villagers?" Sierra gently lowered Uniform to the ground.

"They carry the Le Mans bug, even though it's dormant." Juliet pulled off the boy's helmet. "The wolves won't touch them. Not when they have a feast of pure humans to munch on."

"You mean we're *saved*?"

"Library is saved." Juliet burst into tears. "*We're* in bits."

Sierra looked around. Alpha, Echo and Mike were laid out on the floor, motionless, arms crossed over their torsos.

"Oh God. I'm *so* sorry, girl."

"He ain't gone to meet his maker yet, toots." Al Capone was crouched over Mike. "That serum is even more powerful than yous suspected. The son of a gun is still breathing!"

"They all are!" Jim Bowie tore open Alpha's tunic and put an ear to the boy's ravaged chest. "Get Echo's medical kit! We need bandages. Hot water. Thread to sew up wounds."

"We shall administer to them as best we can!" Charlotte-Emily ran for the door, then hesitated. "Are you positive about the wolves?"

"They won't touch you."

"No matter. We should willingly venture out, whatever perils await."

Juliet knelt next to Mike and felt his pulse. It was faint but steady. The boy's eyes fluttered open.

"Got a terrible sore tummy," he whispered. "Must have been something I ate."

Juliet hugged him and wouldn't let go until Charlotte-Emily returned.

As she treated the boy, Uniform slowly sat up.

"Got to get back... into the fight," he groaned. "Got them right... where I... want them."

He fell back with a clunk and began snoring.

Juliet and Sierra hugged each other in delight.

-61-

Mike woke, lying on a pallet in the barn. His stomach was burning and for the first time in days, he didn't feel hungry.

Alpha and Uniform were sitting against hay bales, swathed in bandages. Echo stood behind them, her head wrapped in gauze. Juliet was holding Mike's hand, her injured leg propped up on a wooden stool.

"Welcome to the land of the living," Alpha grinned feebly.

"Just like a hunter to sleep through the action," Uniform rasped.

Around them, the villagers were packed, shoulder to shoulder. President Lincoln stood at the front.

"We won." His voice was choked with emotion. "Library suffered heavy casualties, but we have proved victorious."

"And the Wholesome army?" Mike slowly pulled himself up.

"Retreating west. Between the wolves and the other villages they have to pass, I do not think any of them will make it back to the Fort."

Tears ran down his wrinkled cheeks.

"For the first time in two centuries, we are free."

"There's still another army heading north." Alpha lifted his arm and winced. "Tango will do all she can to frustrate their efforts, but we have to assume they'll be back."

"And I am confident every village will be waiting."

"Except this yin." Rob Roy limped out of the crowd. "It's totally knacked and the books are gone. We're comin with ye."

"If your offer of settling in the north is still open," Lincoln added anxiously.

"Of course." Alpha tested his leg next. "But you'll have to follow at your own pace. Only the truck will get us to Fort New York State in time to catch Tango."

"I fear that is rather impractical," Charlotte-Emily tutted. "You are most certainly in no condition to travel, never mind brawl. Even taking into account your newfound powers, you must convalesce."

"We'll do that in the back," Uniform replied groggily. "Sierra is unharmed, so she can drive."

"Me?" The girl laughed. "You really do have a death wish."

"Gotta save Tango, farmer."

"That we do." Alpha flexed his fingers. "She's fiercely smart, but I don't see how she can make a difference on her own."

"The mark of a true leader," Lincoln said. "The desire to help everyone."

He pulled a tattered ribbon with a gold pendant attached from around his neck.

"This is a Purple Heart. An award for bravery from a former time." He stepped forwards and slid it over Alpha's head. "Now it is our symbol of office."

"I can't take this," the boy objected. "The fight is over, so you're back in charge."

"I am too old to make the journey," Lincoln polished the locket with his sleeve. "And you are obviously born to command."

Juliet nodded in agreement.

Alpha looked around at the grinning crowd.

"No one is born to be anything, Mr President. I realize that now. I just tried harder than most."

The Threes were helped into the back of the truck.

"Good luck, lads." Rob Roy waved from Big Nose. "I'll follow and make sure the rest of these slow-coaches dinnae dawdle."

"Our sincerest wishes go with you, brave companions." Charlotte-Emily wiped tears from her eyes. "We wholeheartedly salute your doomed endeavor."

"Thanks... I think." Alpha frowned.

Al Capone and Jim Bowie waved as Sierra put her foot on the accelerator and the truck roared out of Library, heading into the hills.

-62-

Echo was quiet for the first few hours, sitting at the very back of the truck. The others were so sick and exhausted they didn't notice at first. Eventually, Juliet crawled over.

"I have to change your dressing."

"Leave it alone."

"I can't. In your weakened state, it might get infected."

"Don't care."

"Let me see your wound, Echo."

"No."

"Do as she says." Alpha slid along the truck bed, grimacing. "What's gotten into you?"

The girl lapsed into silence while Juliet cut the bandages away. Alpha put a hand to his mouth.

"What does it look like?" Echo asked.

"Eh... You got a few scars."

The teenager pushed Juliet aside and scrambled to the front of the truck bed. Mike and Uniform looked away. She leaned over the side and stared into the vehicle's wing mirror.

One side, from eye to chin, was a twisted lump of shiny, pink flesh.

"That's what I thought." The girl sat down and hugged her knees. "They shot half my face off. More than the serum could handle, I guess. No big deal."

Alpha crawled over to her. Echo shuffled away.

"Don't make me chase you around the truck," he pleaded. "It hurts."

"Charlotte-Emily will catch up in a few days." Echo began to put the bandages on again. "They're both sweet on you and they're pretty. I'll be all right."

"*Excuse* me?"

"I'm ugly. I'm *really* ugly."

"You're *different*." The leader tried to make light of the situation. "Uniform is ugly."

"No need to spare my feelings." The boy looked disconsolately out at the landscape, chin on his knee. "Why don't you call me stupid while you're at it?"

"But he's my best friend and I love him."

"Embarrassing me now, Sir."

"I love *you* in a very different way." Alpha reached out to Echo. "You'll always be beautiful to me."

"That's very kind." The girl took his hand and pressed it to her ruined face. "But I finally know how a Dreg feels."

"That word will never be used again." Alpha put his arm round her. "You hear?"

"Still think he's a weak leader?" Mike whispered to Juliet.

"No. He's earned the right to be in charge. But I wish he hadn't." The girl watched Alpha as he held

Echo. His eyes were hollow and his face had the pinched look of someone used to hardship and violence.

"Look what it's done to him."

Tango rode side by side with Commander Reynolds.

"I've not really been anywhere before," the man said chattily. "This is quite exciting."

"Never had the urge to explore?"

"A man should be happy with what he has."

"Especially if he got it from those less fortunate than himself, huh?"

"I'm no botanist, but this seems like a field of wheat." Reynolds disregarded the insult. "Fine and healthy, too."

Echo frowned. To the left, she could see stumps of burned trees. This was the forest they had set on fire; she was sure of it. So, where had the crops come from?

Then it came to her.

The seeds Sierra had dumped over the side of the truck had grown in the space of two weeks. They, too, must have been genetically modified and would take root anywhere.

This was a farmer's paradise.

"I got my bearings," she said. "The Fort is only a few miles away."

"Excellent." Reynolds removed his glasses to wipe off the grime. "Where will the clones be?"

"Sheltering in the agricultural section, along with a heap of automatic weapons. I doubt they'll leave unless someone they trust tells them it's safe to do so."

"Someone like you."

"Someone like me."

"Neutralizing the threat of the serum is my first priority." Reynolds put his glasses back on. "You will show me where it is stored."

"If the clones are smart, they'll have taken the WC-57 back into their sanctuary." Tango eyed the commander's puny build. "You not tempted to take some yourself?" she asked. "It'll make you big and strong."

"And lose my soul? Not a chance." Reynolds looked deeply offended. "It's important that *some* of the race remain human."

"You think that's all there is to being human?"

"I do."

"It is only in our decisions that we are important," Echo quoted. "Jean-Paul Sartre said that."

"He sounds French." The Commander gave a sniff. "Wine, cheese and hairy armpits, if history serves. People like that have nothing to teach me."

"It's your funeral." Tango rolled her eyes. "Fort's right up ahead."

-63-

They reached the familiar hillside and stopped. Above them were the blast doors, as formidable as the girl remembered.

"Now what?" Reynolds dismounted.

"Plenty of light left. I say we go in." Tango got down as well. "Stay out of sight. I'll go to the agriculture section and persuade them to come out. Lead them into an ambush."

The Wholesome army gathered outside the Fort. Tango walked up to the blast doors and put her hands on them.

"Nothing's happening." She feigned surprise. Unlike Reynolds, she knew perfectly well the doors wouldn't open if *she* was near them. After taking the serum Tango was, to all intents and purposes, a mutant herself.

"No matter. I know the master code." The commander stepped up to a console on the wall. "Turn away, please."

"Playing it safe, huh?" The girl reached into her pocket before complying. Reynolds punched in a long string of numbers and the keys bleeped as he did so.

The blast doors slid open. The soldiers drew their weapons and followed the girl through the hanger and down a maze of corridors. Tango reached a door and pushed it slowly open.

"These are bones." Reynolds looked down in revulsion as his boots crushed a skull, releasing a puff of white powder. "What is this cursed place?"

"The food court. The computer won't let the clones out and this is where the bodies get dumped."

The men picked their way through the skeleton strewn hall, covering each other until they were almost at the other side. Reynolds frowned and knelt.

"Something is wrong here. These skeletons are broken and... chewed."

"Did I neglect to mention the monsters who live here too?" Tango sniggered. "I'm a forgetful Type."

"I knew I could not trust you." Reynolds pointed his gun at the girl. "Any last words? Or have you run out of sarcastic comments?"

"I can manage one more," the girl replied coolly. "What kind of commander doesn't recognize a kill zone when he sees it?"

"A *what*?" Reynolds faltered.

"Look up."

The men slowly raised their eyes.

"Lord save us."

The rafters were filled with mutants.

Tango flung herself into the air, somersaulting over the canteen counter, as the creatures opened their huge jaws and dropped from the roof. The Wholesomes opened fire but the mutants were already among them, clawing and biting. One clamped its jaws on a soldier's arm and tore it off.

With a shriek, Reynolds fell on his hands and knees and scuttled away, weaving between the legs of the combatants.

Tango stood up and tried to get the commander in her sights, but the struggling throng obscured her view. A mutant landed on the counter beside her, saliva dripping from its gaping maw.

The girl swung her arm round and fired. Behind the creature, a soldier spun away with a grunt, a hole appearing in his temple.

The monster looked over its shoulder in surprise.

"You're welcome." Tango tipped her hat.

The mutant lowered its head and sniffed the girl. Its eyes widened.

"One of usssssssssssssssss," it hissed.

"I wouldn't go *that* far."

But the creature reached out and softly touched her face. For a second, the girl was sure she saw a flash of sadness in its eyes. On impulse, she pressed the rough hand to her cheek.

"One of usssssssssssssssss," the mutant repeated.

"Yes." Tango felt a lump form in her throat. "One of you."

The creature patted her head like some proud father. Then it jumped into the fray, landing on a human's back and sinking its fangs into the top of the man's head.

"Guess the moment's over." The girl backed away and opened the door of the food court.

She took one last look before she left.

The two parties were locked in a life and death struggle. Gore slicked the walls and blood mingled with the crushed bones, turning the floor into a pink mush. The mutants clawed and bit, using every ounce of their superior strength. But the soldiers were trained and armed. They were beginning to bunch into groups and reinforcements were pouring through the entrance at the other end of the court.

For a moment, Tango was tempted to stay and help the creatures. But they were doomed and she knew it.

Instead, she closed the door and headed for the Division of Youth.

A few minutes later, she reached the corridor with the airlock and gave a sigh of relief.

Mike 32 was on sentry duty outside, automatic weapon in hand.

"Tango 3." He gasped. "You came back."

"Yeah. I got homesick."

"I can hear shooting!"

"Jam the door open with your rifle for a few seconds." Tango wouldn't come closer. "Or else I can't get into the Division of Youth. I'll explain once we're both inside."

The Types gathered in the recreation hall. Tango did a quick headcount.

10 Sierras. 6 Uniforms. 4 Mikes. 3 other Tangos.

No Alphas or Echos.

They gaped at her, not sure of how to act.

Welcome back, Tango. Mrs Brown spoke first. **Never thought I'd see any of the Threes again. May I say, you seem different.**

"You better believe it."

I've missed you. The Types and I aren't really on speaking terms. Hardly surprising, considering what I did to them.

"I need everyone to be quiet while I explain the situation. You too Mrs Brown."

Never was much of a talker.

Tango told them of the danger they faced. The Types sat silently, taking it all in.

Sounds like we're in a pretty pickle.

"Not if you follow my instructions." Tango pulled a recorder from her pocket. "Stole this from Juliet so I could secretly record the sequence Commander Reynolds entered in the console outside."

She pressed the play button and Mrs Brown listened to a succession of different bleeps.

"Can you work out which numbers correspond to these sounds?"

Of course. It's 554894131674.

"Then that's the master code for the entire Fort." Tango tucked the tiny device away. "Using it will allow you to take control of the whole computer system at last, including the blast doors."

"You mean we can get out?" Mike 32 gasped.

"And walk straight into an ambush." Tango didn't beat around the bush. "Those fanatics aren't gonna allow a bunch of clones with automatic weapons into New Eden. Once they've polished off the mutants, they'll come for us."

"We can't even fight back," the boy cursed. "We used up almost all the ammo getting back to the Division of Youth in the first place."

"That's all right. I want you to stay right here until Mrs Brown gives the OK."

She motioned to the other Three Tangos and they trotted over.

"If something happens to me," she whispered. "You must protect the rest of the Types."

"That's Uniform's job."

"There are things a Uniform shouldn't do." It hurt Tango to look at the eight familiar youths standing cockily in one corner. "Things only *we* are capable of."

"What do you mean?"

"Don't be coy. I think you know very well."

Their looks suggested the girls did.

"You don't have to be ashamed or hide your true nature anymore," Tango said softly. "We may never be one of the good guys, but we can still be on their *side*."

She hugged her doubles.

"You must remember that." She kissed each one on the forehead. "Otherwise, I'll have to kill you."

"You sure know how to spoil a reunion, sourpuss."

"That I do, girls."

Tango stepped back and addressed the rest of the group.

"Everybody get their packs and gather in the ante-chamber. Be ready to leave when Mrs Brown gives the order."

Don't forget toothbrushes.

The Types trooped out, leaving Tango and Mrs Brown alone.

How are the rest of the Threes, Tango?

"Dead, for all I know. If they're not, it's thanks to Juliet."

I was *wrong* about her?

"Very."

I wish I could die also.

"The override code will allow you to shut yourself down. But I need some help first."

Of course. I'm sworn to protect the Threes.

"We've got pretty good at looking after ourselves. It's the Types you have to protect now."

I *would* like to make amends. Mrs Brown lowered her voice. **What's your plan, Tango? I'm sure you didn't waltz in here without one.**

The girl told her.

There was silence for a long time.

You really wanna do this?

"Like it or not, I am my mother's daughter."

I'm not sure what you mean.

"I mean, I have no sympathy for the people outside," the girl said. "If you insist on repeating the same mistakes, you can't complain about getting the same results."

I'll follow your instructions.

"Thank you. Now patch me into the speaker system."

Then I can die?

"Be my guest."

Thank you, Tango.

"I know you tried your best, Mrs Brown." The girl said quietly.

"Sleep well."

-65-

"We're almost at the Fort." Uniform grabbed a few stalks of wheat as they flew past. "Gotta say, I'm a mite puzzled about where *this* stuff came from?"

"How good am *I* at farming?" Sierra ground to a halt and stuck her head out of the cab. "I planted a whole crop without getting out of the truck."

"Circle round so we're on the hill above the Fort." Blood had begun seeping through the bandages on Alpha's shoulder. "We'll advance on foot. Anyone not up for it?"

"Me."

"Me too."

"I'll fall over."

"Stop bellyaching," the boy gave an all too rare smile. "I got shot the most."

Sierra kept driving until she was almost at the lip of the hill above the Fort. She helped the others down and the Threes crawled to the edge, then peeped over.

There were a dozen of New York State Fort's trucks below - and hundreds of men loading them with supplies.

"Looks like the occupants were no match for a proper army."

Occasionally, the Threes heard a burst of gunfire coming from the depths of the complex as another group of creatures were weeded out and dispatched.

"I almost feel sorry for them." Sierra shielded her eyes with one hand. "No sign of Tango or the Types."

"If the Wholesomes get back to Fort Virginia with all that stuff, it's curtains for the other villages." Mike rolled onto his back with a moan. "We've lost."

"C'mon, Tango." Uniform clenched a fist. "Don't let us down."

A siren went off.

Mike clasped hands over both ears, trying to block out a sound that brought back painful memories.

Black-clad soldiers poured out of the Fort, looking around in panic. Reynolds appeared in the open doorway, gun in hand. He was shouting orders, but nobody could hear him over the din.

"That's the commander," Juliet pointed. "He obviously doesn't know what's going on."

"Join the club."

The blast doors suddenly slid closed behind him. Reynolds pounded on the metal, to no avail. Darting to the control panel, he began pushing buttons.

The doors remained firmly shut.

The siren faded away and Tango's voice burst from the loudspeakers.

Don't bother, commander, she said. **Mrs Brown and I have taken over Fort New York State and changed the master code.**

"Then stay there, missy!" Reynolds shouted back. "My men and I shall return to Fort Virginia and wipe out the Dregs for good."

You people are incredible. Tango spat. **You still reject anything and anyone that doesn't chime with your narrow views. I'm a damned psychopath and *I'm* better than that.**

"You're a *what*?" Reynolds stammered.

You heard. Which means I've had no qualms about releasing the Le Mans bug from our suspended animation tanks into the air. A parting gift if you like.

The Threes looked at each other in horror.

A terrified hubbub went up in the valley below.

"You wouldn't!" Reynolds waved them into silence. "You and your precious Types would die, too."

They're clones, commander. The plague was specifically designed to wipe out humans. It won't affect them.

The man ran a shaking hand down his face.

Nor will it harm my friends since we've all taken the serum you despise so much. And Dregs are immune, as you know.

The girl gave a sinister giggle.

Oh dear. That means only Wholesomes are susceptible.

A cry went up from the ranks of soldiers.

You have one chance. The lake near your own Fort is polluted with WC-57. If you drive or ride all day and night, you *might* just make it back in time to drink there. Then you'll be immune too.

"It'll turn us into brutes!" Reynolds ranted.

In my eyes, you already are. Better hop to it. Clock's a ticking.

Panicked men leaped into the back of their horses and galloped off. The trucks also roared off, spouting gouts of black smoke and abandoning the unloaded supplies.

"Come back!" Reynolds screamed. "She's bluffing!"

"No, she's not." Juliet reached out and took Mike's hand. "Even if they make it and go back to Fort Virginia, Mrs Chain will never accept them."

"That's pretty ingenious, in a *really* horrible way. What about the people still at the Fort?"

"They'll have to go drink the water too. If not, they'll starve or get eaten by beasts. Mrs Chain will be completely alone. No threat to anyone."

Reynolds watched his men vanish, roaring in fury. Then he vaulted onto his horse and raced after them. Within minutes, the valley was empty.

The Threes climbed down the scree to the blast doors just as they opened again.

Tango stood in the shadows.

"Had a feeling you'd make it," she smiled wearily. "And the villages are finally safe."

The Threes stared at her.

"Don't worry." She flung a rucksack over one shoulder. "I don't expect you to forgive me, so I'll be on my way."

As she pushed past them, Alpha grabbed her arm.

"I would have done the same," he said quietly.

"That's why I had to act first, babe. You couldn't have lived with that guilt. I don't have that problem."

She looked around.

"Wait. Where's Uniform?" Her defiant look vanished. "He's not…?"

"He's fine." The protector slid down the last few feet of grass on his butt. "A bit dented is all."

"You stayed and *fought*?" Tango ran over and helped the boy to his feet. "I thought you'd run away once I was gone."

She blushed.

"Sorry. That was a bit presumptuous of me."

"Being presumptuous kinda pales alongside your other bad qualities." Uniform massaged his leg. "Are you saying you *care* what happens to me?"

"Seems that way." The girl picked up her rucksack again. "Don't quite understand it myself."

"Then why are you leaving? I sorely need some TLC."

"You *want* me to stay?" The girl hesitated.

"I *need* you to stay."

"We all do," Juliet added. "You're one of us."

"Look at what I did. There were *children* at Fort Virginia."

"And now they'll be scaly children with tusks." Uniform put his arms around Tango and held her tight. "Nobody is pure anymore and that's fine by me."

He looked at the other Threes over the girl's shoulder. Exhausted. Hollow eyed and hands stained with blood.

"All the same, I reckon we're the nicest of the damned."

There was a sound behind them. The Threes went for their guns.

"Don't be so trigger happy," Tango sniffed, hugging Uniform back. "It's just some old friends."

The blast doors were opening and Types shuffled nervously out of the hanger, shy and bedraggled. They were led by Mike 32.

"Oh." The boy gazed up at the clear blue sky. "It's everything I hoped it would be."

"Of course. This is New Eden," Mike 3 limped over and shook his hand. "It's your home."

Then Threes stood back and let their brothers and sisters walk into the sunlight.

One Week Later

The Threes survived. And I feel I'm finally one of them. Perhaps it's because we're all outsiders now.

Like Rob Roy, we can't settle for a life that's been mapped out for us. The difference is, he finally found a purpose. We will need to work out ours.

Well... not me. Our future is unwritten. So, I'm going to record it. Library has taught me how important that is.

The History of New Eden

The Threes and the Types sat by the riverbank, feasting. Now that the dogs were gone, game had been quick to return, especially since there were crops to eat. The Mikes had bagged several rabbits and a deer, beside themselves at being able to hunt. The remaining Tangos had already begun building rough cabins.

Sierra galloped into the clearing and dismounted.

"They're coming," she shouted.

Alpha stood up and clapped his hands.

"You've had a few days to acclimatize," he said. "And the people we told you about are arriving. Please make them welcome."

The Types whispered excitedly among themselves.

"There's going to be a change of rules," the teenager continued. "From now on, there will be no more builders or farmers or protectors. You'll all muck in together and do what needs to be done."

"But you'll still lead us, wontcha?" a Uniform piped up. "You're the only Alpha."

"You don't need me." The boy shook his head. "The villagers of Library have been surviving off the land for years. They know more about making a home than I'll ever learn."

"What will *you* do?"

"I'm going north to see what's there. Kinda got sidetracked last time I tried."

He shouted to Echo, sitting on her own at the edge of the clearing.

"Only if you come along, though."

The girl looked around, startled.

"Me?"

"I'm not talking to the tree you're skulking behind."

"I guess I could." The girl smiled for the first time since leaving Library. "It's pretty up there."

"Me and Tango are heading off as well," Uniform announced. "We've a hankering to see what happened to Fort Colorado."

"Isn't that a bit dangerous? Who knows what's waiting out there for you?"

"Not afraid, Sir. Got the fastest gun on the planet to protect me."

"That leaves Fort Texas for Juliet and me." Mike put his arm around the girl. "We'll send you a postcard."

There was a whinny from the edge of the clearing and Rob Roy trotted into view, flanked by Charlotte-Emily, Al Capone and Jim Bowie.

"Something smells awfy nice." The highlander gave a cheery wave. "Dinnae suppose its haggis?"

The Types goggled at them.

"It's not polite to stare, folks," Tango cautioned.

Rob Roy urged his horse forwards. Behind him, the survivors of Library moved cautiously out of the wheat, strung in a long line, sitting awkwardly on their steeds.

They stopped and waited.

Mike 32 got to his feet.

"It's a pleasure to meet you," he announced. "Would you do us the honor of sharing this meal?"

The Types leaped up and helped the villagers from their horses, guiding them to the campfire. Minutes later, they were all chattering animatedly.

The Threes silently gathered their horses and stole away.

"I've got a wee drop of whiskey left in my saddle-bag." Rob Roy broke from the throng and hobbled over to his horse. "Ah feel a toast coming on."

He stopped and stared.

Draped over his saddle was the Purple Heart.

"Aw, ye wee beauty." He put the ribbon round his neck and looked up.

Seven mounted figures were silhouetted on the hill above the Fort.

The boy lifted one hand in salute.

"Peace be with ye, lads and lassies."

"Who are you coming with?" Alpha asked Sierra. "North's gonna be the most fun."

"Boring!" Tango interrupted. "No chance of getting eaten on *that* jaunt."

"Bet you never been to Texas," Juliet cajoled. "Everything's bigger there. Animals too, probably."

"You know what? I reckon I'll stay." The girl gave a wry laugh. "Turns out I wouldn't mind being a farmer after all. Who'd have thought it?"

"At least one of us has sense." Mike reached over and shook her hand. "Look after yourself, Sierra."

"I'm the only one who didn't get shot, remember?"

The girl put two fingers to her lips, then touched the boy's heart with them.

"You'll always be welcome here." Her voice broke. "All of you."

She spurred her mount downhill, heading back to camp.

"Think they'll be ok?" Mike watched as Sierra dismounted next to Rob Roy. "Who knows what other dangers are hidden in New Eden?"

"If they get into trouble, we'll come back and sort it out." Uniform tapped his revolver. "Turns out *that's* what we're good at."

"I feel I should say something." Alpha cleared his throat.

"Waiting for your pearls of wisdom, babe." Tango cupped her ear.

"Nah." The boy wheeled his horse around. "Sometimes words aren't enough."

Uniform smiled.

"Best speech yet, Sir."

Then the Threes turned and rode into the sunset.

END

ABOUT THE AUTHOR

Jan-Andrew Henderson (J.A. Henderson) is the author of 40 children, teenage, YA, adult and non-fiction books. Published in the UK, USA, Canada, Australia and Europe, he has been shortlisted for fifteen literary awards and is the winner of the Doncaster Book Prize, the Aurealis Award and the Royal Mail Award.

www.janandrewhenderson.com